FIFTY STORIES for 8 YEAR OLDS

This edition published in **1990** by Gallery Books,
an imprint of W.H. Smith Publishers, Inc.,
112 Madison Avenue, New York 10016.

Copyright © Grisewood & Dempsey Ltd. 1989

ISBN 0-8317-3278-4

Printed in Yugoslavia

Gallery Books are available for bulk purchase
for sales promotions use. For details write or
telephone the Manager of Special Sales,
W.H. Smith Publishers, Inc., 112 Madison Avenue,
New York, New York 10016. (212) 532-6600.

FIFTY STORIES for 8 YEAR OLDS

Edited by
Marie Greenwood

Illustrated by
Alice Englander

GALLERY BOOKS
An Imprint of W. H. Smith Publishers Inc.
112 Madison Avenue
New York City 10016

ACKNOWLEDGMENTS

Stories retold from traditional sources that in this version are
© Grisewood & Dempsey Ltd are as follows:

The Wild Swans; The Goose Girl; The Sacred Honey Bees; The Tale
of Queen Shaharazad; Pomegranate of the Sea; The Stonecutter;
East of the Sun and West of the Moon; Robin Hood Meets Little
John; The Pickpocket and the Thief; Swan Lake; The Red Shoes;
Gold Tree and Silver Tree; Sinbad and the Old Man of the Sea;
Saint George and the Dragon; Death and the Boy; The Boy who
Found Fear; The Sorcerer's Apprentice; Orpheus in the Underworld;
The Old House; The Envious Neighbor; The Maulvi and the Donkey;
The Passing of King Arthur; Romulus and Remus; Hudden, Dudden and
Donald O'Leary; are retold by Nora Clarke

Brer Fox Goes Hunting; The Dead Wife; The Fox and the Stork;
The Crow; The Milkmaid and her Pail; Brer Fox Invites Brer
Rabbit to Dinner; are retold by Marie Greenwood

The Publishers would like to thank Nora Clarke for her kind assistance
in the making of this book

CONTENTS

THE WILD SWANS

Hans Andersen

Far, far away in the land where swallows fly in our winter time there lived a king who had one daughter, Elisa, and eleven sons. All the children had a wonderful life until their father married a wicked queen. She was his second wife and she made up her mind to hate her stepchildren.

After a while the queen sent Elisa into the country to live with a poor peasant family. After that, she told the king so many wicked lies about the princes that he did not want to have anything to do with them ever again.

"Fly away, out into the world," the queen ordered, "look after yourselves. Fly like great heavy birds who cannot speak." But her magic was not strong enough for her wishes. The princes turned into eleven beautiful white swans who flew away from the palace into the woods. They flew over the peasant's hut where Elisa was sleeping, then they went far away over the dark forests near the sea-shore.

Little Elisa played each day with a green leaf for she had no toys at all. She looked at the sun through a little hole in the leaf and pretended that she could see her brothers' bright eyes and feel their love for her.

When Elisa was sent back to the palace the queen hated her for her beauty and her goodness. Elisa was now fifteen and the queen wanted to turn her into a bird like her brothers but she did not dare to do so because the king himself had sent for his daughter.

Later that day the queen went to her marble bathroom fitted with soft cushions and carpets. She found three toads, kissed them and said to one, "Sit on Elisa's head when she has her bath so that she will become dull like you." Then she said to the second one, "Sit on her face and make her so ugly that her father will not know her." To the third toad she said, "Settle upon her heart so that her mind turns evil and she will suffer pain and misery."

She put the toads into the clear water which turned bright green. Then she called Elisa and made her get into the bath. The toads sat on her head, her face and her chest but Elisa did not seem to notice them. When she stood up three red poppies were floating on the water. Wicked magic had no power over the gentle Elisa.

The evil queen quickly rubbed nasty juices all over poor Elisa and she smeared a horrible cream over her face. She tangled and knotted Elisa's long hair into such a mess that the king was shocked. "Who is this dirty creature?" he demanded. "Get out of my sight." And the poor girl crept away from the palace into the woods. She longed to see her brothers so she planned to search until she found them. On she went until it grew dark. She rested on the soft moss and soon she fell asleep and dreamed of her brothers.

The gentle song of birds and the warm sun woke her and she heard the sound of running water. Up she jumped and went to the water's edge. It was clear and sparkling, but her face reflected there was dirty and ugly. She scooped up some water and washed her face. It was clean and shining again so Elisa threw off her clothes, rubbed herself down in the cool water and at once became beautiful again. She dried herself in the warm sunshine and drank some sparkling water, then she set off into the forest.

All day she wandered until she met an old woman carrying a

basket of delicious berries. "I'm looking for eleven princes riding through the forest," Elisa told her, "have you seen them?" She eyed the berries hungrily.

"I'm afraid not," said the old woman kindly, "but yesterday I saw eleven swans wearing golden crowns. They were swimming in the river over yonder. Eat these berries, my dear, then I'll show you the way there."

Elisa thanked the old woman who then led her to a little hill. She walked down and followed a tiny river at the bottom until it reached the sea-shore. Countless smooth pebbles lay on the sand and Elisa looked at them thoughtfully. "The sea rolls in, day after day," she said. "It never grows tired of making the rough stones smooth. I too must never grow tired of searching for my beloved brothers."

Then, mixed up in some seaweed, she found eleven swan feathers which she picked up and gathered into a small bundle. When had the swans dropped the feathers, she wondered as she watched the rolling waves of the sea.

At sunset Elisa saw eleven wild swans with golden crowns on their heads fly towards the shore. She hid behind a rock as they flew in one after the other like a streaming white ribbon. They landed

close to her and flapped their large wings. Then, as the sun disappeared from sight, the swans also disappeared. Eleven handsome princes, Elisa's brothers, stood there. They laughed and cried and told her how wicked their stepmother had been.

"We fly or swim," her eldest brother said, "like wild swans while the sun is above, but when it sets we turn into humans again. We must look out for a safe landing place for if we are flying up in the clouds at sunset we would fall like stones. We don't live here. We live in a beautiful land across the sea, far away. We are only allowed to make this trip to our homeland once a year and it takes two whole days to cross the ocean safely – so we spend the night on one small rock in the middle of the ocean. Without this rock we would never make the crossing."

He stopped for a moment then said, "We have only two days left. We cannot leave you but how can we take you with us, Elisa?"

They talked and talked but fell asleep without finding an answer. The sound of flapping wings woke Elisa. Her brothers had changed into swans and were flying far above her, but the youngest one stayed behind and laid his head on her lap so she stroked his soft feathers gently.

At dusk the swan-brothers returned. After sunset when they

became humans again they told Elisa their great plan. "Our wings are strong enough to carry you," they said, "if you are brave enough to fly with us. If not, we must leave you here for a whole year."

"Of course I'll come," exclaimed Elisa. "Show me what to do."

So all night they wove a strong mat out of willows and rushes and Elisa lay down on it. When the brothers changed back into wild swans at dawn they seized the mat in their beaks and flew high into the clouds with their dear sister, who was still asleep. When she awoke they were far from land. On and on they flew over the sea and Elisa nibbled some ripe berries her youngest brother had picked for her. The sky darkened. A storm was coming and Elisa could not see a tiny rock anywhere. The brothers could not fly any faster because they were carrying her. She was terrified. If the swans turned into men before they reached the rock they would crash into the sea. Suddenly the swans shot downwards. Elisa closed her eyes. This must be the end! The sun was sinking fast. She opened one eye and saw the rock below. The sun was just disappearing when her feet touched the firm ground and the next moment her brothers stood arm in arm round her. The sea beat fiercely over them but they held firm and chatted softly but cheerfully to make themselves feel brave.

At daybreak the storm had died down and the swans flew away with Elisa. All day palaces, churches, gardens and mountains floated beneath her. "There is Fairy Morgana's palace," her youngest brother whispered, "but no human is allowed there." Elisa was delighted. There were so many lovely sights until at last the swans flew down to a beautiful mountainside and set her down outside a cave hidden by trailing creepers. "Sleep peacefully here tonight," the brothers said, "and perhaps you'll dream of a way to set us free."

And dream she did. She dreamed that she flew to Fairy Morgana's palace and the fairy came to meet her. She was shining and radiant but Elisa thought she looked like the old woman in the forest who had first told her about the swans with the golden crowns.

"You can free your brothers," Morgana said, "but have you courage enough? Look at these stinging nettles. They grow near the cave or in the graveyard. You can only use these special nettles. They will burn and blister your hands. You must not mind that. You must tramp on them with your bare feet and make them into thread. Then you must spin and weave eleven shirts with long sleeves. The spell will break when you throw these shirts over the wild swans. Now listen carefully. From the moment you begin your work until it is finished you must not speak. Any word you utter will fall like a dagger into your brothers' hearts. They will die. Their lives hang upon the silence of your tongue."

She touched Elisa's hand with a nettle. The pain burned her like a flame and she woke up. It was daylight so she rushed out of the cave. Nettles grew everywhere! Her dream was true. Quickly she picked armfuls of nettles and her soft hands were burned and blistered. She trod them down and started to spin the green thread.

At sunset her brothers returned. They were frightened when she didn't welcome them but when they saw her poor hands they knew she must be doing something to help them. Her youngest brother wept and where his tears fell on her hands the burning pain and blistering disappeared.

All night long she worked. She wanted no rest until she had broken the spell on her brothers. Silently she worked next day and finished one shirt. She was making the second when she heard a hunting horn and the barking of hounds. Elisa was frightened. She ran into a cave and hid her bundle of nettles. A huge dog rushed out of the bushes, then another and another. They barked furiously and ran round in circles until a band of hunters rode up. The most handsome one stepped towards Elisa. He thought he'd never seen such a beautiful girl before.

"What are you doing here?" he asked. Elisa shook her head.

"I am the king," said the hunter. "You cannot stay here. If you are virtuous as well as beautiful you shall live in my palace and wear a golden crown." He lifted her upon his horse and rode off over the mountains with the other hunters but Elisa wept and wrung her blistered hands. The king's wonderful palace did not cheer her and she wept silently even when the maids dressed her in rich robes, threaded jewels through her hair and covered her sore hands with silken gloves.

All the courtiers were dazzled by her beauty and the king chose her to be his wife. But the archbishop muttered crossly, "This cave-girl is a witch. She has put a spell on the king's heart for certain."

The king did not listen. He ordered joyful music and dancing, but still Elisa looked sorrowful. He showed her gardens and treasures. She remained sad. Then he led her to a small room hung with green silk. It looked exactly like the cave where the king had found her. One finished shirt was over a chair and on the floor was her precious bundle of nettle yarn. "Do your work if it pleases you," the king said kindly.

At once Elisa smiled. She thought of her brothers and she kissed the king's hand happily. He went out and ordered churchbells to ring to honour their wedding. The cave-girl was to be queen.

The archbishop was still unhappy. He whispered evil things about Elisa and even in church during the wedding he pressed her crown extremely hard upon her head. She made not a sound but smiled sweetly at the king. He was so kind and gentle that Elisa began to love him dearly. She longed to tell him about her brothers, but she dared not.

Every night she slipped away to her little green room and made more shirts. She started the seventh, but found she had no yarn left. She was forced to visit the graveyard to gather some nettles. She crept into the gardens. Some hideous witches sat on the gravestones and watched her with evil eyes. Elisa picked the stinging nettles and tiptoed back to the palace. But the archbishop had seen her. He was sure that the new queen was a witch so he hurried off to tell the king all he had seen. The king did not want to believe the archbishop, but

that night he pretended to fall asleep, then he saw Elisa creep away to her little green room.

Night after night this happened. Elisa went on working until she had ten shirts. She needed more thread so she had to visit the graveyard again. The king and the archbishop followed her. They saw her pass the evil witches sitting there and they thought she was visiting these ugly creatures.

Next day, the king spoke to his people and said, "What shall I do about the queen? You shall judge her."

"Burn her like a witch," they shouted. "Burn her in the fire!"

Elisa was thrown into prison. "Make your nettles into a pillow," the guards shouted, "and use the shirts as your blankets." Just then a swan flew past the barred window. Her youngest brother had found her. Yet she uttered not a sound but went on frantically making the last shirt.

Before dawn the next day, her eleven brothers demanded to see the king but the courtiers said they could not disturb him. The brothers made such a noise that at last the king came out. At that moment the sun rose. The brothers vanished but the king noticed eleven wild swans flying over his palace.

Now Elisa was dressed in a torn robe and pushed into a rough cart. Her lips moved gently as she silently prayed and all the time she went on weaving the eleventh shirt. Crowds hurried beside the cart, screaming and shouting roughly, "Burn the witch. Tear away the spell she is weaving!" But as they stretched out their arms eleven swans flew down. They settled around Elisa and flapped their huge wings. The mob fell back in terror. "Is this a sign from Heaven?" they wondered. "Maybe she isn't a witch!"

The executioner seized Elisa, but she quickly threw the shirts over the swans. Behold, eleven handsome princes stood there. The youngest had one arm and a swan's wing for she had not quite finished weaving his shirt.

"Now I can speak," cried Elisa joyfully. "I am no witch," then she sank exhausted into her brothers' arms.

"She is indeed innocent," the eldest prince said as he told their story. Then a wonderful thing happened. The branches of wood all ready to burn Elisa turned into sweet-smelling red roses. The king picked the finest one and put it in her hand. She opened her eyes and smiled happily. At once churchbells pealed. The crowds cheered and the king and the eleven princes led Elisa back to the palace where they lived happily thereafter.

OLD TOMMY
AND THE SPECTRE

English Traditional

Once upon a time, and a long time ago, a Spectre went wandering through the country looking for a place to live. And on the border, just where England ends and Wales begins, he found the very house he was looking for. It was a pretty house, not too big and not too small; it had a garden with rose bushes and apple trees, and it was handsomely furnished.

The owner of the house, Mr Jones, didn't live in it (he was a merchant and lived in town) but of course he didn't want to keep the house empty. So he decided to let it.

And he did let it; he let it over and over again; but no one would stay in it. Well, how could you expect people to stay, when they couldn't so much as go upstairs without meeting the Spectre coming down? And if they went into the library in the evening, like as not they would see the Spectre seated at the table, turning over the leaves of some big book or other, and muttering to himself. He was enough to scare anyone out of his wits, was that Spectre, with his bluish-whitish body that you could see through, his nodding head, his long green hair, his pale staring eyes, his beak of a nose, and his great mouth with no lips to it. Add to all this that though he had legs and feet, he didn't walk – he *floated*.

Mr Jones got so annoyed about the Spectre that he felt like burning the house down. But his wife said, "Why don't you send for old Tommy?"

"Old Tommy," says Mr Jones, "who's he?"

"He's an old fellow who lives in the village," says Mrs Jones. "People say he has a way with Spectres. He sent one packing out of Robinson's farm, so I'm told."

So Mr Jones went to call on old Tommy, whom he found in his garden, digging up potatoes.

"Tommy," says Mr Jones, "I've a job for you. And if you can make a success of it, I'll pay you handsomely."

"What's the job then?" says old Tommy.

"To get rid of an unwelcome guest," says Mr Jones.

And he tells Tommy about the Spectre.

16

Old Tommy leans on his spade and looks at Mr Jones. There's a twinkle in his bright blue eyes. "I'll have a try at him, sir," says he. "I'll go up to the house tonight. Let me have a good blazing fire in that there liber-rary of yours, and a bottle full of brandy and a glass, and maybe a sandwich or two; and also an empty bottle with a good cork to it, and a stick of sealing wax. Don't forget about the empty bottle and the cork and the sealing wax, for they be the most important of all."

"And you think you can get rid of the thing?" says Mr Jones, greatly relieved.

"Sir," says Tommy. "I don't say as I *can*. All I say is I'll *try*."

So that evening, there was old Tommy seated in an armchair before a bright fire in the library. On a table at his side were the two bottles, one filled with brandy, the other empty, and also a plate holding a plentiful supply of ham sandwiches. For some reason best known to himself Tommy had locked the library door and put the key in his pocket. He had also taken the cork out of the empty bottle and laid it on the table.

"Now," says he with a chuckle, "you can come just as soon as you've a mind to, my friend!"

For a long time nobody did come. It was all very quiet-seeming: just the little tick-tock of the clock on the mantelpiece (which Tommy had wound up) and the soft-sounding flare of the small flames in the fire. Tommy had eaten a sandwich or two, and had taken more than a few sips out of the brandy bottle. Now his head kept nodding and his eyes kept shutting; he was in danger of falling asleep, which of course would never do. He was giving himself a good pinch, when he felt a kind of breezy stir in the air behind him, and glancing over his shoulder he saw the Spectre moving without a sound across the floor.

The Spectre was taller than the tallest man Tommy had ever seen. He had long locks of green hair, and he had nothing on him that you could call anything: only some wisps of bluish-whitish floating clouds. But he had a voice that seemed to fill the whole room, for it was as loud as a storm of wind.

"Well, old Tommy," says the Spectre in that roaring voice of his. "And how do you find yourself this evening?"

"In the pink," says Tommy. "But how do you come to know my name?"

"Oh, easy enough," says the Spectre.

"But I haven't the pleasure of knowing yours," says old Tommy.

"I don't own to one," says the Spectre. "Call me what you please."

"Well then, Mr What-You-Please," says Tommy, "how did you get in here? Not by the door, I do know, because I locked it."

"I got in through the keyhole," says the Spectre.

"Oh no, Mr What-You-Please," says Tommy. "I'm not believing that! A great fellow like you couldn't get through a keyhole!"

"I tell you I *did* get through that keyhole!" says the Spectre, in that loud roaring stormy-windy voice of his.

Tommy shakes his head. He puts on a very serious unbelieving look. "It's no laughing matter when a fellow tells lies," says he.

"*Lies, LIES!*" roars the Spectre, and now his voice was louder than a thunder clap. "WHO'S TELLING LIES?"

"You needn't deafen me," says Tommy. "But you know, a size of a fellow such as you be, to get through a keyhole, just as if you were an ant or a fly – why, it don't make sense! I'd as soon believe you could get into this empty bottle here on the table."

"So I can get into it," roars the Spectre.

"Don't believe it," says Tommy.

"I *can*, I *CAN*," roars the Spectre.

"Don't believe it," says Tommy again.

18

"IS SEEING BELIEVING THEN OR IS IT NOT?" roars the Spectre.

And next moment he shrank to the size of a match stick and gave a skip into the bottle.

In a flash Tommy snatched up the cork and rammed it down into the neck of the bottle. Then he took the stick of sealing wax from the table. He heated the wax at a candle flame till it was dripping all over the place; and then he covered the cork with the melted wax. He made the sign of the cross on the hot wax – and burned his fingers in the doing of it – but what of that? Now, with the bottle tucked under his arm, he was scurrying off out of the house, and down to the bank of a nearby river.

The river was swift-flowing and deep. "Catch as catch can!" shouted Tommy. And he flung the bottle out into the water. For a moment he watched it, bobbing away on the surface of the water. Then it sank. "Just as if someone had pulled it down," said Tommy to himself. "A pleasant journey to you, Mr Spectre!" says he, laughing. "I'm not particular where the bottle carries you, so long as it don't bring you here no more!" And he waved his hand to the river, and turned and went back into the house.

And where did that bottle go? Some people say that it is still lying at the bottom of the river. Others say that the river carried it down to the sea, and that the sea washed it up on to the shore, and that a girl picked it up and opened it, and wished she hadn't. Others again, say that the bottle, with the Spectre inside it, is to this day washing about in the sea, somewhere between Wales and Ireland.

Anyway, one thing is certain. The Spectre never came back to Mr Jones's house.

In his gratitude, Mr Jones offered to let old Tommy live in the house rent free. But Tommy said, "Me? What should I do with that great building round my neck? I'd rather you put me to work in the garden."

So then Mr Jones made Tommy head gardener: which meant that he had a good wage, and a cottage to live in, rent free. And no hard work to do, either, only to boss it over two brisk lads whom Mr Jones put to work under him.

Old Tommy told the two lads all about his adventure with the Spectre. And the two lads told it to their sweethearts. And when they married, the wives told it to their children. And when the children grew up and married they told it to *their* children. So the story was never forgotten. And that is how I am now able to tell it to you.

WHITEWASHING

Mark Twain (from *The Adventures of Tom Sawyer*)

Saturday morning was come, and all the summer world was bright and fresh, and brimming with life. There was a song in every heart; and if the heart was young the music issued at the lips. There was cheer in every face, and a spring in every step. The locust trees were in bloom, and the fragrance of the blossoms filled the air.

Cardiff Hill, beyond the village and above it, was green with vegetation, and it lay just far enough away to seem a Delectable Land, dreamy, reposeful, and inviting.

Tom appeared on the sidewalk with a bucket of whitewash and a long-handled brush. He surveyed the fence, and the gladness went out of nature, and a deep melancholy settled down upon his spirit. Thirty yards of board fence nine feet high! It seemed to him that life was hollow, and existence but a burden. Sighing he dipped his brush and passed it along the topmost plank; repeated the operation; did it again; compared the insignificant whitewashed streak with the far-reaching continent of unwhitewashed fence, and sat down on a tree-box discouraged. Jim came skipping out at the gate with a tin pail, and singing *Buffalo Gals*. Bringing water from the town pump had always been hateful work in Tom's eyes before, but now it did not strike him so. He remembered that there was company at the pump. White, mulatto, and Negro boys and girls were always there waiting their turns, resting, trading playthings, quarrelling, fighting, skylarking. And he remembered that although the pump was only a hundred and fifty yards off Jim never got back with a bucket of water under an hour; and even then somebody generally had to go after him. Tom said:

"Say, Jim; I'll fetch the water if you'll whitewash some."

Jim shook his head, and said:

"Can't, Ma'rs Tom. Ole missis she tole me I got to go an' git dis water an' not stop foolin' 'roun' wid anybody. She say she spec' Ma'rs Tom gwyne to ax me to whitewash, an' so she tole me go 'long an' 'tend to my own business – she 'lowed *she'd* 'tend to de whitewashin'."

"Oh, never you mind what she said, Jim. Gimme the bucket – I won't be gone only a minute. *She* won't ever know."

"Oh, I dasn't, Ma'rs Tom. Ole missis she'd take an' tar de head off'n me. 'Deed she would."

"*She*! she never licks anybody – whacks 'em over the head with her thimble, and who cares for that, I'd like to know? She talks awful, but talk don't hurt – anyways, it don't if she don't cry. Jim, I'll give you a marble. I'll give you a white alley!"

Jim began to waver.

"White alley, Jim; and it's a bully taw."

"My: dat's a mighty gay marvel, *I* tell you. But, Ma'rs Tom, I's powerful 'fraid ole missis."

"And besides, if you will, I'll show you my sore toe."

But Jim was only human – this attraction was too much for him. He put down his pail, took the white alley. In another minute he was flying down the street with his pail and a tingling rear. Tom was whitewashing with vigour, and Aunt Polly was retiring from the field with a slipper in her hand and triumph in her eye.

But Tom's energy did not last. He began to think of the fun he had planned for this day, and his sorrows multiplied. Soon the free boys would come tripping along on all sorts of delicious expeditions, and they would make a world of fun of him for having to work – the very thought of it burnt him like fire. He got out his worldly wealth and examined it – bits of toys, marbles, and trash; enough to buy an exchange of work maybe, but not enough to buy so much as half an hour of pure freedom. So he returned his straitened means to his pocket, and gave up the idea of trying to buy the boys. At this dark and hopeless moment an inspiration burst upon him. Nothing less than a great, magnificent inspiration.

He took up his brush and went tranquilly to work. Ben Rogers hove in sight presently; the very boy of all boys whose ridicule he had been dreading. Ben's gait was the hop, skip, and jump – proof enough that his heart was light and his anticipations high. He was eating an apple, and giving a long melodious whoop at intervals, followed by a deep-toned ding dong dong, ding dong dong, for he was personating a steamboat! As he drew near he slackened speed, took the middle of the street, leaned far over to starboard, and rounded-to ponderously, and with laborious pomp and circumstance, for he was personating the *Big Missouri*, and considered himself to be drawing nine feet of water. He was boat, and captain, and engine-bells combined, so he had to imagine himself standing on his own hurricane-deck giving the orders and executing them.

"Stop her, sir! Ling-a-ling-ling." The headway ran almost out,

and he drew up slowly towards the sidewalk. "Ship up to back! Ling-a-ling-ling!" His arms straightened and stiffened down his sides. "Set her back on the stabboard! Ling-a-ling-ling! Chow! ch-chow-wow-chow!" his right hand meantime describing stately circles, for it was representing a forty-foot wheel. "Let her go back on the labboard! Ling-a-ling-ling! Chow-ch-chow-chow!" The left hand began to describe circles.

"Stop the stabboard! Ling-a-ling-ling! Stop the labboard! Come ahead on the stabboard! Stop her! Let your outside turn over slow! Ling-a-ling-ling! Chow-ow-ow! Get out that head-line! Lively, now! Come – out with your spring-line – what're you about there? Take a turn round that stump with the bight of it! Stand by that stage now – let her go! Done with the engines, sir! Ling-a-ling-ling!"

"Sht! s'sht! sht!" (Trying the gauge-cocks.)

Tom went on whitewashing – paid no attention to the steamer. Ben stared a moment, and then said:

"Hi-yi! You're up a stump, ain't you?"

No answer. Tom surveyed his last touch with the eye of an

artist; then he gave his brush another gentle sweep, and surveyed the result as before. Ben ranged up alongside of him. Tom's mouth watered for the apple, but he stuck to his work. Ben said:

"Hello, old chap; you got to work, hey?"

"Why, it's you, Ben! I warn't noticing."

"Say, I'm going in a swimming, I am. Don't you wish you could? But of course, you'd druther work, wouldn't you? 'Course you would!"

Tom contemplated the boy a bit, and said:

"What do you call work?"

"Why, ain't that work?"

Tom resumed his whitewashing, and answered carelessly:

"Well, maybe it is, and maybe it ain't. All I know is, it suits Tom Sawyer."

"Oh, come now, you don't mean to let on that you like it?"

The brush continued to move.

"Like it? Well, I don't see why I oughtn't to like it. Does a boy get a chance to whitewash a fence every day?"

That put the thing in a new light. Ben stopped nibbling his apple. Tom swept his brush daintily back and forth – stepped back to note the effect – added a touch here and there – criticized the effect again, Ben watching every move, and getting more and more interested, more and more absorbed. Presently he said:

"Say, Tom, let me whitewash a little."

Tom considered; was about to consent; but he altered his mind: "No, no; I reckon it wouldn't hardly do, Ben. You see, Aunt Polly's awful particular about this fence – right here on the street, you know – but if it was the back fence I wouldn't mind, and she wouldn't. Yes she's awful particular about this fence: it's got to be done very careful: I reckon there ain't one boy in a thousand, maybe two thousand, that can do it the way it's got to be done."

"No – is that so? Oh, come now; lemme just try, only just a little. I'd let you, if you was me, Tom."

"Ben, I'd like to, honest injun; but Aunt Polly – well, Jim wanted to do it, but she wouldn't let him. Sid wanted to do it, but she wouldn't let Sid. Now, don't you see how I am fixed? If you was to tackle this fence, and anything was to happen to it –"

"Oh, shucks; I'll be just as careful. Now lemme try. Say – I'll give you the core of my apple."

"Well, here. No, Ben; now don't; I'm afeard –"

"I'll give you all of it!"

Tom gave up the brush with reluctance in his face, but alacrity in his heart. And while the late steamer *Big Missouri* worked and sweated in the sun, the retired artist sat on a barrel in the shade close by, dangled his legs, munched his apple, and planned the slaughter of more innocents. There was no lack of material; boys happened along every little while; they came to jeer, but remained to whitewash. By the time Ben was fagged out, Tom had traded the next chance to Billy Fisher for a kite in good repair; and when he played out, Johnny Miller bought in for a dead rat and a string to swing it with; and so on, and so on, hour after hour. And when the middle of the afternoon came, from being a poor poverty-stricken boy in the morning Tom was literally rolling in wealth. He had besides the things I have mentioned, twelve marbles, part of a jew's harp, a piece of blue bottle-glass to look through, a spool-cannon, a key that wouldn't unlock anything, a fragment of chalk, a glass stopper of a decanter, a tin soldier, a couple of tadpoles, six firecrackers, a kitten with only one eye, a brass doorknob, a dog-collar – but no dog – the handle of a knife, four pieces of orange-peel, and a dilapidated old window-sash. He had had a nice, good, idle time all the while – plenty of company – and the fence had three coats of whitewash on it! If he hadn't run out of whitewash he would have bankrupted every boy in the village.

Tom said to himself that it was not such a hollow world after all. He had discovered a great law of human action, without knowing it, namely, that, in order to make a man or a boy covet a thing, it is only necessary to make the thing difficult to attain. If he had been a great and wise philosopher, like the writer of this book, he would now have comprehended that work consists of whatever a body is obliged to do, and that play consists of whatever a body is not obliged to do. And this would help him to understand why constructing artificial flowers, or performing on a treadmill, is work, whilst rolling nine-pins or climbing Mont Blanc is only amusement. There are wealthy gentlemen in England who drive four-horse passenger-coaches twenty or thirty miles on a daily line, in the summer, because the privilege costs them considerable money; but if they were offered wages for the service that would turn it into work, then they would resign.

THE GOOSE GIRL

Grimm Brothers

When the king of a great kingdom died, the queen took charge of their only child. She was a beautiful girl with long hair as soft as satin.

When she grew up she was betrothed to a prince in a faraway land and soon the time came for their marriage to take place. The queen prepared dresses, jewels, and gold and silver cups for the wedding. She packed everything into two saddlebags then she chose a trusted maid to travel with the princess. The heavy saddlebags were loaded onto the packhorse while the princess was given Falada, a splendid horse which could speak.

On the day they set out, the queen went into her room and cut off a lock of her hair which she wrapped in a scrap of silk. She gave it to her daughter saying, "Take care of this, my dear, for it is a magic charm to keep you from any harm." Then she kissed her tearfully and the princess tucked the silk into her dress. She mounted Falada and rode off with her maid on the long journey to her bridegroom's country.

One warm sunny day as they were riding along the edge of a stream the princess felt thirsty so she said to her maid, "Please get out my golden cup and fetch me a drink of water."

"You don't need gold cups to get a drink," said the maid. "Get off your horse and stoop down by the stream. I'm not going to be a servant and wait on you a moment longer!"

The princess was frightened. She left Falada and knelt over the stream and scooped up a little water. "Alas," she sighed, "what will become of me?" The lock of hair answered her:

> *"Alas, alas! If thy mother knew it,*
> *Sadly, sadly would she rue it."*

The princess was very gentle so she didn't scold her maid when she got up on Falada again, and they rode off in silence.

The day grew so scorching hot that the princess soon felt thirsty again. When they reached another stream she forgot her maid's rude words and said, "Please fetch me a drink in my golden cup."

The maid answered more roughly and rudely than before, "Get down if you want to. I'm not your servant. Get your own drink!"

The princess had to lie down to reach the water and as she took a little drink she whispered, "Whatever is happening to me? I'm afraid of this girl." The lock of hair spoke again:

> *"Alas, alas! If thy mother knew it,*
> *Sadly, sadly would she rue it."*

She leaned over to drink again and the lock of hair fell out of her dress and floated away. She did not notice this but the cunning maid did. Without the charm, the princess would be in her power now, she thought. So when the poor young bride had finished her drink and went to get back onto her horse, the maid said harshly, "I'm taking Falada now. You get up on the packhorse. But first I'll take your royal robes and you can wear mine." She was strong and powerful so the princess obeyed. Then the maid hissed at her, "If you tell anyone about this, even a single word, you will be killed. I promise you!" Falada saw and heard all this and noted it well.

At last they arrived at the bridegroom's court and there was great joy at their coming. The prince rushed to meet them and he lifted the maid down from Falada. She was wearing royal robes so he felt sure she was the one to be his bride. She was led up the steps into the castle but the true princess was told to stay outside in the courtyard with the other servants.

Now the prince's father, the king, happened to look outside and he saw a young and pretty girl standing there. She seemed to be a stranger so he asked the bride if she knew anything about her.

"Oh, she's just a rough girl I brought to keep me company," she said carelessly. "Can you find some work for her? She needn't be idle."

At first the old king couldn't think of any work, then he said, "She can help the lad who takes care of my geese."

So the real princess became a goose girl and she helped Curdken, the goose lad.

Next day the wrong bride spoke prettily to the prince: "Will you do something for me? Order your men to cut off the head of the horse that brought me here. It's badly behaved, dangerous and it tried to throw me off and kick me." Secretly she was afraid that one day Falada might tell the prince all she had done to the princess. Naturally, the prince suspected nothing so he gave the order and poor faithful Falada was killed.

The true princess wept when she heard this and she begged the huntsmen to hang Falada's head in a dark archway that led out of the city. She went through this arch morning and night with the geese and she thought she wouldn't feel so lonely if she could see Falada now and then.

Next day, as she and Curdken left the city with the geese she whispered: "Alas, poor Falada hanging there!" And the horse's head whispered back:

"Alas, princess, if these troubles your mother knew
Her tender loving heart would break in two."

They drove the geese outside and she sat down on a grassy bank. She untied her long hair which glittered like gold and shone like satin. Curdken thought it was beautiful. He wanted some for himself so he went to cut off a lock but the princess pushed him away and cried sweetly:

"Blow, breezes, blow,
Let Curdken's hat go!
Blow, breezes, blow
Let him after it go!
Over hill, dale and rock
Away let it be whirled
Till every golden lock
Is combed, brushed and curled."

At once a strong wind blew Curdken's hat away and he chased after it. By the time he came back the princess had finished combing her hair and had fastened it up again. Curdken was cross, he sulked all day until it grew dark and they took the geese back to the city in silence.

The next morning the princess spoke to Falada's head as they led the geese through the archway and it gave her the same reply:

"Alas, princess, if these troubles your mother knew
Her tender loving heart would break in two."

Once more the princess sat on the grass and let down her lovely hair. It glittered and gleamed so that Curdken was dazzled. He wanted to stroke it but she spoke the same words quickly yet gently to him once more.

At once a sudden gust again blew away Curdken's hat. This time it flew even further over the hills and far away. When he got back, hot and dusty, he was furious to see the lovely hair was all safely tied up.

Later, when the geese had been put away, Curdken went to see the old king.

"I can't have that strange girl with me any longer," he said.

"Why ever not?" the king asked. "She seems so quiet and gentle to me."

"She teases me all day long and never talks to me!"

"There must be some reason for this," said the king, "tell me all about it."

So Curdken talked about Falada the speaking horse, about the goose girl's golden hair and how sudden winds kept blowing his hat away. The king told him to be patient for one more day as he wanted to see these things for himself.

When morning came, the king hid himself behind the dark arch. He saw the goose girl and Curdken coming and sure enough she whispered to Falada: "Alas, poor Falada, hanging there," and the horse's words came back, just as Curdken had said:

"Alas, princess, if these troubles your mother knew
Her tender loving heart would break in two."

The king slipped away and reached the meadow where he hid behind a bush. With his own eyes he marvelled at the goose girl's wonderful hair. All happened as before. Curdken tried to steal a golden curl, the goose girl sang her song and a strange puff of wind blew the hat away. The king stole quietly back to the palace. He was puzzled and upset, so when the goose girl came back that night he asked her what all these strange things meant. She was terrified, and wondered what would happen to her now. Sobbing bitterly, she said, "I dare not tell you or I will be killed."

The king promised that nobody would harm her. He begged so hard and spoke so kindly that in the end she whispered the whole story to him. His heart was filled with pity and he ordered his servants to bring royal robes at once for her. Then he called his son and told him about his false and unworthy bride. When the prince saw the real bride he loved her at once. He admired her patience and gentleness and he wanted to cast out the untrustworthy maid there and then. The king asked him to say nothing for a while as he had thought of a special plan.

On the next day, the king ordered a splendid feast for all his court. The trumpets sounded and the prince sat at the head of the table with the false bride on one side and the true princess on the other. Nobody guessed that this was the little goose girl they'd seen in the meadow. She dazzled everybody by her beauty.

After they had feasted well, the old king said he wanted to tell some old tales. So he told the story of the princess as if it were one he'd heard long ago. When he had finished he turned to the false bride and said, "What would you do to anyone who betrayed her mistress, killed her horse and played false with me and the prince?"

"Such a wretch deserves to be punished severely," she said. "She should be pushed into a barrel with sharp nails stuck inside, then two horses should drag it round the city, street by street till she cries for mercy."

"You are that wretched woman," cried the king. "You have judged yourself and that shall be your punishment!" And so the wicked servant was justly dealt with.

The prince married the true golden-haired princess and they reigned over the kingdom in peace and happiness for the rest of their lives.

THE SACRED HONEY BEES

Greek Legend

Many years ago, in the time of the Ancient Greeks, people believed that Zeus was the chief of all the gods and it was said that he was specially kind to everybody who had looked after him when he was a baby. Honey and goat's milk had been his favourite food: so when Amalthea the goat, who had provided him with milk in his infancy, was very old, he did not allow her to die but he turned her into the lovely group of stars high in the heavens which we call Capricorn. He gave the bees, which provide honey, their lovely gold and ebony bodies and he made their wings tiny but very strong.

Many years later in Greece, it chanced that a slave called Comatas used to take his master's flock of goats each day to the grassy slopes of Mount Helicon. He was very happy in the warm summer months for then he could stay out all day and all night with the goats. He found plenty of berries to eat and he drank the pure sparkling water from the mountain streams when he was thirsty. In the hot midday sun he rested under bushes while the goats grazed peacefully around him. At night he wrapped himself in a shepherd's cloak and slept under the stars. He was as happy as a slave could be and he was pleased to be left on his own. He carved some pipes out of reeds and made up many happy tunes to amuse himself. He felt sure that Mount Helicon was an enchanted place where kind spirits lived. Sometimes he even thought he could hear soft music and see shadowy figures dancing on the mountain top.

Then one night the full moon was shining brightly and he was resting when he heard clearly the sounds of music and dancing. Silently, he rose to his feet and crept nearer to the sounds. To his amazement he saw in the clear moonlight many nymphs or woodland fairies dancing in a circle by a sparkling waterfall. In the middle of the circle there were some lovely goddesses who were singing the sweetest songs Comatas had ever heard.

"Ah," thought Comatas, "this is the reason why I have always thought Mount Helicon must be a magic mountain! What wonderful music. Who can they be?"

Near the waterfall he noticed a small altar. Now it was the

custom at that time to offer gifts to the gods and goddesses on these altars and Comatas wished he had something he could offer that night.

"There are nine singers," he counted, but at that moment a cloud passed over the moon and everything went dark. When it became clear again the singers, the dancers, all had disappeared and Comatas walked back to his flock.

He did not know that the mountain was the favourite sacred meeting place of the Nine Muses. People believed they were the goddesses who gave poetry, music, dancing and other gentle arts to the world. Nor did he know that the woodland nymphs often listened, hidden among the trees, to the sound of his merry piping. Each day now he remembered all that he had seen and heard on that moonlit night and this made him long to put an offering on the altar by the waterfall. But Comatas was a slave. He owned nothing. Even his rough shepherd's cloak belonged to his master. He thought and thought as he watched his flock and then he had an idea. He spent all the days of his life with the goats and he was the only one who looked after and loved them. Perhaps after all this time one little tiny kid might belong to him?

Comatas made up his mind to kill a kid and place it on the altar near the waterfall as an offering to the gods.

It then happened that his master decided to count his goats. He found out at once that one was missing and flew into a terrible rage. "Worthless, dishonest slave," he shouted, "what have you done with my goat?" He forgot that his slave had been a wonderful shepherd for many years and he did not allow Comatas to explain what had happened. He ordered his servants to drag the poor fellow to the village and throw him into a big chest behind the master's house. Then he turned the key and shouted: "You killed my goat to feed yourself. Now you can die of starvation as a punishment."

On the mountain the nymphs looked around for Comatas. They missed the cheerful music from his pipes and each day they wondered where he was. When he did not come back, they decided to send a butterfly to look for him in the village.

The butterfly flitted into the stables and into the barns but it could not find Comatas. It went inside the rich man's house, but there was no sign of the slave. At last, the butterfly came to rest on the big chest and it peeped through the keyhole and spotted Comatas lying there, weak and helpless. At once, it flew back to the nymphs and they thought of a plan to rescue the slave.

The very next day swarm after swarm of bees flew to the village. They buzzed around the chest outside the rich man's house and one by one they flew in through the keyhole. Those clever bees went in with their honey-bags filled to the brim with honey but they were quite empty when they flew out. The bees went on doing this day after day, month after month.

When a whole year had passed by, the master decided to clear out the chest. He ordered his servants to open it up and he felt sure they would find the skeleton of the slave. To everyone's astonishment Comatas greeted them very cheerfully. He was alive and well! He told them that the bees had flown in through the keyhole and built honeycombs all round the chest. He had eaten enough to keep himself alive. The master knew that the bees were greatly loved by Zeus, so he thought that his slave must be loved by the god as well. So he himself lifted his slave out of the chest and ever afterwards Comatas was treated kindly and respectfully.

THE TALE OF QUEEN SHAHARAZAD

Arabian Nights

In Persia long ago there lived a king called Shahriyar. His wife was beautiful and he thought she loved him as much as he loved her. Then he found out that she was planning to kill him so that she could marry someone else. He was furious. In his rage he killed her. Worse was to come. Shahriyar vowed that each day he would marry any girl he chose. Then she would be beheaded the next day.

He kept his wicked promise, so secretly parents started to send their daughters to other places. Before long the only girls left were the two daughters of the Grand Vizier. He did not wish to lose his daughters so when the king demanded another girl he said fearfully, "There are no maidens left, Your Majesty, in any of our cities."

"Bring me a maiden by tomorrow," the king thundered, "or you will lose your head. And she must be beautiful. Now, be off with you."

Sadly the Vizier went home. Now his elder daughter Shaharazad was as clever as she was beautiful. She loved reading all kinds of stories and she had a marvellous memory. At dinner she saw her father's sad face and she knelt before him.

"What troubles you, dear father?" she asked. "Why are you not eating?" The Vizier did not answer but his daughter went on asking questions until he said, "The king will execute me tomorrow because I cannot find a young beautiful girl to take to his palace."

"In Allah's name," Shaharazad cried, "give me to the king, O father! Either I die and your life will be saved – or I will live!"

Her father was horrified. At first he would not agree but finally he knew that clever Shaharazad had thought of a plan so he asked his servants to get everything ready before he took her to the palace. The girl asked her father to allow Dunyazad, her younger sister, to go with her, and he agreed at once.

Next day Shaharazad wore her bridal dress made from cloth-of-gold. A shimmering veil covered her shining black hair. Her teeth were like glistening pearls and silken lashes fluttered around her dark sparkling eyes. She looked so lovely that the servants wept for they were sure they would never see her alive again. Shaharazad did not shed a single tear but her poor father almost died from sorrow when he left her and Dunyazad at the palace.

On the palace steps Shaharazad whispered to her sister:

"Dearest sister, I need your help. Tomorrow I will ask the king to let me see you in his rooms. You must come an hour before the dawn and pretend to say goodbye to me. But first you must offer a cup of sherbet to the king. Then you must beg me to tell you a story before the sun reddens the sky. Remember this carefully, little sister, for it may save our lives."

So next morning Dunyazad went along carrying two cups of cool sherbet and she spoke softly to the king and Shaharazad, "Will you not tell me a story before the sun reddens the sky and makes the land so hot?"

"Gladly I will, if my noble lord agrees," her sister replied. King Shahriyar waved his hand. "A story will pass the time well," he thought, "before I have to execute yet another lovely girl."

Shaharazad began the story called 'The Merchant and the Genie'.

"A merchant was sitting under a tree eating bread and dates. He threw away the date stones and he forgot to say 'Destoor' which means 'excuse me, please, may I do this?' At once a fearsome genie appeared. He had a wickedly curved scimitar in one hand and he shouted at the frightened merchant, 'You've just killed my son. You hit him on the chest with your date stones. Now I will kill you!'

'Mercy,' begged the merchant. 'It was only a little date stone! I have a wife and children at home. Please spare my life.'

'You must die,' said the genie and he threw the merchant on the ground and lifted his scimitar. The merchant wailed and begged for mercy. 'You can take my life,' he cried, 'but allow me to say goodbye to my family. Give me but one year and I swear I'll return here.' The genie lowered his scimitar, muttered to himself, then he disappeared.

The merchant went home. He told his wife and children what had happened. The year flew by and the time came when he had to keep his promise to the genie. His wife and children cried bitterly as he set off. He reached the palm tree and, trembling with fear, he knelt down and waited for death."

Shaharazad stopped speaking. "The sun has risen," she said. "There is no more time."

"But what happened to the poor merchant?" her sister asked.

"It's very strange," she replied. "I'd be happy to tell you the rest of the story if only I had time." And she sighed.

"By Allah," the king said, "I must know if the genie killed that honest man who kept his word."

"Tomorrow I will tell you," replied the girl. "If I'm alive!"

Next morning Dunyazad came with cups of delicious sherbet and she begged Shaharazad to go on with the story. The king agreed, so she continued:

"Two men came walking past the merchant. They were dressed in rich clothes and one led two black dogs with silver chains while the other had a gazelle on a gold chain. They asked the man why he looked so miserable. He told them his story and then the genie suddenly appeared, holding his sharp scimitar over his head.

'Don't be in a hurry to kill this man,' one stranger begged. 'Let me tell you why my wife was turned into this gazelle.'

'And I'll tell you why my brothers were turned into black dogs,' said the other, 'and if you like our stories, O genie, then we'd each like half this merchant's life as our reward.'

The fierce genie agreed to this. He lowered his scimitar and he listened carefully to their stories. He liked them so much that he gave them their reward. The merchant's life was spared!"

Shaharazad stopped here. "I see the sun is rising," she said. "I wish I had time, sweet sister, to tell you about 'The Pickpocket and the Thief'. It is more exciting than this tale about the genie."

"By Allah," exclaimed the king, "I must hear it if it is better than this one. Be ready to tell it tomorrow at the same time!" With that he swept out of the room to meet his ministers.

Shaharazad remembered many stories and she was very clever when she told them. Sometimes she stopped at an exciting moment when she knew the sun was rising. She left Aladdin alone in the dark cave and she stopped when the sea-king had taken the baby prince under the sea in the story of 'The Pomegranate of the Sea'. Another time she stopped when Sinbad the Sailor was sinking on his ship. The king listened eagerly to her tales and each time he could not bear to kill her until he knew what happened next!

For a thousand nights Shaharazad told her tales then on the thousand and first night she did something different. She ended her story completely even though the sun had risen and she did not whet the king's appetite with the title of another. Her sister was frightened. She could not beg for the rest of the story for it was finished. Then she saw that her sister was actually smiling at the king. "For a thousand nights, O King," Shaharazad said, "I have told you stories about people who had amazing adventures. Did they please you? And if you liked them will you now give me some reward?"

King Shahriyar felt overcome. He often gave gold and silver to his subjects when they served him well. Yet this girl had never asked for anything. Furthermore, while she was telling her marvellous stories he had fallen in love with her. But he was worried about breaking his old promise.

"I vowed to kill any girl I married," he said but Shaharazad stopped him gently: "Vows which are evil must not be kept."

"I am ashamed of that vow," the king replied, "and to tell the truth, I could not have executed you for I know you are the best wife a king could have. Can you forgive me? Will you be my true queen? Ask for any reward and it shall be yours."

"Please tell my father, the Grand Vizier, that Dunyazad and I are well," she said joyously, "and promise that no more maidens will die ever again." King Shahriyar promised gladly and he and Queen Shaharazad lived happily for many years thereafter.

PRINCE RABBIT

A. A. Milne

Once upon a time there was a King who had no children. Sometimes he would say to the Queen, "If only we had a son!" and the Queen would answer, "If only we had!" Another day he would say, "If only we had a daughter!" and the Queen would sigh and answer, "Yes, even if we had a daughter, that would be something." But they had no children at all.

As the years went on, and there were still no children in the Royal palace, the people began to ask each other who would be the next King to reign over them. And some said that perhaps it would be the Chancellor, which was a pity, as nobody liked him very much; and others said that there would be no King at all, but that everybody would be equal. Those who were lowest of all thought that this would be a satisfactory ending of the matter, but those who were higher up felt that, though in some respects it would be a good thing, yet in other respects it would be an ill-advised state of affairs; and they hoped, therefore, that a young Prince would be born in the palace. But no Prince was born.

One day, when the Chancellor was in audience with the King, it seemed well to him to speak what was in the people's minds.

"Your Majesty," he said, and then stopped, wondering how best to put it.

"Well?" said the King.

"Have I Your Majesty's permission to speak my mind?"

"So far, yes," said the King.

Encouraged by this, the Chancellor resolved to put the matter plainly. "In the event of Your Majesty's death –" He coughed and began again. "If Your Majesty ever *should* die," he said, "which in any case will not be for many years – if ever – as, I need hardly say, Your Majesty's loyal subjects earnestly hope – I mean they hope it will be never. But assuming for the moment – making the sad assumption –"

"You said you wanted to speak your mind," interrupted the King. "Is that it?"

"Yes, Majesty."

"Then I don't think much of it."

"Thank you, Your Majesty."

"What you are trying to say is, 'Who will be the next King?'"

"Quite so, Your Majesty."

"Ah!" The King was silent for a little. Then he said, "I can tell you who won't be."

The Chancellor did not seek for information on this point, feeling that in the circumstances the answer was obvious.

"What do you suggest yourself?"

"That Your Majesty choose a successor from among the young and the highly born of this country, putting him to whatever test seems good to Your Majesty."

The King pulled at his beard and frowned. "There must be not one test, but many tests. Let all who will offer themselves, provided only they are under the age of twenty and well born. See to it."

He waved his hand in dismissal, and with an accuracy established by long practice, the Chancellor retired backwards out of the palace.

On the following morning, therefore, it was announced that all those who were ambitious to be appointed the King's successor, and who were of high birth and not yet come to the age of twenty, should present themselves a week later for the tests to which His Majesty desired to put them, the first of which would be a running race. Whereat the people rejoiced, for they wished to be ruled by one to whom they could look up, and running was much esteemed in that country.

On the appointed day the excitement was great. All along the course, which was once round the castle, large crowds were massed, and at the finishing point the King and Queen themselves were seated in a specially erected pavilion. And to this the competitors were brought to be introduced to Their Majesties. There were nine young nobles, well built and handsome and (it was thought) intelligent, who were competitors. And there was also one Rabbit.

The Chancellor had first noticed the Rabbit when he was lining up the competitors, pinning numbers on their backs so that the people should identify them, and giving them such instructions as seemed necessary to him. "Now, now, be off with you," he said. "Competitors only, this way." And he made a motion of impatient dismissal with his foot.

"I *am* a competitor," said the Rabbit. "And I don't think it is usual," he added with dignity, "for the starter to kick one of the competitors just at the beginning of an important foot race. It looks like favouritism."

"*You* can't be a competitor," laughed all the nobles.

"Why not? Read the rules."

The Chancellor, feeling rather hot suddenly, read the rules. The Rabbit was certainly under twenty; he had a pedigree which showed that he was of the highest birth; and –

"And," said the Rabbit, "I am ambitious to be appointed the King's successor. Those were all the conditions. Now let's get on with the race."

But first came the introduction to the King. One by one the competitors came up . . . and at the end –

"This," said the Chancellor, as airily as he could, "is Rabbit."

Rabbit bowed in the most graceful manner possible, first to the King and then to the Queen. But the King only stared at him. Then he turned to the Chancellor.

"Well?"

The Chancellor shrugged his shoulders. "His entry does not appear to lack validity," he said.

40

"He means, Your Majesty, that it is all right," explained Rabbit.

The King laughed suddenly. "Go on," he said. "We can always have a race for a new Chancellor afterwards."

So the race was started. And the young Lord Calomel was much cheered on coming in second, not only by Their Majesties, but also by Rabbit, who had finished the course some time before and was now lounging in the Royal pavilion.

"A very good style, Your Majesty," said Rabbit, turning to the King. "Altogether he seems to be a most promising youth."

"Most," said the King grimly. "So much so that I do not propose to trouble the rest of the competitors. The next test shall take place between you and him."

"Not racing again, please, Your Majesty. That would hardly be fair to His Lordship."

"No, not racing. Fighting."

"Ah! What sort of fighting?"

"With swords," said the King.

"I am a little rusty with swords, but I daresay in a day or two –"

"It will be now," said the King.

"You mean, Your Majesty, as soon as Lord Calomel has recovered his breath?"

The King answered nothing, but turned to his Chancellor. "Tell the young Lord Calomel that in half an hour I desire him to fight with this Rabbit –"

"The young Lord Rabbit," murmured the other competitor to the Chancellor.

"To fight with him for my kingdom."

"*And* borrow me a sword, will you?" said Rabbit. "Quite a small one. I don't want to hurt him."

So, half an hour later, on a level patch of grass in front of the pavilion, the fight began. It was a short but exciting struggle. Calomel, whirling his long sword in his strong right arm, dashed upon Rabbit, and Rabbit, carrying his short sword in his teeth, dodged between Calomel's legs and brought him toppling. And when it was seen that the young lord rose from the ground with a broken arm, and that with the utmost gallantry he had now taken his sword in his left hand, the people cheered. And Rabbit, dropping his sword for a moment, cheered too, and then he picked it up and got it entangled in his adversary's legs again, so that again young Lord Calomel crashed to the ground, this time with a sprained ankle. And so there he lay.

Rabbit trotted into the Royal pavilion and dropped his sword in the Chancellor's lap. "Thank you so much," he said. "Have I won?" And the King frowned and pulled at his beard. "There are other tests," he muttered.

But what were they to be? It was plain that Lord Calomel was in no condition for another physical test. What, then, of an intellectual test?

"After all," said the King to the Queen that night, "intelligence is a quality not without value in a ruler."

"Is it?" asked the Queen doubtfully.

"I have found it so," said the King, a trifle haughtily.

"Oh," said the Queen.

"There is a riddle of which my father was fond, the answer to which has never been revealed save to the Royal House. We might make this the final test between them."

"What is the riddle?"

"I fancy it goes like this." He thought for a moment and then recited it, beating time with his hand.

> *"My first I do for your daylight,*
> *Although 'tis neither black nor white.*
> *My second looks the other way,*
> *Yet always goes to bed by day.*
> *My whole can fly and climb a tree,*
> *And sometimes swims upon the sea."*

"What is the answer?" asked the Queen.

"As far as I can remember," said His Majesty, "it is either *Dormouse* or *Raspberry*."

"*Dormouse* doesn't make sense," objected the Queen.

"Neither does *Raspberry*," pointed out the King.

"Then how can they guess it?"

"They can't. But my idea is that young Calomel should be secretly told beforehand what the answer is, so that he may win the competition."

"Is that fair?" asked the Queen doubtfully.

"Yes," said the King. "Certainly. Or I wouldn't have suggested it."

So it was duly announced by the Chancellor that the final test between the young Lord Calomel and Rabbit would be the solving of an ancient riddle-me-ree which in the past had baffled all save those of Royal blood. Copies of the riddle had been sent to the competitors, and in a week from that day they would be called upon to give their answers before Their Majesties and the full court. And with Lord Calomel's copy went a message, which said this:

"*From a Friend.* The answer is *Dormouse*. BURN THIS."

The day came around; and Calomel and Rabbit were brought before Their Majesties; and they bowed to Their Majesties and were ordered to be seated, for Calomel's ankle was still painful to him. And when the Chancellor had called for silence, the King addressed those present, explaining the conditions of the test to them.

"And the answer to the riddle," he said, "is in this sealed paper, which I now hand to my Chancellor, in order that he shall open it as soon as the competitors have told us what they know of the matter."

The people, being uncertain what else to do, cheered slightly.

"I will ask Lord Calomel first," His Majesty went on. He looked at his Lordship, and His Lordship nodded slightly. And Rabbit, noticing that nod, smiled suddenly to himself.

The young Lord Calomel tried to look very wise, and he said, "There are many possible answers to this riddle-me-ree, but the best answer seems to me to be *Dormouse*."

"Let someone take a note of that answer," said the King: whereupon the chief secretary wrote down: "LORD CALOMEL — *Dormouse*."

"Now," said the King to Rabbit, "what suggestion have you to make in this matter?"

Rabbit, who had spent an anxious week inventing answers each more impossible than the last, looked down modestly.

"Well?" said the King.

"Your Majesty," said the Rabbit with some apparent hesitation, "I have a great respect for the intelligence of the young Lord Calomel, but I think in this matter he is mistaken. The answer is not, as he suggests, *Woodlouse*, but *Dormouse*."

"I SAID *Dormouse*," cried Calomel indignantly.

"I thought you said *Woodlouse*," said Rabbit in surprise.

"He certainly said *Dormouse*," said the King coldly.

"*Woodlouse*, I think," said Rabbit.

"'LORD CALOMEL — *Dormouse*,'" read out the chief secretary.

"There you are," said Calomel. "I did say *Dormouse*."

"My apologies," said Rabbit, with a bow. "Then we are both right, for *Dormouse* it certainly is."

The Chancellor broke open the sealed paper and, to the

amazement of nearly all present, read out, "*Dormouse* . . . Apparently, Your Majesty," he said in some surprise, "they are both equally correct."

The King scowled. In some way which he didn't quite understand, he had been tricked.

"May I suggest, Your Majesty," the Chancellor went on, "that they be asked now some question of a different order, such as can be answered, after not more than a few minutes' thought, here in Your Majesty's presence? Some problem in the higher mathematics, for instance, such as might be profitable for a future King to know."

"What question?" asked His Majesty, a little nervously.

"Well, as an example – what is seven times six?" And behind his hand he whispered to the King. "Forty-two."

Not a muscle of the King's face moved, but he looked thoughtfully at the Lord Calomel. Supposing His Lordship did not know!

"Well?" he said reluctantly. "What is the answer?"

The young Lord Calomel thought for some time and then said, "Fifty-four."

"And you?" said the King to Rabbit.

Rabbit wondered what to say. As long as he gave the same answers as Calomel, he could not lose in the encounter, yet in this case, 'forty-two' was the right answer. But the King, who could do no wrong, even in arithmetic, might decide, for the purposes of the competition, that 'fifty-four' was an answer more becoming to the future ruler of the country. Was it, then, safe to say 'forty-two'?

"Your Majesty," he said, "there are several possible answers to this extraordinary novel conundrum. At first sight the obvious solution would appear to be 'forty-two'. The objection to this solution is that it lacks originality. I have long felt that a progressive country such as ours might well strike out a new line in the matter. Let us agree that in future seven sixes are fifty-four. In that case the answer, as Lord Calomel has pointed out, is 'fifty-four'. But if Your Majesty would prefer to cling to the old style of counting, then Your Majesty and Your Majesty's Chancellor would make the answer 'forty-two'."

After saying which, Rabbit bowed gracefully, both to Their Majesties and to his opponent, and sat down again.

The King scratched his head in a puzzled sort of way. "The correct answer," he said, "is, or will be in future, 'fifty-four'."

"Make a note of that," whispered the Chancellor to the chief secretary.

"Lord Calomel guessed this at his first attempt; Rabbit at his second attempt. I therefore declare Lord Calomel the winner."

"Shame!" said Rabbit.

"Who said that?" cried the King furiously.

Rabbit looked over his shoulder with the object of identifying the culprit, but was apparently unsuccessful.

"However," went on the King, "in order that there should be no doubts in the minds of my people as to the absolute fairness with which this competition is being conducted, there will be one further test. It happens that a King is often called upon to make speeches and exhortations to his people, and for this purpose ability to stand evenly upon two legs for a considerable length of time is of much value to him. The next test, therefore, will be —"

But at this point Lord Calomel suddenly cleared his throat so loudly that the King had perforce to stop and listen to him.

"Quite so," said the King. "The next test, therefore, will be held in a month's time, when His Lordship's ankle is healed, and it will be a test to see who can balance himself longest upon two legs only."

Rabbit lolloped back to his home in the wood, pondering deeply.

Now, there was an enchanter who lived in the wood, a man of many magical gifts. He could (it was averred by the countryside) extract coloured ribbons from his mouth, cook plum puddings in a hat, and produce as many as ten handkerchiefs, knotted together, from a twist of paper. And that night, after a simple dinner of salad, Rabbit called upon him.

"Can you," he said, "turn a rabbit into a man?"

The enchanter considered this carefully. "I can," he said at last, "turn a plum pudding into a rabbit."

"That," said Rabbit, "to be frank, would not be a helpful operation."

"I can turn almost anything into a rabbit," said the enchanter with growing enthusiasm. "In fact, I like doing it."

Then Rabbit had an idea. "Can you turn a man into a rabbit?"

"I did once. At least, I turned a baby into a baby rabbit."

"When was that?"

"Eighteen years ago. At the court of King Nicodemus. I was giving an exhibition of my powers to him and his good Queen. I asked one of the company to lend me a baby, never thinking for a moment that — The young Prince was handed up. I put a red silk handkerchief over him and waved my hands. Then I took the

45

handkerchief away . . . The Queen was very distressed. I tried everything I could, but it was useless. The King was most generous about it. He said that I could keep the rabbit. I carried it about with me for some weeks, but one day it escaped. Dear, dear!" He wiped his eyes gently with a red silk handkerchief.

"Most interesting," said Rabbit. "Well, this is what I want you to do." And they discussed the matter from the beginning.

A month later the great standing competition was to take place. When all was ready, the King rose to make his opening remarks.

"We are now," he began, "to make one of the most interesting tests between our two candidates for the throne. At the word 'Go!' they will —" and then he stopped suddenly. "Why, what's this?" he said, putting on his spectacles. "Where is the young Lord Calomel? And what is that second rabbit doing? There was no need to bring your brother," he added severely to Rabbit.

"I am Lord Calomel," said the second rabbit meekly.

"Oh!" said the King.

"Go!" said the Chancellor, who was a little deaf.

Rabbit, who had been practising for a month, jumped on his back paws and remained there. Lord Calomel, who had had no practice at all, remained on all fours. In the crowd at the back the enchanter chuckled to himself.

"How long do I stay like this?" asked Rabbit.

"This is all very awkward and distressing," said the King.

"May I get down?" said Rabbit.

"There is no doubt that Rabbit has won," said the Chancellor.

"Which rabbit?" cried the King crossly. "They're both rabbits."

"The one with the white spots behind the ears," said Rabbit helpfully. "May I get down?"

There was a sudden cry from the back of the hall. "Your Majesty?"

"Well, well, what is it?"

The enchanter pushed his way forward. "May I look, Your Majesty?" he said in a trembling voice. "White spots behind the ears? Dear, dear! Allow me!" He seized Rabbit's ears and bent them this way and that.

"Ow!" said Rabbit.

"It is! Your Majesty, it is!"

"Is what?"

"The son of the late King Nicodemus, whose country is now joined to your own. Prince Silvio."

"Quite so," said Rabbit airily, hiding his surprise. "Didn't any of you recognize me?"

"Nicodemus only had one son," said the Chancellor, "and he died as a baby."

"Not died," said the enchanter, and forthwith explained the whole sad story.

"I see," said the King, when the story was ended. "But of course that is neither here nor there. A competition like this must be conducted with absolute impartiality." He turned to the Chancellor. "Which of them won that last test?"

"Prince Silvio," said the Chancellor.

"Then, my dear Prince Silvio —"

"One moment," interrupted the enchanter excitedly. "I've just thought of the words. I *knew* there were some words you had to say."

He threw back his red silk handkerchief over Rabbit and cried, "Hey presto!"

And the handkerchief rose and rose and rose . . . And there was Prince Silvio!

You can imagine how loudly the people cheered. But the King appeared not to notice that anything surprising had happened.

"Then, my dear Prince Silvio," he went on, "as the winner of this most interesting series of contests, you are appointed successor to our throne."

"Your Majesty," said Silvio, "this is too much." And he turned to the enchanter and said, "May I borrow your handkerchief for a moment? My emotion has overcome me."

So on the following day Prince Rabbit was duly proclaimed heir to the throne before all the people. But not until the ceremony was over did he return the enchanter's red handkerchief.

"And now," he said to the enchanter, "you may restore Lord Calomel to his proper shape."

And the enchanter placed his handkerchief on Lord Calomel's head and said, "Hey presto!" and Lord Calomel stretched himself and said, "Thanks very much." But he said it rather coldly, as if he were not really very grateful.

So they all lived happily for a long time. And Prince Rabbit married the most beautiful Princess of those parts, and when a son was born to them there was much feasting and jollification. And the King gave a great party, whereat minstrels, tumblers, jugglers and suchlike were present in large quantities to give pleasure to the company. But, in spite of a suggestion made by the Princess, the enchanter was not present.

"But I hear he is so clever," said the Princess to her husband.

"He has many amusing inventions," replied the Prince, "but some of them are not in the best of taste."

"Very well, dear," said the Princess.

BLACK BEAUTY

Anna Sewell (from the novel *Black Beauty)*

I was now beginning to grow handsome, my coat had grown fine and soft, and was bright black. I had one white foot and a pretty white star on my forehead. I was thought very handsome; my master would not sell me till I was four years old; he said lads ought not to work like men, and colts ought not to work like Horses till they were quite grown up.

When I was four years old, Squire Gordon came to look at me. He examined my eyes, my mouth, and my legs; he felt them all down, and then I had to walk and trot and gallop before him; he seemed to like me and said, "When he has been well broken in he will do very well." My master said he would break me in himself, as he should not like me to be frightened or hurt, and he lost no time about it, for the next day he began.

Every one may not know what breaking in is, therefore I will describe it. It means to teach a Horse to wear a saddle and bridle, and to carry on his back a man, woman or child; to go just the way they wish, and to go quietly. Besides this, he has to learn to wear a collar, a crupper, and a breeching, and to stand still while they are put on; then to have a cart or a chaise fixed behind, so that he cannot walk or trot without dragging it after him; and he must go fast or slow, just as his driver wishes. He must never start at what he sees, nor speak to other Horses, nor bite, nor kick, nor have any will of his own, but always do his master's will, even though he may be very tired or hungry; but the worst of all is, when his harness is once on, he may neither jump for joy nor lie down for weariness. So you see this breaking in is a great thing.

I had long been used to a halter and a head-stall, and to be led about in the fields and lanes quietly, but now I was to have a bit and bridle; my master gave me some oats as usual, and after a good deal of coaxing he got the bit into my mouth and the bridle fixed, but it was a nasty thing. Those who have never had a bit in their mouths cannot think how badly it feels; a great piece of cold hard steel as thick as a man's finger to be pushed into one's mouth, between one's teeth, and over one's tongue, with the ends coming out at the corners of your mouth, and held fast there by straps over your head, under your throat, round your nose, and under your chin; so that no way in the world can you get rid of the nasty hard thing; it is very bad! At least I thought so; but I knew my mother always wore one when she went out, and so what with the nice oats, and what with my master's pats, kind words, and gentle ways, I got to wear my bit and bridle.

Next came the saddle, but that was not half so bad; my master put it on my back very gently, while old Daniel held my head; he then made the girths fast under my body, patting and talking to me all the time; then I had a few oats, then a little leading about; and this he did every day till I began to look for the oats and the saddle. At length, one morning, my master got on my back and rode me around the meadow on the soft grass. It certainly did feel queer; but I must say I felt proud to carry my master, and as he continued to ride me a little every day, I soon became accustomed to it.

The next unpleasant business was putting on the iron shoes; that too was very hard at first. My master went with me to the smith's forge, to see that I was not hurt or got any fright. The blacksmith took my feet in his hand one after the other, and cut away some of the hoof. It did not pain me, so I stood still on three legs until he had done them all. Then he took a piece of iron the shape of my foot, and clapped it on, and drove some nails through the shoe quite into my hoof, so that the shoe was firmly on. My feet felt very stiff and heavy, but I got used to it.

And now having got so far, my master went on to break me to harness; there were more new things to wear. First, a stiff heavy collar just on my neck, and a bridle with great side-pieces against my eyes, called blinkers, and blinkers indeed they were, for I could not see on either side, but only straight in front of me; next there was a small saddle with a nasty stiff strap that went right under my tail; that was the crupper. I hated the crupper – to have my long tail doubled up and poked through that strap was almost as bad as the bit. I felt like kicking, but of course I could not kick such a good master, and so in time I got used to everything, and could do my work as well as my mother.

I must not forget to mention one part of my training, which I have always considered a very great advantage. My master sent me for a fortnight to a neighbouring farmer's, who had a meadow which was skirted on one side by the railway. Here were some Sheep and Cows, and I was turned in among them.

I shall never forget the first train that ran by. I was feeding quietly near the pales which separated the meadow from the railway, when I heard a strange sound at a distance, and before I knew whence it came – with a rush and a clatter, and a puffing of smoke – a long black train of something flew by, and was gone almost before I could draw my breath. I turned and galloped to the farther side of the meadow as fast as I could go, and there I stood snorting with astonishment and fear. In the course of the day many other trains went by, some more slowly; these drew up at the station close by, and sometimes made an awful shriek and groan before they stopped. I thought it very dreadful, but the Cows went on eating very quietly, and hardly raised their heads as the black, frightful thing came puffing and grinding past. For the first few days I could not feed in peace; but as I found that this terrible creature never came into the field, or did me any harm, I began to disregard it, and very soon I cared as little about the passing of a train as the Cows and Sheep did.

Since then I have seen many Horses much alarmed and restive at the sight or sound of a steam engine; but, thanks to my good master's care, I am as fearless at railway stations as in my own stable. Now if anyone wants to break in a young Horse well, that is the way.

My master often drove me in double harness, with my mother, because she was steady and could teach me how to go better than a strange Horse. She told me the better I behaved the better I should be treated, and that it was wisest always to do my best to please my master. "But," said she, "there are a great many kinds of men; there are good, thoughtful men, like our master, that any Horse may be proud to serve, and there are cruel men, who never ought to have a Horse or a Dog to call their own. Besides, there are a great many foolish men, ignorant and careless, who never trouble themselves to think; these spoil more Horses than all, just for want of sense; they don't mean it, but they do it for all that. I hope you will fall into good hands; but a Horse never knows who may buy him, or who may drive him, it is all a chance for us; but do your best wherever it is, and keep up your good name."

POMEGRANATE OF THE SEA

Arabian Nights

In faraway Persia long ago a rich king lived in a palace by the sea. He had everything he wanted except for one thing. He had neither a son nor a daughter to take over his kingdom and he felt very sad indeed.

One day he was sitting in his garden when a merchant came up to him and asked him to buy a slave girl he had with him. When the king lifted her veil he was astonished. She was so beautiful, with long black hair, cherry-red lips and big dark eyes.

"If only she would fall in love with me," he thought, "I'd be a happy man." He gave much gold to the merchant and the lovely slave stayed behind with him in the palace by the sea.

The king spoke gently to her but she said not a word. He gave her jewels, rich gowns and slave girls to wait on her. They led her to a beautiful room and at once she went to the wide window and gazed out across the sea. Yet still she did not utter a sound. They brought baskets of fruit and the king himself picked out the best and sweetest fruits and popped them into her mouth. She swallowed them down but not a sound passed her lips.

It was the same the next day. The king was angry. He wanted to force her to speak somehow but when he looked at her she was so lovely that his anger disappeared. Instead, he decided to marry her. So the slave girl became a queen. She gazed at the king with her beautiful dark eyes when the wedding took place but not a word did she utter, not even at the magnificent wedding feast in the palace.

"I'd be the happiest man in the world," thought the king, "if only my beautiful wife would speak to me."

In time the queen gave birth to a fine baby boy. The king was delighted. "This little prince will be king one day," he said proudly to the queen. "But can you not say one word of love to me? Will you make a sign if you cannot speak for I love you above all else." He lifted his lute and sang sweetly to her.

She lifted her head. She looked straight at the king for the first time. At last she spoke. Her voice was soft, sweet and musical.

"O King, you have been patient for so long. Now I will tell you

53

my story. My name is Jallanar which means 'Pomegranate Flower'.
My father was the king-of-the-sea, but I quarrelled with my brother
when he became the new king. I would not live in the sea any longer
so I left him, my mother and my sisters, and I rose out of the waves.
I sat on a rock until a merchant came along. He tied me up and
tried to make me marry him. He was cruel and I hated him. I kicked
him hard one day, so he planned to sell me as a slave. And you
bought me, O King."

"That was the best deed I have ever done," smiled the king.

"If you had treated me unkindly," the queen continued, "I
would have left you. I could have thrown myself back into the sea
from this window at any time. You were so gentle and kind that I
started to love you. Yet I kept silent to see if your love would fade
away and you would treat me as a slave girl again."

"I am your slave now," the king said happily. "Everything I
have is yours. What can I give you? What do you long for?"

"I long for one thing only," she said. "I wish to see my family. I
want them to see our little son."

"I'll send messengers at once," the king said but the queen
shook her head. "They cannot walk on the sea," she told him. "I will

call my family myself. Will you stay hidden and listen to our talk?"

The king gladly gave his promise and hid behind a stone pillar. Jallanar went outside on the terrace. She lit a small fire with scented wood then she blew the smoke over the sea. She whispered some magic words and gave a low sweet whistle.

At once huge waves rose up and crashed on the terrace walls. A tall young man dressed in wonderful robes stepped out of the foam. A stately old lady and five lovely girls followed him. The king peeped out. He was surprised to see that their clothes were dry as they walked on the waves to the palace steps by the terrace.

"My daughter," said the old lady, "we are happy to see you, safe and well. We miss you so much. Please come back to the land-of-the-sea with us."

"Please come," begged the girls. "Our quarrel is over."

The poor king trembled as he listened. Would she leave him?

Then Jallanar spoke, "I love you all dearly but I have learnt to love the king-of-the-land who has treated me so well. We have a son now. I cannot leave my child nor take him away for he will be the next king of this rich and peaceful country."

"We rejoice that you are happy," said her mother quietly as Jallanar went to the king's hiding place. "I was worried lest they persuaded you to leave me," he whispered. Then Jallanar led him to meet the sea-king, her mother and her sisters. The king-of-the-land ordered his servants to prepare a splendid feast. Later on, Jallanar asked her family to bless the new little prince. His grandmother and Jallanar's sisters blessed him gently then his uncle took him in his arms. As soon as the sea-king held the baby he turned and walked down the steps into the sea.

"The prince! Our baby! We'll never see him alive again," exclaimed the king. "Do not worry," said Jallanar, "remember that I came from the sea so our son is part of the sea-family too. My brother will not let any harm come to him, I promise you!"

Soon the sea-king walked back across the sea and gave the baby back to his mother. "Your little son is safe now from sea dangers," he told the worried king. "He will be able to walk on land and sea. And for you, I have brought some presents." The sea-king dropped pearls and diamonds at the feet of the king-of-the-land.

The sea-people stayed in the palace for many days then they returned to the sea. The king, Jallanar and the little prince lived happily together and each year the sea-king and his family walked over the waves to visit them in the palace by the sea.

THE STONECUTTER

Japanese Traditional

Many years ago there lived a stonecutter in Japan. His job was to slice huge slabs of stone out of the rock in the mountain near his home. He was a good workman for he understood all about the different kinds of stones which his customers needed. Some wanted them for houses, for roofs and even for gravestones. There was plenty of work for him and each day when he walked to the rock with his pick he was happy and cheerful. People told him a spirit who could make men rich lived in the mountain but he only smiled and said he'd never seen or heard such a spirit.

One day the stonecutter delivered a gravestone to a rich man's house. He looked around and his eyes widened in surprise when he saw so many beautiful things. Slowly he went back to work and it

seemed to him that his pick had suddenly become heavier and the rock was harder to cut.

"If I were a rich man," he sighed, "I'd have a soft bed with silk cushions and satin curtains. How happy I'd be!"

"Your wish is granted," a voice whispered. "You shall be a rich man." When he heard this, the stonecutter looked around but he could not see anybody.

"It must be my imagination," he thought. "Ah well, I think I'll pack up and go home. I don't feel like doing any more work today."

Off he went down the mountain. But what a surprise he had! His little home was no longer there. Instead there was a grand palace. He rushed inside and in every room he found splendid furniture and to his great joy there was a wonderful bed waiting for him. From that time on he forgot all about stonecutting.

It was now summertime in Japan and the sun blazed fiercely every day. One morning the stonecutter was so hot that he decided to stay inside his palace. He peeped through the silk curtains to see what was going on in the street below. At that moment a pretty chair was passing by. It was carried by servants dressed in blue and silver and inside the chair sat a prince. Another servant held a golden umbrella over his head to shade him from the strong sunshine.

"If I were a prince," the stonecutter sighed, "I'd have a chair and a servant to hold a gold umbrella over me. How happy I'd be!"

"Your wish is granted," a voice answered. "You shall be a prince."

And that is what happened. Servants dressed in scarlet and gold carried his chair, and over his head a servant held a gold umbrella trimmed with diamonds and rubies.

However, he soon became discontented and wondered what he should wish for now. His face was getting browner even though the umbrella was held over his head all day. The grass around his palace was brown too, even though the servants poured water over it each morning. He shouted crossly, "The sun is so powerful. If only I were the sun."

"Your wish is granted. You shall be the sun." It was the voice of the mountain spirit which answered him.

So he became the sun and he loved the power of his rays. He darted round the world and burned the faces of princes and scorched their grass. But before long he grew tired of shining all the time and wondered what to do next. Then a cloud drifted past. It covered his face and he could not see the earth. He shone and he shone then he shouted angrily, "This little cloud is covering me. It is more powerful than I, the mighty sun! If only I were a cloud."

"Your wish is granted. You shall be a cloud," the mountain spirit answered.

At once the stonecutter became a cloud floating easily between the earth and the sun. He played games and covered up the sun's face to tease him. Then he noticed that the grass became green and the flowers started to bloom as he shaded the earth from the sun's hottest rays and sent down cooling showers. He felt very pleased with himself but once again he grew tired of this and instead of gentle rains he poured out heavy storms for days and weeks without stopping. The rivers overflowed their banks. People's houses fell down. Their crops were destroyed and they soon had no food. Towns and cities were ruined by the rains and only the huge rock in the mountain was left standing, solid and unmoving.

"That rock seems to be stronger than I am," said the cloud. "Ah me, if only I were the rock, how happy I would be."

"Your wish is granted," the mountain spirit called. "You shall be the rock."

The stonecutter felt very proud as he stood on the mountainside. He need not worry about heavy rain or baking sunshine because he was so strong and powerful: "This is the best wish of all," he said to himself.

A few days later he heard a strange noise. When he looked down he saw that a stonecutter was pushing some tools into the rock. Into him! And at that moment he felt a funny feeling running right through him and a big piece of stone broke off. It crashed to the ground and the workman started to chip away at him again.

"So," shouted the rock, "is a small man stronger than a huge rock? Oh, if only I were a man! How happy I would be."

The mountain spirit laughed sweetly and answered:

"Your wish is granted. You shall be a man all over again."

Well, he did become a man and a stonecutter once more.

It was hard work cutting the rock and then pulling the stone down the mountainside. His bed in his little house was hard and it did not have any silk cushions or curtains. He was often burned brown by the sun's strong rays but he had plenty of work and his customers paid him well, so he always had enough money to buy food and clothes – and a paper umbrella! He did not want to change into anything else, he decided, for he was happy as he was.

Strange to say, he never heard the voice of that mountain spirit again.

EAST OF THE SUN AND WEST OF THE MOON

Norwegian Traditional

Once upon a time a farmer and his wife lived in a broken-down cottage. Their ten children never had enough food or clothes. All of them were handsome, but the youngest girl was the prettiest of them all.

One night there was a dreadful storm. The wind was howling and the rain was beating against the windows so the family huddled together round a miserable little fire. Suddenly somebody tapped three times on the window. The father opened the door and a great White Bear was standing there.

"Good evening," said the White Bear politely. The man gasped in surprise. "I'd like you to give me your youngest daughter," White Bear said, "and if you agree, you and your family will be rich for evermore."

"I'd like that," the man replied, "but I'll have to ask my daughter. Please wait here."

Well, the youngest daughter said a loud "No". So the father went outside and asked the White Bear to come back another night. Then he told his daughter what a marvellous time they could have if only she would agree to go away with the White Bear. "It will be good for you too," he said. In truth, he said this so many times that at last she changed her mind. She washed and mended her ragged clothes, brushed her hair until it shone and got everything ready so that she could set out on this exciting adventure.

White Bear came back a few nights later. She climbed on his back with her little bundle and off they went into the forest.

After a time White Bear said, "Are you scared, pretty maiden?"

"Not even a little bit," she answered and White Bear grunted, "If you hold tight to my fur, there won't be any danger, I promise you."

They went on until they came to a high mountain. White Bear knocked on it and a door opened. They went into a castle blazing with lights. Every room was full of gold and silver and fine furniture and the girl stared in amazement. They stopped at a table which was covered with delicious food and White Bear lowered her gently

to the floor. "Take this silver bell," he said. "Ring it whenever you want anything and it will appear at once."

She was hungry after her long journey so she had a good meal and then she felt sleepy. She thought she would like to go to bed so she rang the bell. In a second she found herself in a beautiful warm room with the prettiest bed she had ever seen all ready for her. She undressed and put out the lights. Then she was aware that a man had come in and was standing by the door. She could not see him clearly as it was so dark. She slept soundly and when she woke at daybreak, he was gone.

She spent many contented days exploring the magnificent castle. Each night she slept in the lovely bed and the man would stand in the doorway, but he always disappeared before daybreak, so she never saw his face.

After some time she began to feel sad and lonely.

"What is the matter?" asked White Bear, "Is there something you want?"

"I'm sorry," the girl said, "you've been so very kind to me, but it is dull and quiet here. I miss my brothers and sisters very much."

"Well," White Bear said kindly, "perhaps I can help you. I'll take you to see them, but you must promise one thing. You must not talk to your mother unless the family are with you. She will take your hand and ask you to go into another room with her. You must not do this or you will make both of us miserable. Promise me this one thing!"

The girl promised, so one Sunday White Bear came to the castle to collect her. She jumped on his back and they journeyed for a long time until they reached a big white farmhouse. Her brothers and sisters, wearing rich clothes, were laughing and chatting in the beautiful gardens.

"This is your father's house now," White Bear said. "Go and talk to your family but don't forget your promise, whatever you do!"

"Of course I won't forget," she said as she skipped away. Her parents cried with joy when they saw her. "Look, dearest daughter," they said, "we have everything we need now and it is all thanks to you."

"Where do you live? Are you happy? Who is White Bear?" They asked many questions. That afternoon White Bear's words came true. Her mother wanted to talk to her alone. The girl would not go at first, but her mother kept asking and asking until at last she went with her.

"Tell me what you do all the time, dear daughter," her mother asked. So the girl told her about the wonderful castle, then she sighed, "It is so lonely there all day and I never see the man who comes each night because my room is too dark and he disappears when the sun rises."

"Oh," cried her mother, "it must be a wicked troll! But this is what you must do. Take this piece of candle and hide it in your dress. Light it when the man is asleep but take care. You must not let any candle wax drop on him."

The girl hid the candle and that night White Bear carried her off again.

They travelled many miles and White Bear suddenly stopped. "Your mother spoke to you, didn't she?" he said. "I hope you haven't done anything foolish."

"No, no," the girl answered, "I haven't done anything at all!"

After they reached the castle, she went to bed as usual and the man lay down inside the door and went to sleep. At midnight she got out of bed, lit her candle and crept towards him. When the tiny light shone on his face she saw that it was the most handsome prince in the world! She bent over and kissed him gently, but as she did so, three drops of wax fell on his shirt. He awoke instantly. "What have you done?" he cried sadly. "I warned you, didn't I! My stepmother is a troll. She bewitched me, so I am White Bear all day and a prince at night. She lives East of the Sun and West of the Moon and I must go to her horrible castle now. Her magic will make me marry a princess with a nose three ells long. We will be parted now for ever."

"Let me go with you!" the girl pleaded over and over again. But he shook his head. "Tell me how to find you then," she begged. "Surely I am allowed to look for you?"

"You cannot find me, East of the Sun and West of the Moon," she heard him whisper before the candle went out and she fell asleep.

When she woke the castle had gone. She was lying in a dark wood wearing the ragged dress she had brought from her old home. She jumped to her feet and without wasting any time at all, she set out to search for the prince.

For many long days she walked until she came to a huge rock. An old woman was sitting near it, holding a golden apple.

"Can you tell me how to get to a castle East of the Sun and West of the Moon?" the girl asked politely. "A prince lives there and his troll-stepmother wants him to marry a princess with a nose three ells long."

"How do you know this?" asked the old woman. "Are you the girl he wants to marry?" When she nodded her head the woman went on: "I know the castle is East of the Sun and West of the Moon, and a long way from here. You'd better borrow my horse and ride to my neighbour. She can tell you something more. And you'd better take this golden apple. It may be useful to you."

The girl thanked her and rode many miles until she came to another rock where another old lady was sitting with a gold carding-comb. The girl asked the same questions and she heard the same answers: "The castle you seek is East of the Sun and West of the Moon. You'd better use the horse and ride to my neighbour. And take this carding-comb. It may come in useful."

Once more the girl rode on until she saw a third old woman. She was spinning on a golden spinning-wheel and the girl heard her say softly: "East of the Sun and West of the Moon. Ride on to the East Wind, he may blow you to the castle. You can take this spinning-wheel along with you."

Day after day she rode along until at last she found the East

Wind. "Please can you help?" she asked. "I seek a castle East of the Sun and West of the Moon."

"I've heard of it," East Wind said, "but I've never blown so far as that. Brother West Wind is stronger than I am, I'll take you to see him." She got on his back and quickly they found West Wind. "I'm afraid I've never blown East of the Sun or West of the Moon," West Wind said, "but I'll carry you to South Wind for he is very strong and blows far and wide. Maybe he can tell you where to go. Jump on my back and hold tight."

Off they went and very quickly they reached South Wind who shook his head when West Wind asked him what he knew about a prince in a castle.

"I've wandered to many places," he said, "but I've never seen this castle. Brother North Wind is the oldest and strongest wind – he knows everything! I'll take you to him if you'll jump on my back."

The girl sat wearily on his back and before long they felt the icy breath of North Wind. They almost froze when he shouted, "What do you want, South Wind?"

"This is the girl who should marry the prince in the castle East of the Sun and West of the Moon. Have you been there? Can you tell her where to go? The poor girl is so tired and weary."

"Yes," said North Wind, "but it will be dangerous because I blow very hard."

"I'm not afraid," said the girl. "I only want to get there to find the prince."

So North Wind huffed and puffed and the girl clung to him. She felt bitterly cold and her teeth chattered but at last North Wind blew her gently into the castle garden which lay East of the Sun and West of the Moon.

The girl took out the golden apple and suddenly the princess with the long nose came up to her. "How much money do you want for that apple?" she asked.

"Money cannot buy it," said the girl.

"What do you want then?" asked the princess, "I'll give you anything you wish for."

"If I may see the prince tonight, you can take the apple," the girl said. "That's easy enough," the princess replied, but she smiled cruelly behind her hand when the girl gave her the golden apple.

Happily the girl visited the prince that night, but he was asleep. She shook him but she could not wake him up, and at daybreak the long-nosed princess pushed her outside. The girl took out the golden carding-comb and the princess now wanted this. She promised to let the girl visit the prince in exchange for the comb, and the girl agreed. But again that night the prince lay sleeping. She shook him, she cried loudly, but he did not move and at daybreak the princess pushed her roughly outside again.

Then the girl started to spin on her golden spinning-wheel and the princess wanted that as well. Once more the girl agreed to exchange the spinning-wheel for a chance to see the prince. But the prince had grown suspicious, and that night he only pretended to drink what the princess offered him, for he felt sure she was giving him a sleeping-potion. He was wide awake this time when the girl went to his room and was overjoyed to see her. "My brave girl," he said, "you alone can save me, for tomorrow I am to marry the long-nosed princess, but I have thought of a plan."

He whispered in her ear so that nobody except the girl could hear and next morning, he spoke boldly to his troll-stepmother:

"I wish to wear this fine shirt at my wedding," he said, "but there are three spots of wax on it. I'll only marry the one who can clean them off. Can the princess do this?" He knew, you see, that trolls cannot touch wax.

"How easy," the princess thought and she seized the shirt. She scrubbed and she scrubbed but those spots grew bigger and bigger. The troll-stepmother grabbed it. "I'll show you how to do it," she said. But the more she rubbed the blacker the spots looked. She called all the trolls in the castle to help but they made the shirt blacker than the blackest soot.

"You're good for nothing," the prince cried. "That beggar-girl over there can wash better than any of you," and he gave the shirt to the girl. As soon as she dipped it into the water it became as white as snow. "We'll be married now," the prince said joyfully. "You dropped the wax so I knew you were the only one who could wash it away. Thank you for everything you've done for me."

The troll-stepmother was so angry she exploded on the spot and the troll-princess and all the little trolls disappeared in a puff of smoke.

North Wind blew the prince and his bride gently away from the castle East of the Sun and West of the Moon to their own home where they lived happily with their family for many peaceful years.

ROBIN HOOD MEETS LITTLE JOHN

A Robin Hood Story

Robin Hood and his band of outlaws lived in Sherwood Forest many years ago.

One day, Robin felt restless. "Will," he called to his trustiest friend, "I'm going through the forest to see what is happening out there. Don't come with me but keep your ears open for my horn. If you should hear three blasts then I need help. Come quickly then!"

"We'll certainly do that," replied Will, "but have a care, good master."

It was a lovely day when Robin set off. He followed a narrow path which led him to the banks of a wide stream. A big tree trunk had fallen over the water and it made a rough and ready bridge. It looked dangerous for it was slippery and bumpy but Robin was not worried. He climbed up and the trunk started to sway and creak. He balanced himself carefully then slowly he edged forward. He took two or three steps then he stopped in surprise. Another man was coming over this makeshift bridge from the other side. He looked at least seven feet tall! He had broad strong shoulders, a thick beard and he was carrying a heavy blackthorn staff. Both men glared at each other.

Slowly they walked to the middle of the tree trunk. Then they stopped.

"Step aside," Robin said commandingly, "or go back, whichever you like."

"Who are you to give me orders?" came the reply. "I'll only give way to a better man than myself. Go back yourself."

"Better man!" Robin spluttered. "I'll soon show you! You'll feel my arrows if you're not careful and into the water you'll go."

"That's a cowardly thing to say," said the man, "when you can see plainly that I am not carrying a bow and arrows."

"I'm no coward," Robin said. "I see you have a staff. Give me time to make one. We'll see then who will cross this bridge first."

Robin went back to the bank and cut himself an oak staff six feet long. "The first to tumble into the water is the loser," called Robin.

The men twirled their staffs and the fight began. Robin swung his staff. His opponent caught the fearful blow on his blackthorn staff and in return gave a blow that should have knocked Robin out, but at the last moment he swerved. His shoulder was hurt but not his head. He lunged forward, his staff hit the stranger's ribs but he only grunted, "This fight is getting better! You're warming me up nicely. Watch out for your head!" Robin ducked and landed another fierce blow. The bridge shook as the men fought violently. They moved back, then forwards. It looked as if the fight would never end when Robin landed a huge blow and his opponent wobbled and almost fell into the water. As he struggled to keep on his feet, his stick swung round and caught Robin by surprise. He yelled as his feet shot out from under him. Into the water he splashed, head over heels.

"Dear me," laughed the big man, "I fear you are getting wet, my boy!" Robin coughed and spluttered as he stood up. Then he saw the funny side of it all. His green jerkin was covered with mud.

"You beat me in a fair fight," he said. "You have a strong arm."

"Here, let me pull you out of the water," the big man said.

Together the men rested on the bank, still panting and puffing. "Well," the man announced, "you've taken your defeat bravely. You remind me of someone who lives in this forest. I've been told he is as brave as a lion and twice as cunning. Have you heard of him? His name is Robin Hood."

Robin smiled to himself as he lifted up his hunting horn and blew three short blasts. "What are they for?" the stranger asked curiously but Robin didn't reply.

Soon there came a rustling from the bushes. The stranger looked round in alarm as about twenty men dressed in Lincoln green rushed towards them. He seized his staff, jumped to his feet and got ready to fight all over again. Will stared at Robin. "You are wet from head to foot!" he exclaimed.

"Yes," said Robin, "this fellow gave me a beating on yonder tree and tumbled me head over heels into the stream."

"Come on, lads," cried Will. "We'll give him the same!"

The outlaws sprang to the attack but the stranger defended himself so well that several of them soon had to move away, but they managed at last to hold him down. They carried him to the bank and tossed him far into the water.

"Dear friend," said Robin mockingly, "I fear you are soaked!"

The man took Robin's helping hand and climbed on to the bank. The others burst out laughing and he shook his fist at them.

"Come along," he cried, "I'll fight you one, two, five at a time. Nobody laughs at me!" and he moved towards them.

Robin held on to his arm. "You laughed at me!" he said. "Let the fighting end here. We both have had a soaking. Honour is satisfied."

"All right," he said slowly, "but tell me, who are you?"

"First of all, tell us about yourself," replied Robin.

"John Naylor is my name, I'm looking for Robin Hood. I want to join his band and I hope to put my hand in his."

"Put your hand here then," said Robin as he held out his own.

"You are Robin Hood!" John Naylor exclaimed. "Impossible!"

"I am he, and gladly you can join my band."

Will stepped forward. "There's something we must do, Robin. We must give this bonny fellow a new name. From now on, as he's so tall, let us call him Little John!"

"This has been a day of adventure," laughed Robin Hood. "I have a sore head and sore ribs but I have found a new and true friend – Little John."

THE SILLY KING

Terry Jones

King Herbert XII had ruled wisely and well for many years. But eventually he grew very old and, although his subjects continued to love him dearly, they all *had* to admit that as he had grown older he had started to do *very* silly things. One day, for example, King Herbert went out of his palace and walked down the street with a dog tied to each leg. Another time, he took off all his clothes and sat in the fountain in the principal square, singing selections of popular songs and shouting "Radishes!" at the top of his voice.

Nobody, however, liked to mention how silly their king had become. Even when he hung from the spire of the great cathedral, dressed as a parsnip and throwing Turkish dictionaries at the crowd below, no one had the heart to complain. In private they would shake their heads and say: "Poor old Herbert – whatever will he do next?" But in public everyone pretended that the King was as grave and as wise as he had always been.

Now it so happened that King Herbert had a daughter whom, in a moment of slightly more silliness than usual, he had named Princess Fishy – although everyone called her Bonito. Rather conveniently, the Princess had fallen in love with the son of their incredibly rich and powerful neighbour, King Rupert, and one day it was announced that King Rupert intended to pay a state visit to King Herbert to arrange the marriage.

"Oh dear!" said the Prime Minister. "Whatever shall we do? Last time King Herbert had a visitor, he poured custard over his head and locked himself in the broom cupboard."

"If only there was someone who could make him act sensibly," said the Lord Chancellor, "just while King Rupert's here at any rate."

So they put up a notice offering a thousand gold pieces to anyone who could help. And from the length and breadth of the land came doctors offering their services, but it was all no use. One eminent doctor had a lotion which he said King Herbert must rub on his head before going to bed, but King Herbert drank it all on the first night, and was very ill. So a second eminent doctor produced a powder to cure the illness caused by the first doctor, but King Herbert put a match to it, whereupon it exploded and blew his eyebrows off. So a third doctor produced a cream to replace missing eyebrows, but King Herbert put it on his teeth and they all turned bright green overnight.

Not one of the doctors could make King Herbert less silly, and he just got ill from their lotions and potions and creams and powders.

Eventually the day of the state visit arrived, and King Herbert was still swinging from the chandeliers in the throne room and hitting people with a haddock.

Everyone was very agitated. The Prime Minister had chewed his nails right down to nothing, and the Lord Chancellor had gnawed through his chain of office, but no one had any idea of what to do. Just then the Princess Fishy stood up and said: "Since no one else can help, let me try."

"Don't talk nonsense, Bonito!" said the Prime Minister. "Fifty of the most eminent doctors in the land have failed to cure the King, what could *you* possibly do?"

"I may not be able to cure the King," said the Princess, "but if I could show you how to turn an egg into solid gold, then would you do as I said?"

And the Lord Chancellor said: "Princess, if you could indeed show us how to turn an egg into solid gold, then we should certainly do as you told us."

"For shame!" said the Princess. "Then you should do as I say now. I can no more turn an egg into solid gold than you can, but even if I could it wouldn't prove that I could help my father."

Well, the Lord Chancellor and the Prime Minister looked at each other and, because they had no ideas themselves, and because they had no other offers of help, they agreed to do what the Princess told them.

Shortly afterwards, King Rupert arrived. There were fanfares of trumpets; drums rolled; the people cheered, and they looked for King Rupert's son, but they couldn't see him. King Rupert was dressed in gold and rode a white horse, and on his head he bore the richest crown anyone had ever seen. The Lord Chancellor and the Prime Minister met him at the gates of the town and rode with him down the main street.

Suddenly, just as they were about to enter the palace, an old woman rushed out of the crowd and threw herself in front of King Rupert's horse.

"Oh, King Rupert!" she cried. "Dreadful news! An army of fifty thousand soldiers is marching through your country!"

King Rupert said: "Surely that cannot be!" But just then a messenger in King Rupert's own livery rode up on a horse and cried: "It's true, Your Majesty! It's more like a million of them – I've never seen so many!"

King Rupert went deadly pale and fell off his horse in a faint.

They carried him into the throne room, where King Herbert was standing on his head, balancing a box of kippers with his feet. Eventually, King Rupert regained consciousness, and found his son and the Princess looking down at him.

"I am afraid we are homeless now, my dear," said King Rupert to the Princess. "An army of fifty million soldiers has overrun our country. Do you think your father will let us stay here to live?"

"Of course he will," said the Princess. "Only you mustn't mind if he's a bit silly now and again."

"Of course not," said King Rupert, "we're all a bit silly now and again."

"That's true," said the Prince. "For example, the old lady who stopped you outside the palace was none other than the Princess here, but you didn't recognize her."

"Indeed I did not," said King Rupert.

"And the messenger was none other than your own son," said the Princess, "and yet you didn't even recognize him."

"Indeed I did not," said King Rupert.

"Moreover," said the Princess, "you didn't even stop to consider how you could defeat that army of a million soldiers."

"I have no need to consider it," said King Rupert. "How could I possibly deal with an army of such a size?"

"Well, for a start you could pour a kettle of boiling water over them," said the Princess, "for they're only an army of soldier ants."

Whereupon King Rupert laughed out loud at his own silliness, and agreed that the Princess should marry the Prince without delay, and he didn't even mind when King Herbert poured lemonade down his trousers and put ice-cream all over his crown.

THE SQUIRE'S BRIDE

Norwegian Traditional

There was once a rich squire with a mint of silver in the barn and gold aplenty in the bank. He farmed over hill and dale, was ruddy and stout, yet he lacked a wife. So he had a mind to wed.

After all, since I am rich, he thought, I can pick and choose whatever maid I wish.

One afternoon the squire was wandering down the lane when he spotted a sturdy lass toiling in the hayfield. And he rubbed his grizzled chins, muttering to himself, "Oh aye, I fancy she'd do all right, and save me a packet on wages too. Since she's poor and humble she'll take my offer, right enough."

So he had her brought to the manor house where he sat her down, all hot and flustered.

"Now then, gal," he began, "I've a mind to take a wife."

"Mind on then," she said. "One may mind of much and more."

She wondered whether the old buffer had his sights set on her; why else should she be summoned?

"Aye, lass, I've picked thee out. Tha'll make a decent wife, sure enough."

"No thank you," said she, "though much obliged, I'm sure."

The squire's ruddy face turned ruby red; he was not used to people talking back. The more he blathered, the more she turned him down, and none too politely either. Yet the more she refused, the more he wanted what he could not have. With a final sigh, he dismissed the lass and sent for her father; perhaps the man would talk some sense into his daughter's head.

"Go to it, man," the squire roared. "I'll overlook the money you owe me and give you a meadow into the bargain. What d'ye say to that?"

"Oh, aye, Squire. Be sure I'll bring her round," the father said. "Pardon her plain speaking; she's young yet and don't know what's best."

All the same, in spite of all his coaxing and bawling, the girl was adamant – she would not have the old miser even if he were made of gold! And that was that.

When the poor farmer did not return to the manor house with the girl's consent, the squire stormed and stamped impatiently. And next day he went to call on the man.

"Settle this matter right away," he ranted on, "or it'll be the worse for you. I won't bide a day longer for my bride."

There was nothing for it. Together the master and the farmer hatched a plan: the squire was to see to all the wedding chores – parson, guests, wedding feast – and the farmer would send his daughter at the appointed hour. He would say nothing of the wedding to her, but just let her think that work awaited her up at the big house.

Of course, when she arrived she would be so dazzled by the wedding dress, afeared of the parson and awed by the guests that she would readily give her consent. How could a farm girl refuse the squire? And so it was arranged.

When all the guests had assembled at the manor and the white wedding gown laid out and the parson, in black hat and cloak, settled down, the master sent for a stable lad. "Go to the farmer," he ordered, "and bring back what I'm promised. And be back here in two ticks or I'll tan your hide!"

The lad rushed off, wondering what the promise was. In no time at all he was knocking on the farmer's door.

"My master's sent me to fetch what you promised him," panted the lad.

"Oh, aye, dare say he has," the farmer said. "She's down in the meadow; you'd better take her then."

Off ran the lad to the meadow and found the daughter raking hay.

"I've come to fetch what your father promised the squire," he said all out of breath.

It did not take the girl long to figure out the plot.

So that's their game, she thought, a twinkle in her eye. "Right, then, lad, you'd better take her then. It's the old grey mare grazing over there."

With a leap and a bound the lad was on the grey mare's back and riding home at full gallop. Once there he leapt down at the door, dashed inside and called up to the squire.

"She's at the door now, Squire."

"Well done," called down the master. "Take her up to my old mother's room."

"But, master –"

73

"Don't but me, you scoundrel," the old codger roared. "If you can't manage her on your own, get someone else to help."

On glimpsing the squire's angry face he knew it was no use arguing. So he called some farmhands and they set to work. Some pulled the old mare's ears, others pushed her rump; they heaved and shoved until finally they got her up the stairs and into the empty room. There they tied the reins to a bedpost and let her be.

Wiping the sweat from his brow, the lad now reported to the squire.

"That's the darndest job I've ever done," he complained.

"Now send the wenches up to dress her in the wedding gown," said the squire.

The stable lad stared.

"Get on with it, dung-head. And tell them not to forget the veil and crown. Jump to it!"

Forthwith the lad burst into the pantry to tell the news.

"Hey, listen here, go upstairs and dress the old mare in wedding clothes. That's what the master says. He must be playing a joke on his guests."

The cooks and chambermaids all but split their sides with laughter. But in the end they scrambled up the stairs and dressed the poor grey mare as if she were a bride. That done, the lad went off once more to the squire.

"Right, lad, now bring her downstairs. I'll be in the drawing room with my guests. Just throw open the door and announce the bride."

There came a noisy clatter and thumping on the stairs as the old grey mare was prodded down; at last she stood impatiently in the hallway before the door. Then, all at once, the door burst open and all the guests looked round in expectation.

What a shock they got!

In trotted the old grey mare dressed up as a bride, with a crown sprawling on one ear, veil draped over her eyes, and gown covering her rump. Seeing the crowd, she let out a fierce neigh, turned tail and fled out of the house.

The parson spilled his glass of port all down his purple front; the squire gaped in amazement, the guests let out a roar of laughter that could be heard for miles around.

And the squire, they say, never went courting again.

As for the girl, some say she married, some say not. It matters little. What is certain is that she lived happily ever after.

BRER FOX GOES HUNTING

Joel Chandler Harris

Long ago an old man called Uncle Remus lived on a plantation in the southern states of America. He used to tell stories about Brer Rabbit and Brer Fox to a little boy.

One evening, he settled down in his big chair out on the veranda and he said:

"I recall a time when Brer Fox and Brer Rabbit got mighty friendly. Brer Fox would sometimes call on Brer Rabbit and they would sit up and smoke their pipes together. It was a mighty strange sight to see those two so close – but it wasn't to last." He paused for a moment and then the story began.

One day Brer Fox came along all rigged out to go hunting and asked Brer Rabbit to join him. Brer Rabbit, however, was feeling lazy and said he had other things to do, and sloped off for a nap.

Brer Fox was disappointed, but he went away by himself. He was gone all day and had a rare old time bagging game.

As evening drew in, Brer Rabbit woke up from his nap and thought, "Well, I reckon it's time old Brer Fox was coming home. I'll go and meet him."

Then up Brer Rabbit got and went and climbed a tree to watch out for Brer Fox.

Well, he hadn't been there long when, sure enough, he saw Brer Fox tripping through the woods whistling merrily to himself. Now, old Brer Rabbit, he leapt from the tree and lay on the road as if he were stone dead.

When Brer Fox came up to Brer Rabbit he stared at him a minute, then he turned him over and looked mighty closely at him, then said he, "This here rabbit is dead. He looks as if he's been dead a mighty long time. He's dead, but he's fat – he's the fattest rabbit I ever did see – but he's been dead too long, I'd better not take him home."

Brer Rabbit, he stayed mighty quiet.

Brer Fox was sore tempted, but he went his way and left old Brer Rabbit lying there on the road.

Now, Brer Rabbit, he opened one eye and when he saw Brer

Fox disappearing into the distance he got up in real haste and ran round through the woods and overtook Brer Fox walking along the road. Then Brer Rabbit, he lay down as if he were stone-cold dead.

Then Brer Fox, he came up to Brer Rabbit and stared. He thought a bit then he said, "This is another mighty fat dead rabbit. These here rabbits are just going to waste. I'll leave my game here and go back and get that other rabbit – my, everyone is going to be mighty impressed with all the game I've caught." With that, he dropped his game bag from his shoulder and went back down the road after the other dead rabbit.

Now, Brer Rabbit jumped up mighty quick, grabbed Brer Fox's game bag and made for home.

Next time Brer Rabbit met up with Brer Fox, he called out:

"What did you catch the other day, Brer Fox?"

"I caught a handful of common sense, Brer Rabbit," said he.

Then old Brer Rabbit, he gave a loud laugh and said, "If I'd known you were after that I'd have given you some of mine."

Old Uncle Remus leant back in his chair and peered at the little boy over his spectacles. "So clever old Brer Rabbit had tricked Brer Fox yet again – and I don't believe they were such good friends for a long, long time."

77

THE LAST OF THE DRAGONS

E. Nesbit

Of course you know that dragons were once as common as motor-omnibuses are now, and almost as dangerous. But as every well-brought-up prince was expected to kill a dragon, and rescue a princess, the dragons grew fewer and fewer, till it was often quite hard for a princess to find a dragon to be rescued from. And at last there were no more dragons in France and no more dragons in Germany, or Spain, or Italy, or Russia. There were some left in China, and are still, but they are cold and bronzy, and there were never any, of course, in America. But the last real live dragon left was in England, and of course that was a very long time ago, before what you call English History began. This dragon lived in Cornwall in the big caves amidst the rocks, and a very fine big dragon, quite seventy feet long from the tip of its fearful snout to the end of its terrible tail. It breathed fire and smoke, and rattled when it walked, because its scales were made of iron. Its wings were like half-umbrellas – or like bat's wings, only several thousand times bigger. Everyone was very frightened of it, and well they might be.

Now the King of Cornwall had one daughter, and when she was sixteen, of course she would have to go and face the dragon: such tales are always told in royal nurseries at twilight, so the Princess knew what she had to expect. The dragon would not eat her, of course – because the prince would come and rescue her. But the Princess could not help thinking it would be much pleasanter to have nothing to do with the dragon at all – not even to be rescued from him.

"All the princes I know are such very silly little boys," she told her father. "Why must I be rescued by a prince?"

"It's always done, my dear," said the King, taking his crown off and putting it on the grass, for they were alone in the garden, and even kings must unbend sometimes.

"Father, darling," said the Princess presently, when she had made a daisy chain and put it on the King's head, where the crown ought to have been. "Father, darling, couldn't we tie up one of the silly little princes for the dragon to look at – and then *I* could go and

78

kill the dragon and rescue the Prince? I fence much better than any of the princes we know."

"What an unladylike idea!" said the King, and put his crown on again, for he saw the Prime Minister coming with a basket of newlaid Bills for him to sign. "Dismiss the thought, my child. I rescued your mother from a dragon, and you don't want to set yourself up above her, I should hope?"

"But this is the *last* dragon. It is different from all other dragons."

"How?" asked the King.

"Because he *is* the last," said the Princess, and went off to her fencing lessons, with which she took great pains. She took great pains with all her lessons – for she could not give up the idea of fighting the dragon. She took such pains that she became the strongest and boldest and most skilful and most sensible princess in Europe. She had always been the prettiest and nicest.

And the days and years went on, till at last the day came which was the day before the Princess was to be rescued from the dragon. The prince who was to do this deed of valour was a pale prince, with large eyes and a head full of mathematics and philosophy, but he had unfortunately neglected his fencing lessons. He was to stay the night at the palace, and there was a banquet.

After supper the Princess sent her pet parrot to the Prince with a note. It said: "Please, Prince, come on to the terrace. I want to talk to you without anybody else hearing. – The Princess."

So, of course, he went – and he saw her gown of silver a long way off shining among the shadows of the trees like water in starlight. And when he came quite close to her he said:

"Princess, at your service," and bent his cloth-of-gold-covered knee and put his hand on his cloth-of-gold-covered heart.

"Do you think," said the Princess earnestly, "that you will be able to kill the dragon?"

"I will kill the dragon," said the Prince firmly, "or perish in the attempt."

"It's no use your perishing," said the Princess.

"It's the least I can do," said the Prince.

"What I'm afraid of is that it'll be the most you can do," said the Princess.

"It's the only thing I can do," said he, "unless I kill the dragon."

"Why you should do anything for me is what I can't see," said she.

"But I want to," he said. "You must know that I love you better than anything in the world."

When he said that he looked so kind that the Princess began to like him a little.

"Look here," she said, "no one else will go out tomorrow. You know they tie me to a rock, and leave me – and then everybody scurries home and puts up the shutters and keeps them shut till you ride through the town in triumph shouting that you've killed the dragon, and I ride on the horse behind you weeping for joy."

"I've heard that that is how it is done," said he.

"Well, do you love me well enough to come very quickly and set me free – and we'll fight the dragon together?"

"It wouldn't be safe for you."

"Much safer for both of us for me to be free, with a sword in my hand, than tied up and helpless. *Do* agree."

He could refuse her nothing. So he agreed. And next day everything happened as she had said.

When he had cut the cords that tied her to the rocks they stood on the lonely mountainside looking at each other.

"It seems to me," said the Prince, "that this ceremony could have been arranged without the dragon."

"Yes," said the Princess, "but since it has been arranged with the dragon –"

"It seems such a pity to kill the dragon – the last in the world," said the Prince.

"Well, then, don't let's," said the Princess; "let's tame it not to eat princesses but to eat out of their hands. They say everything can be tamed by kindness."

"Taming by kindness means giving them things to eat," said the Prince. "Have you got anything to eat?"

She hadn't, but the Prince owned that he had a few biscuits. "Breakfast was so very early," said he, "and I thought you might have felt faint after the fight."

"How clever," said the Princess, and they took a biscuit in each hand. And they looked here and they looked there, but never a dragon could they see.

"But here's its trail," said the Prince, and pointed to where the rock was scarred and scratched so as to make a track leading to the mouth of a dark cave. It was like cart-ruts in a Sussex road, mixed with the marks of seagulls' feet on the sea-sand. "Look, that's where it's dragged its brass tail and planted its steel claws."

"Don't let's think how hard its tail and its claws are," said the Princess, "or I shall begin to be frightened – and I know you can't tame anything, even by kindness, if you're frightened of it. Come on. Now or never."

She caught the Prince's hand in hers and they ran along the path towards the dark mouth of the cave. But they did not run into it. It really was so very *dark*.

So they stood outside, and the Prince shouted: "What ho! Dragon there! What ho within!" And from the cave they heard an answering voice and great clattering and creaking. It sounded as though a rather large cotton-mill were stretching itself and waking up out of its sleep.

The Prince and the Princess trembled, but they stood firm.

"Dragon – I say, Dragon!" said the Princess. "Do come out and talk to us. We've brought you a present."

"Oh, yes – I know your presents," growled the dragon in a huge rumbling voice. "One of those precious princesses, I suppose? And I've got to come out and fight for her. Well, I tell you straight, I'm not going to do it. A fair fight I wouldn't say no to – a fair fight and no favour – but one of these put-up fights where you've got to lose – No. So I tell you. If I wanted a princess I'd come and take her, in my own time – but I don't. What do you suppose I'd do with her, if I'd got her?"

"Eat her, wouldn't you?" said the Princess in a voice that trembled a little.

"Eat a fiddle-stick end," said the dragon very rudely. "I wouldn't touch the horrid thing."

The Princess's voice grew firmer.

"Do you like biscuits?" she asked.

"No," growled the dragon.

"Not the nice little expensive ones with sugar on the top?"

"*No*," growled the dragon.

"Then what *do* you like?" asked the Prince.

"You go away and don't bother me," growled the dragon, and they could hear it turn over, and the clang and clatter of its turning echoed in the cave like the sound of the steam-hammers in the Arsenal at Woolwich.

The Prince and Princess looked at each other. What *were* they to do? Of course it was no use going home and telling the King that the dragon didn't want princesses – because His Majesty was very old-fashioned and would never have believed that a new-fashioned dragon could ever be at all different from an old-fashioned dragon.

They could not go into the cave and kill the dragon. Indeed, unless he attacked the Princess it did not seem fair to kill him at all.

"He must like something," whispered the Princess, and she called out in a voice as sweet as honey and sugar-cane.

"Dragon – Dragon dear!"

"WHAT?" shouted the dragon. "Say that again!" and they could hear the dragon coming towards them through the darkness of the cave. The Princess shivered, and said in a very small voice:

"Dragon – Dragon dear!"

And then the dragon came out. The Prince drew his sword, and the Princess drew hers – the beautiful silver-handled one that the Prince had brought in his motor-car. But they did not attack; they moved slowly back as the dragon came out, all the vast scaly length of him, and lay along the rock – his great wings half-spread and his silvery sheen gleaming like diamonds in the sun. At last they could retreat no further – the dark rock behind them stopped their way – and with their backs to the rock they stood swords in hand and waited.

The dragon drew nearer and nearer – and now they could see that he was not breathing fire and smoke as they had expected – he came crawling slowly towards them wriggling a little as a puppy does when it wants to play and isn't quite sure whether you're cross with it.

And then they saw that great tears were coursing down its brazen cheek.

"Whatever's the matter?" said the Prince.

"Nobody," sobbed the dragon, "ever called me 'dear' before!"

"Don't cry, dragon dear," said the Princess. "We'll call you 'dear' as often as you like. We want to tame you."

"I *am* tame," said the dragon – "that's just it. That's what nobody but you has ever found out. I'm so tame that I'd eat out of your hands."

"Eat what, dragon dear?" said the Princess. "Not biscuits?"

The dragon slowly shook its heavy head.

"Not biscuits?" said the Princess tenderly. "What, then, dragon dear?"

"Your kindness quite undragons me," it said. "No one has ever asked any of us what we like to eat – always offering us princesses, and then rescuing them – and never once, 'What'll you take to drink the King's health in?' Cruel hard I call it," and it wept again.

"But what would you like to drink our health in?" said the Prince. "We're going to be married today, aren't we, Princess?"

She said that she supposed so.

"What'll I take to drink your health in?" asked the dragon. "Ah, you're something like a gentleman, you are, sir. I don't mind if I do, sir. I'll be proud to drink your and your good lady's health in a tiddy drop of" – its voice faltered – "to think of you asking me so friendly like," it said. "Yes, sir, just a tiddy drop of puppuppuppuppupetrol – tha – that's what does a dragon good, sir –"

"I've lots in the car," said the Prince, and was off down the mountain like a flash. He was a good judge of character, and he knew that with this dragon the Princess would be safe.

"If I might make so bold," said the dragon, "while the gentleman's away – p'raps just to pass the time you'd be so kind as to call me Dear again, and if you'd shake claws with a poor old dragon that's never been anybody's enemy but his own – well, the last of the dragons'll be the proudest dragon there's ever been since the first of them."

It held out an enormous paw, and the great steel hooks that

were its claws closed over the Princess's hand as softly as the claws of the Himalayan bear will close over the bit of bun you hand it through the bars at the Zoo.

And so the Prince and Princess went back to the palace in triumph, the dragon following them like a pet dog. And all through the wedding festivities no one drank more earnestly to the happiness of the bride and bridegroom than the Princess's pet dragon – whom she had at once named Fido.

And when the happy pair were settled in their own kingdom, Fido came to them and begged to be allowed to make himself useful.

"There must be some little thing I can do," he said, rattling his wings and stretching his claws. "My wings and claws and so on ought to be turned to some account – to say nothing of my grateful heart."

So the Prince had a special saddle or howdah made for him – very long it was – like the tops of many tramcars fitted together. One hundred and fifty seats were fitted to this, and the dragon, whose greatest pleasure was now to give pleasure to others, delighted in taking parties of children to the seaside. It flew through the air quite easily with its hundred and fifty little passengers – and would lie on the sand patiently waiting till they were ready to return. The children were very fond of it and used to call it dear, a word which never failed to bring tears of affection and gratitude to its eyes. So it lived, useful and respected, till quite the other day – when someone happened to say, in his hearing, that dragons were out-of-date, now so much new machinery had come in. This so distressed him that he asked the King to change him into something less old-fashioned, and the kindly monarch at once changed him into a mechanical contrivance. The dragon, indeed, became the first aeroplane.

THE YOUNG KING

Oscar Wilde

It was the night before the day fixed for his coronation, and the young King was sitting alone in his beautiful chamber. His courtiers had all taken their leave of him, bowing their heads to the ground, according to the ceremonious usage of the day, and had retired to the Great Hall of the Palace, to receive a few last lessons from the Professor of Etiquette; there being some of them who had still quite natural manners, which in a courtier is, I need hardly say, a very grave offence.

The lad – for he was only a lad, being but sixteen years of age – was not sorry at their departure, and had flung himself back with a deep sigh of relief on the soft cushions of his embroidered couch, lying there, wild-eyed and open-mouthed, like a brown woodland Faun, or some young animal of the forest newly snared by the hunters.

And, indeed, it was the hunters who had found him, coming upon him almost by chance as, bare-limbed and pipe in hand, he was following the flock of the poor goatherd who had brought him up, and whose son he had always fancied himself to be. The child of the old King's only daughter by a secret marriage with an artist – he had been, when but a week old, stolen away from his mother's side, as she slept, and given into the charge of a common peasant and his wife, who were without children of their own, and lived in a remote part of the forest, more than a day's ride from the town.

And it seems that from the very first moment he entered the Court he had shown signs of that strange passion for beauty that was destined to have so great an influence over his life. Those who accompanied him to the suite of rooms set apart for his service, often spoke of the cry of pleasure that broke from his lips when he saw the delicate raiment and rich jewels that had been prepared for him, and of the almost fierce joy with which he flung aside his rough leathern tunic and coarse sheepskin cloak. He missed, indeed, at times the freedom of the forest life, and was always apt to chafe at the tedious Court ceremonies that occupied so much of each day, but the wonderful palace – *Joyeuse*, as they called it – of which he now found himself lord, seemed to him to be a new world fresh-fashioned for his delight.

Upon his journeys of discovery, as he would call them – and, indeed, they were to him real voyages through a marvellous land, he would sometimes be accompanied by the slim, fair-haired Court pages with their floating mantles, and gay ribands; but more often he would be alone, feeling through a certain quick instinct, which was almost a divination, that the secrets of art are best learned in secret, and that Beauty, like Wisdom, loves the lonely worshipper.

All rare and costly materials had certainly a great fascination for him, and in his eagerness to procure them he had sent away many merchants, some to traffic for amber with the rough fisher-folk of the north seas, some to Egypt to look for that curious green turquoise which is found only in the tombs of kings, and is said to possess magical properties, some to Persia for silken carpets and painted pottery, and others to India to buy gauze and stained ivory, moonstones and bracelets of jade, sandalwood and blue enamel and shawls of fine wool.

But what had occupied him most was the robe he was to wear at his coronation, the robe of tissued gold, and the ruby-studded crown, and the sceptre with its rows and rings of pearls. Indeed, it was of this that he was thinking tonight, as he lay back on his luxurious couch, watching the great pinewood log that was burning itself out on the open hearth. The designs, which were from the hands of the most famous artists of the time, had been submitted to him many months before, and he had given orders that the artificers were to toil night and day to carry them out, and that the whole world was to be searched for jewels that would be worthy of their work. He saw himself in fancy standing at the high altar of the Cathedral in the fair raiment of a King, and a smile played and lingered about his boyish lips, and lit up with a bright lustre his dark woodland eyes.

Outside he could see the huge dome of the Cathedral, looming like a bubble over the shadowy houses, and the weary sentinels pacing up and down on the misty terrace by the river. Far away, in an orchard, a nightingale was singing. A faint perfume of jasmine came through the open window. He brushed his brown curls back from his forehead, and taking up a lute, let his fingers stray across the cords. His heavy eyelids drooped, and a strange languor came over him. Never before had he felt so keenly, or with such exquisite joy, the magic and mystery of beautiful things.

When midnight sounded from the clock-tower he touched a bell, and his pages entered and disrobed him with much ceremony, pouring rose-water over his hands, and strewing flowers on his pillow. A few moments after that they left the room; he fell asleep.

And as he slept he dreamed a dream, and this was his dream. He thought he was standing in a long, low attic, amidst the whir and clatter of many looms. The meagre daylight peered in through the grated windows, and showed him the gaunt figures of the weavers bending over their cases.

The young King went over to one of the weavers, and stood by him and watched him.

And the weaver looked at him angrily and said, "Why art thou watching me? Art thou a spy set on us by our master?"

"Who is thy master?" asked the young King.

"Our master!" cried the weaver, bitterly. "He is a man like myself. Indeed, there is but this difference between us – that he wears fine clothes while I go in rags, and that while I am weak from hunger he suffers not a little from overfeeding."

"The land is free," said the young King, "and thou art no man's slave."

"In war," answered the weaver, "the strong make slaves of the weak, and in peace the rich make slaves of the poor. We must work to live, and they give us such mean wages that we die. We toil for them all day long, and they heap up gold in their coffers, and our children fade away before their time, and the faces of those we love become hard and evil. We tread out the grapes, and another drinks the wine. We sow the corn, and our own board is empty. We have chains, though no eye beholds them; and we are slaves, though men call us free."

"Is it so with all?" he asked.

"Ay. It is so with all," answered the weaver. "But what are these things to thee? Thou art not one of us. Thy face is too happy." And he turned away scowling, and threw the shuttle across the loom, and the young King saw that it was threaded with a thread of gold.

And a great terror seized upon him, and he said to the weaver, "What robe is this that thou art weaving?"

"It is the robe for the coronation of the young King," he answered.

And the young King gave a loud cry and woke, and lo! he was in his own chamber, and through the window he saw the great honey-coloured moon hanging in the dusky air.

And he fell asleep again, and dreamed, and this was his dream. He thought that he was lying on the deck of a huge galley that was being rowed by a hundred slaves.

The slaves were naked, but for a ragged loincloth, and each man was chained to his neighbour. The hot sun beat brightly upon them, and the negroes ran up and down the gangway and lashed them with whips of hide. They stretched out their lean arms and pulled the heavy oars through the water. The salt spray flew from the blades.

At last they reached a little bay, and began to take soundings.

As soon as they had cast anchor and hauled down the sail, the negroes went into the hold and brought up a long rope-ladder, heavily weighted with lead. The master of the galley threw it over the side, making the ends fast to two iron stanchions. Then the negroes seized the youngest of the slaves and knocked his gyves off, and filled his nostrils and his ears with wax, and tied a big stone round his waist. He crept wearily down the ladder, and disappeared into the sea. A few bubbles rose where he sank.

After some time the diver rose up out of the water, and clung panting to the ladder with a pearl in his right hand. The negroes seized it from him, and thrust him back.

Again and again he came up, and each time that he did so he brought with him a beautiful pearl. The master of the galley weighed them, and put them into a little bag of green leather.

The young King tried to speak, but his tongue seemed to cleave to the roof of his mouth, and his lips refused to move. The negroes chattered to each other, and began to quarrel over a string of bright beads. Two cranes flew round and round the vessel.

Then the diver came up for the last time, and the pearl that he brought with him was fairer than all the pearls of Ormuz, for it was shaped like the full moon, and whiter than the morning star. But his face was strangely pale, and as he fell upon the deck the blood gushed from his ears and nostrils. He quivered for a little, and then he was still. The negroes shrugged their shoulders, and threw the body overboard.

And the master of the galley laughed, and, reaching out, he took the pearl, and when he saw it he pressed it to his forehead and bowed. "It shall be," he said, "for the sceptre of the young King."

And when the young King heard this he gave a great cry and woke, and through the window he saw the long grey fingers of the dawn clutching at the fading stars.

And he fell asleep again, and dreamed, and this was his dream. He thought that he was wandering through a dim wood, hung with strange fruits and with beautiful poisonous flowers. The adders hissed at him as he went by, and the bright parrots flew screaming from branch to branch. Huge tortoises lay asleep upon the hot mud. The trees were full of apes and peacocks.

On and on he went, till he reached the outskirts of the wood, and there he saw an immense multitude of men toiling in the bed of a dried-up river. They swarmed up the crag like ants. They dug deep pits in the ground and went down into them. Some of them cleft the rocks with great axes; others grabbled in the sand. They tore up the cactus by its roots, and trampled on the scarlet blossoms. They hurried about, calling to each other, and no man was idle.

From the darkness of a cavern Death and Avarice watched them, and Death said, "I am weary; give me a third of them and let me go."

But Avarice shook her head. "They are my servants," she answered.

And Death said to her, "What has thou in thy hand?"

"I have three grains of corn," she answered; "what is that to thee?"

"Give me one of them," cried Death, "to plant in my garden; only one of them, and I will go away."

"I will not give thee anything," said Avarice, and she hid her hand in the fold of her raiment.

And Death laughed, and took a cup, and dipped it into a pool of water, and out of the cup rose Ague. She passed through the great multitude, and a third of them lay dead. A cold mist followed her, and the water-snakes ran by her side.

And when Avarice saw that a third of the multitude was dead she beat her breast and wept. She beat her barren bosom, and cried aloud. "Thou hast slain a third of my servants," she cried. "What is my valley to thee, that thou shouldst tarry in it? Get thee gone and come here no more."

"Nay," answered Death, "but till thou hast given me a grain of corn I will not go."

But Avarice shut her hand, and clenched her teeth. "I will not give thee anything," she muttered.

And Death laughed, and took up a black stone, and threw it into the forest, and out of a thicket of wild hemlock came Fever in a robe of flame. She passed through the multitude, and touched them, and each man that she touched died. The grass withered beneath her feet as she walked.

And Avarice shuddered, and put ashes on her head. "Thou art cruel," she cried; "thou art cruel. There is famine in the walled cities of India, and the cisterns of Samarcand have run dry. There is famine in the walled cities of Egypt, and the locusts have come up from the desert. The Nile has now overflowed its banks, and the priests have nursed Isis and Osiris. Get thee gone to those who need thee, and leave me my servants."

"Nay," answered Death, "but till thou hast given me a grain of corn I will not go."

"I will not give thee anything," said Avarice.

And Death laughed again, and he whistled through his fingers, and a woman came flying through the air. Plague was written upon her forehead, and a crowd of lean vultures wheeled round her. She covered the valley with her wings, and no man was left alive.

And Avarice fled shrieking through the forest, and Death leaped upon his red horse and galloped away, and his galloping was faster than the wind.

And the young King wept, and said: "Who were these men, and for what were they seeking?"

"For rubies for a king's crown," answered one behind him.

And the young King started and, turning round, he saw a man habited as a pilgrim and holding in his hand a mirror of silver.

And he grew pale, and said: "For what king?"

And the pilgrim answered: "Look in this mirror and thou shalt see him."

And he looked in the mirror, and, seeing his own face, he gave a great cry and woke, and the bright sunlight was streaming into the room, and from the trees of the garden and pleasaunce the birds were singing.

And the Chamberlain and the high officers of State came in and made obeisance to him, and the pages brought him the robe of tissued gold, and set the crown and sceptre before him.

And the young King looked at them, and they were beautiful. More beautiful were they than aught that he had ever seen. But he remembered his dreams, and he said to his lords: "Take these things away, for I will not wear them."

And the courtiers were amazed, and some of them laughed, for they thought that he was jesting.

But he spake sternly to them again, and said: "Take these things away, and hide them from me. Though it be the day of my coronation, I will not wear them. For on the loom of sorrow, and by the white hands of Pain, has this robe been woven. There is Blood in the heart of the ruby, and Death in the heart of the pearl." And he told them his three dreams.

And when the courtiers heard them they looked at each other and whispered, saying: "Surely he is mad; for what is a dream but a dream, and a vision but a vision? They are not real things that one should heed them. And what have we to do with the lives of those who toil for us?"

And the Chamberlain spake to the young King, and said, "My lord, I pray thee set aside these black thoughts of thine, and put on this fair robe, and set this crown upon thy head. For how shall the people know thou art a king if thou hast not a king's raiment?"

And the young King looked at him. "Is it so, indeed?" he

questioned. "Will they not know me for a king if I have not a king's raiment?"

"They will not know thee, my lord," cried the Chamberlain.

"I had thought that there had been men who were kinglike," he answered, "but it may be as thou sayest. And yet I will not wear this robe, nor will I be crowned with this crown, but even as I came to the place so will I go forth from it."

And he bade them all leave him, save one page whom he kept as his companion, a lad a year younger than himself. Him he kept for his service, and when he had bathed himself in clear water, he opened a great painted chest, and from it he took the leathern tunic and rough sheepskin coat that he had worn when he had watched on the hillside the shaggy goats of the goatherd. These he put on, and in his hand he took his rude shepherd's staff.

And the little page opened his big blue eyes in wonder, and said smiling to him, "My Lord, I see thy robe and thy sceptre, but where is thy crown?"

And the young King plucked a spray of wild briar that was

climbing over the balcony, and bent it, and made a circlet of it, and set it on his own head. "This shall be my crown," he answered.

And thus attired he passed out of his chamber into the Great Hall, where the nobles were waiting for him.

And the nobles made merry, and some of them cried out to him, "My lord, the people wait for their king, and thou showest them a beggar," and others were wroth and said, "He brings shame upon our State, and is unworthy to be our master." But he answered them not a word, but passed on, and went down the bright porphyry staircase, and out through the gates of bronze, and mounted upon his horse, and rode towards the Cathedral.

And the people laughed and said, "It is the king's fool who is riding by," and they mocked him.

And he drew rein and said, "Nay, but I am the King." And he told them of his three dreams.

And a man came out of the crowd and spake bitterly to him, and said, "Sir, knowest thou not that out of the luxury of the rich cometh the life of the poor? By your pomp we are nurtured, and your vices give us bread. To toil for a master is bitter, but to have no master to toil for is more bitter still. Thinkest thou that the ravens will feed us? And what cure hast thou for these things? Wilt thou say to the buyer, 'Thou shalt buy for so much,' and to the seller, 'Thou shalt sell at this price?' I trow not. Therefore go back to thy Palace and put on thy purple and fine linen. What hast thou to do with us, and what we suffer?"

"Are not the rich and the poor brothers?" asked the young King.

"Ay," answered the man, "and the name of the rich brother is Cain."

And the young King's eyes filled with tears, and he rode on through the murmurs of the people, and the little page grew afraid and left him.

And when he reached the great portal of the Cathedral, the soldiers thrust their halberts out and said, "What dost thou seek here? None enters by this door but the King."

And his face flushed with anger, and he said to them, "I am the King," and waved their halberts aside and passed in.

And when the old Bishop saw him coming in his goatherd's dress, he rose up in wonder from his throne, and went to meet him, and said to him, "My son, is this a king's apparel? And with what crown shall I crown thee, and what sceptre shall I place in thy hand?

Surely this should be to thee a day of joy, and not a day of abasement."

"Shall Joy wear what Grief has fashioned?" said the young King. And he told him his three dreams.

And when the Bishop had heard them he knit his brows, and said, "My son, I am an old man, and in the winter of my days, and I know that many evil things are done in the wide world. But canst thou make these things not to be? Wilt thou take the leper for thy bedfellow, and set the beggar at thy board? Shall the lion do thy bidding, and the wild boar obey thee? Is not He who made misery wiser than thou art? Wherefore I praise thee not for this that thou hast done, but I bid thee ride back to the Palace and make thy face glad, and put on the raiment that beseemeth a king, and with the crown of gold I will crown thee, and the sceptre of pearl will I place in thy hand. And as for thy dreams, think no more of them. The burden of this world is too great for one man to bear, and the world's sorrow too heavy for one heart to suffer."

"Sayest thou that in this house?" said the young King, and he strode past the Bishop and climbed up the steps of the altar, and stood before the image of Christ.

He stood before the image of Christ, and on his right hand and on his left were the marvellous vessels of gold, the chalice with the yellow wine, and the vial with the holy oil. He knelt before the image of Christ, and the great candles burned brightly by the jewelled shrine, and the smoke of the incense curled in thin blue wreaths through the dome. He bowed his head in prayer, and the priests in their stiff copes crept away from the altar.

And suddenly a wild tumult came from the street outside, and in entered the nobles with drawn swords and nodding plumes, and shields of polished steel. "Where is the dreamer of dreams?" they cried. "Where is this King, who is apparelled like a beggar – this boy who brings shame upon our State? Surely we will slay him, for he is unworthy to rule over us."

And the young King bowed his head again, and prayed, and when he had finished his prayer he rose up, and turning round he looked at them sadly.

And lo! through the painted windows came the sunlight streaming upon him, and the sunbeams wove round him a tissued robe that was fairer than the robe that had been fashioned for his pleasure. The dead staff blossomed, and bore lilies that were whiter than pearls. The dry thorn blossomed, and bore roses that were redder than rubies.

He stood there in the raiment of a king, and the gates of the jewelled shrine flew open, and from the crystal of the many-rayed monstrance shone a marvellous and mystical light. He stood there in a king's raiment, and the Glory of God filled the place, and the saints in their carven niches seemed to move. In the fair raiment of a king he stood before them, and the organ pealed out its music, and the trumpeters blew upon their trumpets, and the singing boys sang.

And the people fell upon their knees in awe, and the nobles sheathed their swords and did homage, and the Bishop's face grew pale and his hands trembled. "A greater than I hath crowned thee," he cried, and he knelt before him.

And the young King came down from the high altar, and passed home through the midst of the people. But no man dared look upon his face, for it was like the face of an angel.

THE PICKPOCKET AND THE THIEF

Arabian Nights

In the ancient city of Cairo there once lived two rascals, Akil the pickpocket and Haram the thief. Each wanted to marry the same girl, who was rich and charming. The pickpocket stole by day so he sang love songs to her at night. The thief did his wicked work in the dark so he sang to her in the daytime. The rascals did not meet each other so they did not know that the pretty girl was seeing the two of them at different times! She smiled sweetly but would not agree to marry one or the other because neither would tell her what sort of work he did, no matter how many questions she asked. This is not surprising, is it?

As luck would have it the thief and the pickpocket met at the girl's front door one morning. "This is my lady-friend's house," Akil said grandly. "Your friend!" sneered Haram. "You're wrong there. She is mine. I'm planning to marry her soon. She'd never marry a ne'er-do-well like you!"

"Ne'er-do-well!" screamed Akil. "Who are you to call me names?" and with that the two of them started a tremendous fight. They forgot all about the sweet songs for the lovely lady. They knocked each other over, tore off turbans, shouted and rolled over and over in the dust until they saw that a crowd was gathering round. They didn't want this because street-fighting was not allowed. Besides, somebody might know they were robbers and tell the guards! So they picked themselves up, dusted themselves down and walked off, arm in arm. They pretended they'd been having a friendly tussle but in their hearts they hated each other. "Let's find a quieter place to fight," hissed Akil as they walked along. "We'll never settle this by a fight," Haram whispered, "but you'll never marry my sweet girl, I promise you."

"You shall not have her," Akil muttered, "you're as clumsy as a squashed tomato. I don't wish to boast but I'm the finest pickpocket in the city of Cairo." He pinched Haram's arm hard.

"What rubbish," whispered Haram as they strolled along, still pretending to be good friends. "You miserable dog! Anybody can pick pockets. I rob houses and that is much more difficult. You're as

96

clumsy as a pig! You'd fall over your great feet and make far too much noise to be a thief."

Before long Akil and Haram were quarrelling furiously. This time they argued about which of them was the most rascally rascal!

By now they had reached the market-place and were near the stalls where the money-changers were busy changing coins and gold for the merchants. Akil nudged Haram. "Can you see that old man over there? The one walking behind the stalls with a bag of money? Just watch me steal that bag," he boasted.

"What?" said Haram. "Steal a bag with all these men standing around?" He only stole things in the dark so he felt nervous in the bright sunshine. "The guards will spot you. You must be mad!"

"Ho, ho, scared are you?" laughed Akil nastily. "The guards who frighten you will be a help to me. Just you watch carefully."

Akil slithered close to the old man. His hands moved as light as a feather but as quick as lightning, and he undid the string round the old man's waist. He slid off the bag and brought it back, bulging with money, to Haram. "That was a smart piece of work," Haram said, "but I'm not sure if it was very clever work."

"Tut, tut, that was beginner's work!" Akil grinned. "Now I shall get the guards to help me!" He pulled Haram into a quiet corner and made him stand in front of him while he opened the bag and counted the money inside. There were five hundred gold pieces there. He took ten of them for himself then he put all the rest back. Next, he took a large copper ring with his initials scratched on it off his finger and put this into the bag. Then he crept back and ever so quietly he tied the bag back onto the old man's belt. When he had done this safely, he rushed in front of the poor old man and began shouting and waving his arms angrily.

"You wicked old fellow," he screamed. "Robber! Thief that you are! You've played your tricks once too often though. Give me back my bag or you'll have to face the Kadi, our judge, in the court."

The good man did not know what to think. He did not make a fuss or put up a struggle even when Akil dragged him along the street by his beard. They reached the hall where the Kadi always sat on market days to settle quarrels and troubles.

Akil pushed the old man down on his knees in front of the Kadi. Then he yelled and pretended to be mad with anger. "This man is a wicked pickpocket, O Kadi. Three times he has robbed me, a poor innocent merchant! He must be punished."

"I swear I've never seen this man before," the old man said over and over again in a sad quivery voice but Akil shouted even louder until at last the Kadi told him to be quiet!

"The rightful owner will know exactly what is inside the bag," the Kadi declared, "so, old man, I'll ask you first to tell me."

"Your Worship," the unhappy man said, "it holds five hundred gold pieces. I carried them here this morning."

"That's a lie," shouted Akil. "You thief, you dog! I tell you it holds four hundred and ninety gold coins and a copper ring with my initials."

"Open the bag," the Kadi ordered and when the guards did so, of course this is exactly what was inside. Akil was given the bag and away he went whistling cheekily while the poor innocent old man was punished, having lost his money as well!

Haram was waiting for Akil and they quickly moved away from the market-place. "I must say that you've played a very neat trick," Haram said. "Getting a judge and the guards to help you to steal that money was very clever. But I fancy I am cleverer than you, even so." He took Akil by the arm and went on, "You fooled that old man. You fooled the Kadi and his guards but if you come out with me tonight we'll fool the Sultan himself in the palace."

The two ne'er-do-wells arranged to meet at midnight, but while Akil waited for Haram in a dark doorway he shook with fright. He liked to steal in daylight with plenty of people round him but here the alleys and narrow streets were dark and empty. He jumped in surprise when Haram suddenly and silently stood by his side.

"Come this way," Haram whispered, and they went to a small back lane which ran along one side of the Sultan's gardens. Akil saw that Haram was carrying a rope ladder. He was horrified but he did not want Haram to see that he was scared. He held one end of this ladder and Haram threw the other end up to the top of the garden wall. The hooks on the ladder held firm to the stones so our bold rascals quickly climbed up. They sat on the top to get their breath back then they hauled up the ladder and dropped it over the top. Silently they climbed down into the Sultan's garden. There was no turning back now and even Haram shivered when the watchman came strolling along waving a bright lantern. They crouched behind some bushes until the man was out of sight then they hurried to the palace where they managed to find an open window.

Inside, everything was dark and they had to feel their way along gloomy passages and up and down stairs. Akil was so

frightened he almost forgot to breathe. His legs felt like jelly when Haram led him into a wonderful bedroom lit by golden lamps. It was the Sultan's room and the Sultan himself lay asleep on a silken bed. A pageboy was sitting next to him and he rubbed the Sultan's legs and feet whenever he could catch hold of them for the Sultan was twisting and turning on his bed.

"There's nothing to be afraid of," whispered Haram. "Hide behind this curtain and don't make a sound. You spoke to the Kadi. Now I'm going to speak to the Sultan."

Akil was too scared to utter any word whatsoever. He watched as Haram, moving as gently as a butterfly, crept behind the pageboy. He put his hand over the boy's mouth then he tied him up. He wrapped the boy's turban round his lips to gag him then he bundled him into a corner without making the tiniest sound. Then Haram sat down beside the Sultan's bed. He stroked the Sultan's feet gently and carefully at first. Then he stroked and slapped, slapped and stroked harder and harder until after a time the Sultan yawned and half woke up. "O wonderful Sultan, my dearest master," said Haram in a voice exactly like the pageboy's, "you do

99

not seem very sleepy so perhaps you'd like me to tell you a story."

"Please do," said the Sultan and he yawned again.

"Well," began Haram in the pageboy's voice, "there was once a thief called Haram and a pickpocket called Akil. They did not know that they both loved the same charming girl and they were angry when they found out the truth. Each decided to show the other what a brilliant thief he was." Behind the curtain, Akil gasped in horror as Haram told the whole story about the bag, the Kadi and the old man. Haram went on to explain how they'd got into the palace and what had happened to the little pageboy. "Most wise and wonderful Sultan," he said softly, "you may judge who is the cleverer one for you are all-wise and all-knowing."

But the Sultan did not open his eyes. He laughed many times at Haram's tale then he said sleepily, "I do not talk about such things in the middle of the night," and he gave a loud snore.

Akil and Haram crept out of the palace and climbed over the garden wall. They pulled the rope ladder down and scampered off home.

Next morning the Sultan and his servants were astonished to find the little pageboy tied up and gagged in a corner of the royal bedroom. Slowly, the Sultan began to remember the strange story that somebody had told him during the night. He ordered the guards to search the palace and tell him what the thieves had stolen.

"Nothing is missing, O Sultan," they told him and the Sultan gave a little smile. That rascal had certainly told him a good story. He gave a bigger smile, then he chuckled louder and louder until all his chins wobbled and he had to hold his aching sides!

"Send messengers to every part of Cairo," he said when he had stopped laughing. "Tell them to seek out that rascally pair of thieves, Akil and Haram. Tell them that I, wisest of all Sultans, have forgiven them. Indeed, if they come to the palace – by the front gate this time please – I'll give them a reward."

The Sultan really was a wise and kind ruler so he sent a messenger to the Kadi with a reward for the poor old man. Instead of five hundred gold pieces, the old man went home with a thousand pieces and a new leather bag!

Before long the story was told in every house in Cairo and of course, it reached the ears of the rich charming young lady who had started it all. "At last I know what those two young men do," she laughed. "I love them both. They are clever and smart but somehow I think it would be wiser not to marry either of them." So she didn't!

THE ENCHANTED TOAD

Judy Corbalis

There was once a king who had a daughter called Princess
Grizelda. Princess Grizelda was rather quiet and didn't say very
much but she was very very stubborn and determined once she had
decided on something.

The Queen, her mother, had left their home at the palace many
years before, when Grizelda was a small girl, to seek her fortune as a
racing driver, so the king had had to bring up his daughter himself.

"Grizelda," he said to her one day, "I have a serious problem to
discuss with you. Come into the blue drawing room."

The Princess sighed, put down her bow and arrows and
followed him.

"What is it, Papa?"

"Grizelda," said the king, "it's time you were married."

"But I'm only fourteen, Papa," protested the princess.

"What do you mean – 'only fourteen'?" said the king crossly.
"Fourteen's quite old enough to be married."

"But I don't *want* to be married, Papa."

"Well, sooner or later you'll have to be," said the king, "so why
not now?"

"I don't know if I ever want to be married, Papa."

"What nonsense!" shouted the king. "Everyone wants to be
married. Why I was married at twenty and your mother was
married at fifteen."

"I know, Papa," said the princess, "and when she was eighteen
she went off to race cars and we haven't seen her since."

"Well, she always sends you a birthday present," said the king
defensively.

"Yes, I know, but I'd rather *see* her sometimes."

"Grizelda," said the king, "you are not to talk about Mama. You
know it only upsets me. I'm not going to listen if you do. And I want
you, in fact, I'm ordering you, to start thinking about who you want
to marry. Because if you don't come up with some good suggestions
yourself, I shall have to choose for you."

And he stormed out of the blue drawing room.

"Oh dear," said Grizelda to herself. "Now I really *do* have a problem."

She thought about all the neighbouring princes but she really couldn't face the thought of marrying any of them.

"Well," asked the king at dinner, "have you decided, Grizelda?"

"Really, Papa, you only asked me about it five hours ago."

The king stamped his foot and his soup plate rattled.

"Five hours is long enough for anyone," he thundered.

"Not for me, Papa," said the princess calmly. "And you've spilt your soup."

"Oh, be quiet!" shouted the king and he slammed out of the royal dining room.

The princess ate the rest of her dinner in thoughtful silence.

Next day she had breakfast in her room, got dressed in her best golden dress and slipped outdoors in her blue silk cloak.

"Your Highness," said the Court Usher as she passed him on the stairs, "have you remembered that His Majesty has asked several kings and queens from neighbouring kingdoms to lunch with him today? He particularly wanted Your Highness to be present."

The princess nodded.

"Thank you for reminding me," she said, and to herself she thought, "He's asked them because he thinks they might be interested in marrying me off to one of their sons."

And she carried on downstairs even faster.

She stayed in the gardens for an hour or two, then slipped back into the palace and up to her bedroom unnoticed. She had just enough time to sort out one or two things before lunch.

There was a blast of trumpets from downstairs.

"That'll be the heralds announcing the arrival of the other monarchs," said Princess Grizelda aloud and she smoothed her golden dress, picked up something in her hand and set off for the main staircase and the royal reception room.

"The Princess Grizelda," announced the Court Usher.

"My dear!" cried the king and he walked up and embraced her warmly. "Behave yourself, please," he muttered in her ear.

"I always do, Papa," said the princess.

"And this," announced the king, leading her forward, "is my daughter, Grizelda, my only child, who will, naturally, inherit the kingdom in due course and who, I really feel, is just of an age to be married."

The royal guests smiled at her. The princess smiled back. She took a deep breath.

"Papa," she said loudly, taking a step forward, "I've found a husband for myself."

"Really, Grizelda?" said the king. "I am surprised. And who is the lucky young man going to be?"

"It isn't a *young man*, Papa," said the princess. "I met him in the garden this morning and brought him in to lunch with me."

The king was curious.

"Let him come in!" he commanded, "so we can all see this mysterious fellow. Met him in the garden, indeed! These young girls are so fanciful."

The princess went out to the hallway, picked up a small box she had deposited there and carried it in.

"Well?" demanded the king. "Where is he then?"

The princess lifted the lid of the box.

"Here, Papa."

The king looked in the box.

"It's a toad!!"

"Yes, I know, Papa. I've fallen in love with it and I'm going to marry it."

"GRIZELDA!" thundered the king.

"Lunch is served, Sire," announced the footman appearing at the door.

One of the visiting kings leaned over to Grizelda's father and whispered in his ear, "I shouldn't discourage her too hard if I were you. It will almost certainly be a prince under enchantment."

The king was doubtful.

"Are you sure?"

"They always are," said the visiting king. "Let her have him on the table at lunch and have your Court Wizard change him back later on."

"What a splendid idea," said the king. "Thank you. I hadn't thought of that."

"There have been dozens of cases exactly like it," pointed out the visiting king.

So the Princess Grizelda took her toad in to lunch and it sat by her golden plate as she fed it with tiny scraps of her own food.

The visitors left in the early afternoon. Grizelda shook hands with them all and smiled prettily. The toad looked at them with its unblinking eyes.

The king felt a light touch on his shoulder.

"Don't forget. Get the enchanter in right away," murmured his friend.

The king nodded.

"And many thanks," he said gratefully.

"Don't mention it," said the visiting king.

The princess took her toad into the library. She was examining its warts when the herald arrived with a message that she and the toad were wanted in the throne room.

"The throne room!" The princess was impressed. "Something special must be happening."

"His Majesty is in full regalia," announced the herald importantly.

"Really? It must be something vital then. I wonder what it can be?" said the princess, and picking up her toad she set off along the palace corridor.

The throne room door was opened by the Chief Usher. Inside the room were the King, the Lord Chamberlain, the Court Jester, the Chief Judge and the Court Enchanter. The Court Enchanter was considered to be one of the best wizards in the world. He was always going off to perform difficult spells or to change people back into their normal shapes or to magick someone or something somewhere. People said he could conjure up all sorts of wonderful things and nobody wanted to get on the wrong side of him because it was reputed that he had once put a bad spell on someone who had offended him and caused lizards to jump out of her mouth every time she opened it.

Grizelda went into the room.

"Good afternoon, Papa," she greeted him, and she smiled and nodded at his retinue.

"Good afternoon, my dear," said the king and, looking at the toad, he said, obviously making a great effort, "and how is my future son-in-law this afternoon?"

"Oh, very well, thank you, Papa."

"Good," said the king.

"Would you like to stroke him, Papa?"

"No, no thanks!" said the king hastily. "Ah, I'm sure he's, ah, very, ah, friendly, yes, I'm sure he's got a wonderful nature and so on, but, ah, I don't think I'll stroke him just yet, Grizelda."

"Now," he went on, "the reason I've brought you down here is because I happen to believe your toad, that is, my son-in-law to be, is really a prince under enchantment."

The Princess Grizelda was very disappointed.

"Oh no, Papa, I hope not!"

"Now look here," said the king. "Don't be ridiculous, Grizelda. I mean you can get toads anywhere but princes are another thing altogether. I'll get you another toad as a wedding present if you want. And that's a promise. Now bring that toad over here and put him on the small table."

Grizelda put her toad down in front of the enchanter.

The enchanter looked at her with his piercing green eyes.

"Stand back, Your Highness," he ordered. Then, taking a huge red silk handkerchief from one pocket of his robe, and a wand from the other, he dropped the handkerchief over the toad, threw a powder from another pocket into a glass of water, poured the water over the handkerchief, then waved his wand over it muttering strangely to himself all the time.

There was a sudden flash of pink smoke and a dull boom, the handkerchief and the toad disappeared, and in its place stood a white rabbit.

The princess was overjoyed.

"A rabbit! Oh, Papa, how wonderful! I've always wanted a rabbit."

"Not for a *husband!*" bellowed the king, enraged.

And to the enchanter he said nastily, "You'll have to do something considerably better than that!"

The enchanter turned his piercing green eyes towards the king.

"Patience, Your Highness. These things are very skilled and take time."

"I can see that," said the king bitterly.

The enchanter pulled out another handkerchief, a blue one this time, and laid it over the rabbit.

"Oh no, please don't, please don't." The princess was distressed.

The enchanter put his hand deep in his robe, pulled out a tiny top hat, and presented it to her.

"Here you are," he said gravely. "Put your hand in there."

Grizelda could only get two fingers into the hat because it was so small. Feeling something soft and furry, she pulled at it.

Out popped the tiniest baby rabbit she had ever seen.

"For you," said the enchanter. "A present to make up for losing this one."

"Oh thank you!" cried Princess Grizelda and she put the baby rabbit back in the hat for safe keeping and put the hat in her pocket.

The enchanter was busy with his spell. He had taken out a large book from behind the throne, a book Grizelda was sure had never been there before, and was studying it intently.

Suddenly he leaned forward towards the king.

"Excuse me, Your Majesty," he said, reached behind the king's ear and pulled out a large lemon.

"Oh dear," he said, and reaching behind the king's other ear, pulled out an enormous black spider.

"Stop it *at once!*" commanded the king. "And that's an order."

"Sorry, Your Majesty," murmured the enchanter. "I just thought you'd like to know they were there."

"Thank you for that consideration," said the king. "Now get on with the job."

The enchanter plucked a star from out of the air above his head, laid it on the blue handkerchief, twirled three times round on his toes, and shouted "Abracadabra!"

There was a blinding flash of green light and, lo and behold, a beautiful red sportscar appeared before them.

"My gosh!" breathed Grizelda.

The Lord Chancellor leaned forward enviously. "I'd like that," he sighed.

The king looked very hard at the enchanter. "I see: a sportscar."

"Well, yes," said the enchanter. "I told Your Majesty these things take time."

"Look," said the king through clenched teeth, "I cannot have a sportscar as a son-in-law. The princess cannot marry a *sportscar*."

His voice rose to a shriek. "WHOEVER HEARD OF A KINGDOM RULED BY A SPORTSCAR?"

"A passing bagatelle, Your Majesty," said the enchanter hastily. "We're almost there now."

"It's a very beautiful sportscar," pointed out the princess.

"Grizelda . . .," said the king warningly.

The Lord Chamberlain broke in. "Your Majesty, the enchanter is about to try again."

"He'd better," said the king.

The enchanter took out a checked tablecloth from the back pocket of his robe and flung it over the sportscar.

The Lord Chamberlain sighed. "What a pity."

The king shot him a furious look.

The enchanter lifted three lizards out of a banqueting dish on the regalia table and laid them on the cloth. He took a vial of red liquid from his sleeve, shook it over the lizards and waved his wand low over them.

A tongue of flame shot into the air. Everybody screamed and jumped back.

The smoke cleared and there before them lay – a fish finger.

"NO, NO, NO, NO," groaned the king. "THERE IS NO SUCH THING AS A KINGDOM RULED BY A FISH FINGER! I'm *not* having a fish finger as a son-in-law. I'd rather have a toad. Take him away!" he shouted, pointing at the enchanter. "Off with his head and bring it to me on a plate! It'll be a pleasure, I can tell you."

"Papa!" The princess was deeply shocked. "What a *terrible* thing to say."

The enchanter burst into tears. He reached into his other sleeve and brought out a placard saying,

'WIFE AND SIX CHILDREN TO SUPPORT'.

"You won't get my sympathy *that* way," said the king. "My mind is made up. Take him away!"

The Princess Grizelda jumped to her feet and stood in front of her father.

"I won't have it, Papa," she cried sternly. "This was all your idea in the first place and it wasn't even your toad. It was mine. Of course you're not going to chop off his head. You're going to give him one last chance to succeed and, if he doesn't, you're going to send him on a month's holiday."

"That's just encouraging him to fail," said the king.

"Honestly, Sire," said the enchanter, "it was just a temporary setback. I've prepared my next and final spell now. I *am* in the entertainment business, Sire, after all."

"Entertainment!" exploded the king. "You call this entertainment?"

"Stop it, at once, both of you," ordered the princess. And turning to the enchanter she said, "Would you please try again now?"

"And you'd better get it right this time," snorted the king.

"I will," the enchanter assured them.

He pulled a purple silken cloth with golden stars on it from the Chief Judge's trouser leg and laid it over the fish finger. Then he reached inside his own mouth, pulled out a tonsil and laid that on the cloth.

"Yuk!" said the king. "How disgusting!"

"But effective, Sire," replied the enchanter. "And now, please, absolute silence."

He bent down on his knees, crossed his fingers, his toes, and his eyes and breathed on the tonsil.

The tonsil quivered and grew and grew. The purple cloth with golden stars rose and flapped and shook until it seemed to fill the room. There was a boom of thunder and a light like the sun dazzled them all.

"How beautiful!" murmured the princess to herself.

Suddenly there was a jolt and a bang and without warning they all flew up to the ceiling and fell to the ground again. The room grew dark.

"Sorry about this," came the enchanter's voice through the gloom. "We're nearly there."

A misty cloud was gathering in the middle of the room. A dim human shape was forming inside it.

The enchanter sighed inaudibly with relief, the king muttered aloud, "At last!"

And the Princess Grizelda said to herself, "I do hope he's nice and he likes having fun."

The cloud began to dispel, the light slowly returned to normal and the figure emerged more clearly until it stood visible to them all.

"GOOD HEAVENS!" bellowed the king. "It's Marguerite!"

"Hello, darling," said the figure.

"Mother!" shouted Grizelda and threw herself into the stranger's arms.

"And where have *you* been for the last eleven years then, if it's not a rude question?" asked the king.

"Oh, Arthur," said the queen, holding Grizelda tightly, "don't go on and on, please. I thought you'd be so pleased to see me again. I've been away seeking my fortune, of course. I'm an extremely famous racing driver."

"Well, I've never heard of you," announced the king, "and I've checked the racing lists every time there's been a Grand Prix."

"Oh, Arthur. Did you!" The queen was touched. "That is romantic of you."

The king blushed.

"But," went on the queen, "I raced under an assumed name of

course, otherwise people might have thought my winning was favouritism. And, Grizelda," she continued, "it's so wonderful to see you at last, my darling. I've wanted and wanted to come back, but I knew I couldn't until I'd proved myself. And I've finally done it."

The Princess Grizelda clung tighter to her mother's neck.

"Oh, Mama, I'm so glad you're back at last."

"What I don't understand," said the king, "is if you've reached the peak of your career, what on earth you were doing in the palace garden disguised as a toad. And then to put me through that dreadful business of the rabbit and the sportscar and the fish finger! It's a wonder I'm not grey with worry and strain."

"Well, I couldn't help it," explained the queen. She turned to the enchanter. "It was a terribly strong spell. You did marvellously well to break it at all."

The enchanter looked modest.

"It was nothing, Your Highness."

"It was everything to *me*," the queen assured him. "I could have just about coped with spending the rest of my life as a pet rabbit or a sportscar and at least I would have been at the palace. But a fish finger! I ask you? Here one day and gobbled up the next. I was quite terrified. I was shaking in my breadcrumbs."

"Oh, Mama," breathed Grizelda, "just imagine if the enchanter had failed and we'd eaten you up for tea."

Her eyes filled with tears at the thought.

"Well, we didn't," said the king cheerfully, "so stop crying, Grizelda."

He came and put his arm round the queen and kissed her cheek.

"I'm so glad you've come back."

"I shall never go off again now, I can tell you," promised the queen, "though I had some fun while I was racing."

"Will you tell me all about it?" asked Grizelda eagerly.

"Later," promised the queen.

"We must have a banquet and a party to celebrate your return," said the king, "but there's still one thing I don't understand. How did you come to be a toad?"

"Well," explained the queen, "I was racing very well indeed and clearly I was going to win the major prize. The only person who was anywhere near as good as I was, was a driver who had been a wizard and had given it up for racing, but he was still not up to my standard. And when I had won the competition and it came to the presentation of the prizes, he was so jealous that he cast a spell over me and changed me into a toad, and it took me seven months to hop back here to the palace and then it wasn't till this morning, when Grizelda found me, that anyone noticed me at all, and, of course, you know the rest of the story."

"Amazing," said the king.

"That wizard should be punished," said the Chief Judge.

"He will be," promised the king. "I shall make a point of it."

"Well, if everyone is happy now," put in the enchanter, "I'd quite like to be getting off home to my family . . ."

"Just a moment," said the king sternly. "You promised me a husband for the princess and I haven't got one. She can't marry her mother."

"With respect, Sire," said the enchanter, "*you* asked me if I could change a toad into a prince and I said I'd do my best. I rather thought," he went on huffily, "that I'd done better than my best, but of course if Your Majesty disagrees . . ."

"Absolutely. You've done *marvellously*," cried the queen, "and I shall personally see about a reward in due course."

The enchanter smiled gratefully.

"I still don't know how I'm going to get Grizelda a husband though," muttered the king.

"A husband!" The queen was incredulous. "What on earth does she want a *husband* for? She's only fourteen."

"I don't," put in Grizelda hastily.

"I should think *not*," said the queen. "I've never heard such nonsense. I married young, and look what happened to me. You're surely not encouraging her, Arthur?"

"Well, what else is she going to do?" asked the king defensively.

"What do you want to do, Grizelda?" asked her mother.

Grizelda thought for a bit.

"Well, Mama," she said finally, "what I'd like to do first is to stay here with you for a while and play with my rabbit, and the toad Papa has promised me, and then there is something I'd really like to do."

"And what is that?"

"I hope you won't think it's silly," said the princess, "but I'd simply *love* to be an astronaut. I've always wanted to be one."

"I've never heard of anything so ridiculous," said the king.

"I think it's a wonderfully exciting idea," said the queen, "and you should certainly be allowed to try it. And now, Arthur," she continued, turning to the king, "if it's possible, and I'm sure it should be, I'd love something to eat. I'm so sick of slugs and snails and worms."

"Oh, my dear," cried the king remorsefully, "of course, of course. I'm so sorry. I completely forgot about it in the shock of the moment. Yes. At once. Let's all three of us have a special celebration meal together tonight. I'm so delighted to have you back again."

"And so am I, Mama," murmured the Princess Grizelda, snuggling up to her mother.

"It seems to me," said the enchanter to himself, "that this time I've made an entirely satisfactory job of things."

And wrapping his cloak tightly round himself, he waved a hasty goodbye to everyone and slipped out of the palace off home to his own supper.

SWAN LAKE

Russian Traditional

In Germany a very long time ago, a prince called Siegfried lived with his mother the queen in a wonderful castle built in white marble. He was a happy carefree young man who had many friends and one day he invited all of them to the castle for a party to celebrate his twenty-first birthday.

At the party, Siegfried's mother said gently:

"This is a happy day, my son. Enjoy it with your friends. However, I must remind you of something. Today you have become a man, and tomorrow you must choose a wife."

"But, dearest mother," said Siegfried, "I know several princesses. How shall I know who will be the best wife for me?"

"Tomorrow," she replied, "I am giving another party for you and I have invited the daughters of many of my noble friends. When you kiss the hand of a girl, I will know that you have chosen your bride. Now let the feasting continue."

The party went on until the light began to fade. "Let's have one last dance before we go home," called Benno, Siegfried's best friend, and just then a flight of swans appeared in the sky and some of the guests wanted to chase after them, for in those days people liked to hunt swans.

"Follow me," shouted Benno.

With whoops and shouts the men left the castle and rushed to the woods. It was a pleasant evening and Benno led them to a lovely lake where the sun's last rays sparkled on the rippling waters. On the far side the flock of swans had come to rest and they were spreading their wings. The men pulled out their bows and arrows and got ready to aim. But the swans vanished. The men rubbed their eyes and they wondered if the fading sunlight had been playing tricks on them. "Where is Prince Siegfried?" asked Benno, suddenly. No one could see the prince, so Benno sent the men to look for him. "I'll stay here by the lake in case he comes a different way," he said.

Left alone, Benno heard the sound of wings and the flock of swans flew out of the water. When they landed on the grass they changed into beautiful girls who were wearing long white dresses

with wreaths of white and silver feathers in their hair. Benno was startled. At that moment his friends came running along the paths with Siegfried in front of them. The girls were frightened. Quickly they tried to hide among the trees but their white dresses glimmered in the moonlight. The hunters, who thought they were looking at the swans, lifted their bows ready to fire. Siegfried started to take aim as well and at that moment a bright light shone on them from the ruins of a church at the edge of the lake. The men dropped their arrows in surprise and the prince gasped as the loveliest girl he had ever seen glided towards him and held up her hand.

"My name is Odette," she said. "Please put away your weapons and do not harm me or my friends."

"Have no fear," said Siegfried breathlessly, "we will not hurt you. But where have you come from? We were following a flock of swans that flew over the castle. They landed on this lake, but where are they now?"

"Alas, gentle prince," Odette explained. "I am a queen, but an evil magician called Von Rothbard put a spell upon me and my ladies-in-waiting. We are changed into swans each and every day from dawn until sunset. At night we become humans again and can dance and sing together."

"What a terrible spell!" Siegfried exclaimed. "Is there no way to put an end to it?"

"The magician watches us day and night," Odette told him. "He turns himself into an owl and flies with us wherever we go."

Siegfried paced up and down and his friends moved closer to him. They saw how troubled he was.

"Is there nothing we can do?" asked Benno in a low voice.

"The evil spell will only be broken," said Odette, "if you can find a man who has never loved anyone. He must then promise to love me, and me alone, for ever."

Now Siegfried had fallen in love with Odette the moment he saw her. "I have never loved a girl," he said fiercely. "I will kill this owl and set you free. Then I will ask you to marry me."

Odette shook her head. "Noble prince," she said. "In order to kill Von Rothbard, you must also be willing to give up your life for me. I cannot allow you to do this. Besides, you will find your bride tomorrow at your mother's court."

"I will choose no one except you," said Siegfried. "My life is yours."

"But I will be a swan at that time. I'll only be able to fly round the castle walls," she said. "Von Rothbard will do anything to trick you into declaring your love for someone else. You must take great care."

"I won't be tricked by this wicked fellow," Siegfried cried, but even as he was speaking, Odette ran to her friends. Dawn was breaking and they became swans again. An owl hooted and the light in the church went out.

Next day, many guests arrived at the castle and once more, there was music and dancing. The queen sat on her golden throne and watched her son as he chatted or danced politely with each girl in turn. However, all the time he kept thinking about Odette. He turned to his mother and whispered in her ear, "I'm sorry. I do not wish to marry any of these girls." Before the queen could say a word, the trumpets sounded to announce that some more guests had arrived. One of them was dressed so that he looked like a black swan and holding his arm was a lovely girl, his daughter.

Siegfried could not believe his eyes. Was it Odette? He rushed across the hall and he was in such a hurry to greet her, he did not notice that a pure white swan was beating her wings against the windows.

"That is Odile," the swan tried to warn Siegfried. "She is the magician's daughter. He has made her look like me. Watch out for the Black Swan. It is Von Rothbard himself!"

But the prince looked only at Odile. He praised everything about her and he did not see the evil look in the Black Swan's eyes. Siegfried asked Odile to dance for he was sure she was Odette, his swan-queen. At the end of the dance he kissed her hand to show his mother that he had chosen this girl to be his bride.

"You wish to marry my daughter?" asked Von Rothbard, the Black Swan.

"She is my only true love whom I will love for ever," declared Siegfried. Instantly, every light in the hall went out. There was a roll of thunder followed by a horrible laugh. And an owl flew round the prince's head. Some of the guests started to scream. Poor Siegfried knew at once that he had been tricked. In despair, he ran outside and into the woods.

At sunset, the swans gathered round the lake and became

young girls again. They were dancing and singing when Odette appeared, sad and miserable. "Sweet friends," she said. "I fear the magician has used his worst spell. He has tricked Siegfried and made him say he will love Odile forever." The girls were distressed, for now they would be swans for evermore.

"There is one way out," said Odette gently. "I will kill myself now while I am a human."

"You cannot do this," they cried, but she walked steadily to the water. She was about to cast herself into the lake when Siegfried came crashing through the woods. His face was sorrowful and his eyes streamed with tears.

"Odette!" he called. "The magician fooled me. I thought his daughter, Odile, was you. I love only you. Can you ever forgive me? I will give up my wretched life and Von Rothbard will die. You must be saved."

The lights shone out from the ruins of the church once more and the air was filled with sweet music. Odette smiled radiantly as he spoke: "There is nothing to forgive, dear prince. Von Rothbard the Wicked has done this terrible thing to us."

Siegfried held out his arm and Odette moved one step towards him then she turned and threw herself into the cold waters of the lake. At that moment an owl flew from the trees and fluttered round the prince's head. The young girls huddled together: they were terrified and instead of soft music there was the sound of crashing drums and clashing cymbals. The prince stared in horror as the waters closed over Odette's head. Then he drew his dagger and, quick as a flash, he stabbed himself. The owl crashed to the ground. The magician was dead at last and the swan-maidens were freed from the evil spell. Alas, Siegfried lay dying on the grass. He had killed the wicked Von Rothbard it was true, but he had killed himself as well.

But in all the old stories it is said that the fairies and nymphs were so happy that the wicked magician could not do any more harm that they wanted to reward Siegfried in some way. So they carried him to a wonderful place under the lake where Odette was waiting for him. With great joy, she welcomed him so she and her prince were together once more, never to be parted again.

And nowadays we can see and hear this story as well as read it, because Tchaikovsky, a great Russian composer, wrote some music specially for 'Swan Lake' and turned it into a famous ballet. Perhaps you'll see it one day!

THE KING WHO DECLARED WAR ON THE ANIMALS

Joan Aiken

Once there was a poor young nobleman who had nothing in the world but a ruined castle in the forest, a horse, and a hound. So he was obliged to go hunting every day, in order to get his food. However he looked after his animals with great care, brushing and combing them every evening, giving them the same food as he had himself, and chopping wood to make a fire so that they should be warm at night. In consequence of this they loved him dearly.

One day the young lord went hunting with his hound in a densely thicketed part of the forest. He tied his horse to a tree outside this bushy patch and left him grazing.

Presently a fox came by and stopped to admire the horse.

"My word, brother, you seem fat and glossy! Your master must look after you well."

"Indeed he does," said the horse. "Everything he has, I share."

"May I sit here and keep you company?" asked the fox.

"By all means," replied the horse politely. So the fox sat down by him and chatted until the young lord came back with a stag which he had shot. He was rather astonished to see the fox, and raised his gun, at which the fox exclaimed,

"Don't shoot, my dear sir! Rather, take me into your service, and I'll keep an eye on your horse for you while you are off hunting. Good gracious! What a risky thing to leave a horse tied up here, when there are so many wolves and bears in the forest!"

The young lord thought this was sensible advice; he allowed the fox to come home with him, running alongside his hound. And when they arrived at the castle the fox was given a share of the supper and a place by the fire. "I certainly am in luck!" she thought.

Next day while the young lord went hunting the fox kept watch. Presently a hungry bear came along and began to sniff round the frightened horse.

"Hey, you bear! Leave the horse alone!" called out the fox. "If you will only sit down patiently and wait, our master, who is the most generous man in the world, will certainly give you a good supper when he comes back. Isn't that so, horse?"

"Yes indeed," said the horse, who was sweating with anxiety. "Everything he has, we share."

So the bear sat down and waited, and when the young lord returned he was persuaded to take the bear into his service. The bear had supper and a bed for the night, and next morning he helped the fox mount guard over the horse.

While they chatted, a mouse ran up to them.

"Be off!" shouted the bear. "Can't you see you are making the horse nervous?"

"Oh, kind sirs! Please let me stay with you! Life is so hard in the forest these days, and you all look so well-fed and contented."

"But what can *you* do for our master?" said the bear in disgust.

"Oh, I daresay I can be useful in some way," replied the mouse. "It isn't everyone who can go through a keyhole, after all."

So when the young lord came back he was persuaded to take the mouse, too, into his service.

Next day a mole asked to be allowed to join them.

"Really!" said the fox. "I fail to see what use a miserable little blind mole can be!"

"Oh, you'd be surprised how much I can do," said the mole. "Why, I and a few of my friends can plough up a field as fast as two men and two teams of horses."

So the mole was permitted to go home with them and share their food and fire.

Next day a great buzzard asked if she might join them.

"I am extremely strong," she said. "I can pick up a horse and rider in my talons and carry them right across the forest."

And a wild cat came by.

"I can amuse you all with my purring and my playful ways."

So the cat and the buzzard were added to their company, and the young lord looked after them all, fed them and kept them warm. And they were all exceedingly fond of him.

But one day when the lord was off hunting the fox said:

"Friends, *we* are all happy and contented, but our master sometimes seems rather sad and downcast. It has come into my mind that he needs a wife, one of his own kind, to keep him company. Where can one be found?"

"The other day when I flew over the palace of the king," said the buzzard, "I noticed that he has a very beautiful daughter. Why don't I fetch her to be our master's wife?"

This seemed a good plan to them all.

The buzzard flew to the king's palace, waited, perching in an oak tree, until the princess came out for her evening stroll, and then picked her up and carried her back to the forest, holding her as carefully as if she were made of rose petals.

The young lord was overjoyed to see what a beautiful wife his friends had found for him. Since he looked after her as carefully as he did the rest, the princess too was happy to share their life in the forest.

But her father the king was angry at the loss of his daughter; he asked a wise woman to find out what had become of her.

The wise woman filled a bowl with water and looked into it. Then she said,

"Your daughter is living in the forest with a young nobleman. If you will give me half your treasure I will fetch her back for you."

"Very well," said the king.

So the wise woman, taking a whip in her hand, seated herself on a small carpet and lashed it with the whip until it rose in the air and carried her to the forest. There she saw the princess, walking outside the ruined castle with all the animals keeping guard.

"Would you like to listen to some fine stories?" said the wise woman. "I know stories about heroes, stories about magicians, stories about birds and beasts, summer and winter, the sun, the moon, and the stars."

The princess was very fond of stories, so she was eager to listen to the wise woman.

"Sit beside me on my carpet, then, and I will tell you about the golden apple and the nine peahens."

But when the princess sat down beside her on the carpet, the wise woman snatched up her whip and lashed the carpet with it; next minute they were far away, flying back to the king's palace. And the king shut his daughter in a tower, lest she be stolen again.

The poor young lord was grief-stricken at the loss of his bride, and the animals were very downcast in sympathy.

"Friends, we must get her back," said the fox. "You, cat, must go and play about in the garden of the tower, but don't let the princess's women catch you."

So the striped cat made her way to the garden of the tower. There she played most beautifully, pouncing on leaves and grasses as they blew in the wind, pretending to chase her own tail. "Oh, the pretty creature!" exclaimed the waiting-women. "Let us catch her to amuse our mistress." But, try as they would, they were unable to catch the cat.

"Let me out, just for a moment," called the princess, who was watching from the window. "I am sure she will come to me."

"Only for a moment, then," said the women. "For if the king your father knew, it would be as much as our place was worth."

So they undid the door and the princess stepped into the garden. And the buzzard, who had been waiting hidden in the branches of an oak tree, swooped down, picked her up as carefully as if she were made of rose petals, and carried her back to the forest.

The king was furious at being tricked again, and by nothing more than a pair of animals, at that.

In his rage he declared war on the whole animal tribe, swearing that he would exterminate the lot of them, and recapture his

daughter at the same time. So he collected a huge army with men, horses, and guns, and set out for the forest.

"Now what are we going to do?" said the bear.

"We must defend ourselves as best we can," said the fox. "Each one of you must call as many companions as possible. I myself can summon five hundred foxes. How about you?" she asked the bear.

"Oh, I think I can count on about a hundred," said the bear.

"And you, dear cat?"

"About eight hundred," said the cat.

"And you, little mouse?"

"Eight thousand, for sure."

"And you, friend mole?"

"Oh, three thousand at least."

"And you, O great buzzard?"

"I fear not more than two or three hundred."

So each animal went to fetch his companions, while the fox made a plan of battle.

The king's army marched until nightfall; then they made camp. But during the night the mice invaded their camp and gnawed through all the halters, saddle-girths, and reins, while the bears, foxes, and cats growled and howled around the outskirts of the camp with a sound fearful enough to make your blood run cold. The king's horses, finding their halters cut through, made off in terror. Next day not a horse was to be seen.

"You must continue on foot, then," said the angry king to his soldiers. "You will have to pull the great guns yourselves, since there are no horses."

So they went on with great difficulty. Next night the mice came again, and gnawed through the soldiers' belts and sword-straps, so they had no means of keeping their swords and their breeches on. Moreover the moles dug hundreds of tunnels under their line of march. When they tried to stumble on, the heavy guns sank up to their barrels in the ground; meanwhile the buzzards hovered overhead, hurling down great rocks on the struggling men.

"Oh, well, let us turn back," said the king at last. "I can see God himself must be against us, since I have declared war on the animals. I will just have to give up my daughter!"

So he went back to his palace and sent a message telling the princess that she and her husband were forgiven. And they came to the palace with all their animals and lived happily together for many years.

HOW THE LEOPARD GOT HIS SPOTS

Rudyard Kipling

In the days when everybody started fair, Best Beloved, the Leopard lived in a place called the High Veldt. 'Member it wasn't the Low Veldt, or the Bush Veldt, or the Sour Veldt, but the 'sclusively bare, hot, shiny High Veldt, where there was sand and sandy-coloured rock and 'sclusively tufts of sandy-yellowish grass. The Giraffe and the Zebra and the Eland and the Koodoo and the Hartebeest lived there; and they were 'sclusively sandy-yellow-brownish all over; but the Leopard, he was the 'sclusivest sandiest-yellowest-brownest of them all – a greyish-yellowish catty-shaped kind of beast, and he matched the 'sclusively yellowish-greyish-brownish colour of the High Veldt to one hair. This was very bad for the Giraffe and the Zebra and the rest of them; for he would lie down by a 'sclusively yellowish-greyish-brownish stone or clump of grass, and when the Giraffe or the Zebra or the Eland or the Koodoo or the Bush-Buck or the Bonte-Buck came by he would surprise them out of their jumpsome lives. He would indeed! And, also, there was an Ethiopian with bows and arrows (a 'sclusively greyish-brownish-yellowish man he was then), who lived on the High Veldt with the Leopard; and the two used to hunt together – the Ethiopian with his bows and arrows, and the Leopard 'sclusively with his teeth and claws – till the Giraffe and the Eland and the Koodoo and the Quagga and all the rest of them didn't know which way to jump, Best Beloved. They didn't indeed!

After a long time – things lived for ever so long in those days – they learned to avoid anything that looked like a Leopard or an Ethiopian; and bit by bit – the Giraffe began it, because his legs were the longest – they went away from the High Veldt. They scuttled for days and days and days till they came to a great forest, 'sclusively full of trees and bushes and stripy, speckly, patchy-blatchy shadows, and there they hid: and after another long time, what with standing half in the shade and half out of it, and what with the slippery-slidy shadows of the trees falling on them, the Giraffe grew blotchy, and the Zebra grew stripy, and the Eland and the Koodoo grew darker, with little wavy grey lines on their backs like bark on a tree trunk;

123

and so, though you could hear them and smell them, you could very seldom see them, and then only when you knew precisely where to look. They had a beautiful time in the 'sclusively speckly-spickly shadows of the forest, while the Leopard and the Ethiopian ran about over the 'sclusively greyish-yellowish-reddish High Veldt outside, wondering where all their breakfasts and their dinners and their teas had gone. At last they were so hungry that they ate rats and beetles and rock-rabbits, the Leopard and the Ethiopian, and then they had the Big Tummy-ache, both together; and then they met Baviaan – the dog-headed, barking Baboon, who is Quite the Wisest Animal in All South Africa.

Said Leopard to Baviaan (and it was a very hot day), "Where has all the game gone?"

And Baviaan winked. *He* knew.

Said the Ethiopian to Baviaan, "Can you tell me the present habitat of the aboriginal Fauna?" (That meant just the same thing, but the Ethiopian always used long words. He was a grown-up.)

And Baviaan winked. *He* knew.

Then said Baviaan, "The game has gone into other spots; and my advice to you, Leopard, is to go into other spots as soon as you can."

And the Ethiopian said, "That is all very fine, but I wish to know whither the aboriginal Fauna has migrated."

Then said Baviaan, "The aboriginal Fauna has joined the aboriginal Flora because it was high time for a change; and my advice to you, Ethiopian, is to change as soon as you can."

That puzzled the Leopard and the Ethiopian, but they set off to look for the aboriginal Flora, and presently, after ever so many days, they saw a great, high, tall forest full of tree trunks all 'sclusively speckled and sprottled and spottled, dotted and splashed and slashed and hatched and cross-hatched with shadows. (Say that quickly aloud, and you will see how *very* shadowy the forest must have been.)

"What is this," said the Leopard, "that is so 'sclusively dark, and yet so full of little pieces of light?"

"I don't know," said the Ethiopian, "but it ought to be the aboriginal Flora. I can smell Giraffe, and I can hear Giraffe, but I can't see Giraffe."

"That's curious," said the Leopard. "I suppose it is because we have just come in out of the sunshine. I can smell Zebra, and I can hear Zebra, but I can't see Zebra."

124

"Wait a bit," said the Ethiopian. "It's a long time since we've hunted 'em. Perhaps we've forgotten what they were like."

"Fiddle!" said the Leopard. "I remember them perfectly on the High Veldt, especially their marrow-bones. Giraffe is about seventeen feet high, of a 'sclusively fulvous golden-yellow from head to heel; and Zebra is about four and a half feet high, of a 'sclusively grey-fawn colour from head to heel."

"Umm," said the Ethiopian, looking into the speckly-spickly shadows of the aboriginal Flora-forest. "Then they ought to show up in this dark place like ripe bananas in a smoke-house."

But they didn't. The Leopard and the Ethiopian hunted all day; and though they could smell and hear them, they never saw one of them.

"For goodness' sake," said the Leopard at tea-time, "let us wait till it gets dark. This daylight hunting is a perfect scandal."

So they waited till dark, and then the Leopard heard something breathing sniffily in the starlight that fell all stripy through the branches, and he jumped at the noise, and it smelt like Zebra, and it felt like Zebra, and when he knocked it down it kicked like Zebra, but he couldn't see it. So he said, "Be quiet, O you person without any form. I am going to sit on your head till morning, because there is something about you that I don't understand."

Presently he heard a grunt and a crash and a scramble, and the Ethiopian called out, "I've caught a thing that I can't see. It smells like Giraffe, and it kicks like Giraffe, but it hasn't any form."

"Don't you trust it," said the Leopard. "Sit on its head till the morning – same as me. They haven't any form – any of 'em."

So they sat down on them hard till bright morning-time, and then Leopard said, "What have you at your end of the table, Brother?"

The Ethiopian scratched his head and said, "It ought to be 'sclusively a rich fulvous orange-tawny from head to heel, and it ought to be Giraffe; but it is covered all over with chestnut blotches What have you at *your* end of the table, Brother?"

And the Leopard scratched his head and said, "It ought to be 'sclusively a delicate greyish-fawn, and it ought to be Zebra; but it is covered all over with black and purple stripes. What have you been doing to yourself, Zebra? Don't you know that if you were on the High Veldt I could see you ten miles off? You haven't any form."

"Yes," said the Zebra, "but this isn't the High Veldt. Can't you see?"

"I can now," said the Leopard. "But I couldn't all yesterday. How is it done?"

"Let us up," said the Zebra, "and we will show you."

They let the Zebra and the Giraffe get up; and Zebra moved away to some little thorn-bushes where the sunlight fell all stripy, and Giraffe moved off to some tallish trees where the shadows fell all blotchy.

"Now watch," said the Zebra and the Giraffe. "This is the way it's done. One – two – three! And where's your breakfast?"

Leopard stared, and Ethiopian stared, but all they could see were stripy shadows and blotched shadows in the forest, but never a sign of Zebra and Giraffe. They had just walked off and hidden themselves in the shadowy forest.

"Hi! Hi!" said the Ethiopian. "That's a trick worth learning. Take a lesson by it, Leopard. You show up in this dark place like a bar of soap in a coal-scuttle."

"Ho! Ho!" said the Leopard. "Would it surprise you very much to know that you show up in this dark place like a mustard-plaster on a sack of coals?"

"Well, calling names won't catch dinner," said the Ethiopian. "The long and the little of it is that we don't match our backgrounds. I'm going to take Baviaan's advice. He told me I ought to change; and as I've nothing to change except my skin I'm going to change that."

"What to?" said the Leopard, tremendously excited.

"To a nice working blackish-brownish colour, with a little purple in it, and touches of slaty-blue. It will be the very thing for hiding in hollows and behind trees."

So he changed his skin then and there, and the Leopard was more excited than ever; he had never seen a man change his skin before.

"But what about me?" he said, when the Ethiopian had worked his last little finger into his fine new black skin.

"You take Baviaan's advice too. He told you to go into spots."

"So I did," said the Leopard. "I went into other spots as fast as I could. I went into this spot with you, and a lot of good it has done me."

"Oh," said the Ethiopian, "Baviaan didn't mean spots in South Africa. He meant spots on your skin."

"What's the use of that?" said the Leopard.

"Think of Giraffe," said the Ethiopian. "Or if you prefer

stripes, think of Zebra. They find their spots and stripes give them per-fect satisfaction."

"Umm," said the Leopard. "I wouldn't look like Zebra – not for ever so."

"Well, make up your mind," said the Ethiopian, "because I'd hate to go hunting without you, but I must if you insist on looking like a sun-flower against a tarred fence."

"I'll take spots, then," said the Leopard; "but don't make 'em too vulgar-big. I wouldn't look like Giraffe – not for ever so."

"I'll make 'em with the tips of my fingers," said the Ethiopian. "There's plenty of black left on my skin still. Stand over!"

Then the Ethiopian put his five fingers close together (there was plenty of black left on his new skin still) and pressed them all over the Leopard, and wherever the five fingers touched they left five little black marks, all close together. You can see them on any Leopard's skin you like, Best Beloved. Sometimes the fingers slipped and the marks got a little blurred; but if you look closely at any

Leopard now you will see that there are always five spots – off five fat black finger-tips.

"Now you *are* a beauty!" said the Ethiopian. "You can lie out on the bare ground and look like a heap of pebbles. You can lie on the naked rocks and look like a piece of pudding-stone. You can lie out on a leafy branch and look like sunshine sifting through the leaves; and you can lie right across the centre of a path and look like nothing in particular. Think of that and purr!"

"But if I'm all this," said the Leopard, "why didn't you go spotty too?"

"Oh, plain black's best for me," said the Ethiopian. "Now come along and we'll see if we can't get even with Mr One-Two-Three-Where's-your-Breakfast!"

So they went away and lived happily ever afterwards, Best Beloved. That is all.

Oh, now and then you will hear grown-ups say, "Can the Ethiopian change his skin or the Leopard his spots?" I don't think even grown-ups would keep on saying such a silly thing if the Leopard and the Ethiopian hadn't done it once – do you? But they will never do it again, Best Beloved. They are quite contented as they are.

THE RED SHOES

Hans Andersen

There was once a little girl called Karen who was very pretty but very poor as well. In warm weather she went barefoot but in winter she wore heavy wooden clogs which rubbed her ankles and made them sore. In the village the shoemaker's mother found some scraps of red cloth. She tried her best to make a pair of shoes for Karen but they looked clumsy even though they fitted her quite well.

On the very day of her mother's funeral the old lady gave Karen the red shoes. They were not suitable to wear at a funeral but Karen could not go barefoot so she put them on. She wore her ragged dress as she walked behind her mother's miserable coffin outside the church.

Just then a big carriage passed by with an old lady sitting inside. When she saw the sad little girl she felt so sorry for her that she went at once to see the church minister.

"Give me that child and I will take care of her," she said.

Karen felt sure the old lady liked her because of the red shoes. But, the old lady said they were ugly and must be burnt in the stove. Karen was given clean new clothes and she learnt to read and sew. Everyone said she was pretty, but her mirror whispered:

"You are more than pretty, you are beautiful."

Sometime later, the queen travelled round the country with her little daughter, the princess. When they arrived at a castle near Karen's village, people streamed out to see them. Karen went too and she had a wonderful view of the little princess who was standing on a stool by the window. She was wearing a lovely white dress and the prettiest red shoes made from softest Moroccan leather. Karen sighed enviously. There was nothing in the world she wanted as much as another pair of red shoes.

When Karen was old enough to be confirmed in church a new dress and new shoes were needed. The old lady took Karen to the best shoemaker in the nearby town who measured her foot. There were glass cabinets filled with the finest shoes around the shop but the old lady could not see very well so she did not take much interest in them. Karen did though! She spotted a pair of red shoes exactly like those of the little princess. How beautiful they were! The shoemaker said he'd made them for a rich man's daughter but they didn't fit her feet.

"They shine very well," the old lady said. "Do they fit you?"

"Perfectly," said Karen. So the old lady paid for them and Karen kept quiet. She knew red was not the proper colour to wear to church, but she could not resist the lovely shoes and knew that the old lady had not seen the colour clearly.

Everyone in the church stared at Karen's feet. She felt all the statues were staring as well. The organ played; the choir sang sweetly. Solemnly the Bishop laid his hands on her head but she could only think proudly about her beautiful red shoes!

Everybody told the old lady about Karen's red shoes and she said crossly, "Don't do that again. You must wear black shoes in church."

When Sunday came Karen looked at her red shoes. She looked at the black ones. She looked at the red ones again and put them on! She and the old lady walked to church and at the gate an old soldier asked if he might dust their shoes and Karen put her foot forward.

"What pretty dancing shoes! Take care they do not slip off!" he said as he touched the soles lightly and secretly.

Inside the church everybody stared at Karen's feet. She thought of nothing except red shoes. She did not sing. She even forgot to say the Lord's Prayer. When she walked outside, red shoes seemed to float around her. The coachman was waiting with the carriage and the old lady climbed in. Karen was following her when the old soldier called out, "Oh look, what pretty dancing shoes!"

Happily Karen skipped a few dancing steps. Then she took a few more. And her feet would not stop! Round and round the churchyard she danced until the coachman jumped down. He grabbed her and it was funny to see her feet dancing in the air. He pushed her into the carriage but her feet went on dancing and she gave the old lady some very nasty kicks before the coachman managed to wrench off the red shoes!

Later on, the old lady became very ill. The doctors agreed that she was dying. She could not be left alone so Karen was told to stay with her. Then an invitation for a grand ball arrived. Karen looked at the sick old lady. She also looked at her red shoes. She put them on. Then off to the ball she went!

She began to dance, but when she wanted to move to the right, the shoes danced to the left. She wanted to dance up the ballroom,

but the shoes danced down the stairs and into the street. They danced her out of the city straight into the dark forest.

Something shone at her and she thought it was the moon. But it was the old soldier who cackled, "Look! What pretty dancing shoes!" She was terrified. She tried to pull off her shoes. They would not move. She tore her stockings but her shoes stuck to her feet and away she danced. Over hills, over fields, by day and by night, in rain and sunshine, dance she did. And dance she must! She danced into the churchyard and tried to rest on a gravestone but her feet carried her to the church. A shining white spirit stood by the door holding a sword. "You shall dance," it said coldly. "You'll dance in your red shoes for ever. And if you dance past any vain proud folk, show them what has happened to you."

"Have pity on me," cried Karen but the red shoes carried her away.

One morning she danced past a door that she remembered well. She heard soft music then she saw a coffin covered with flowers. The one who had been so kind to her was dead and Karen had left her all alone.

Dance she must. And dance she did! Those shoes took her over rough places until her feet and legs were bleeding. She was exhausted, but she danced on until one day she reached a lonely cottage and she tapped on the window.

"I know the executioner lives here," she called. "Come outside. I cannot come in for I must keep on dancing."

A big man opened the door. "Do you know who I am?" he asked. "I cut off the heads of wicked men."

"Cut off my feet, I pray you," begged Karen, "to show that I'm truly sorry. You see, I loved these red shoes more than anything, more than the sweet lady who gave me a home. I left her alone when she needed me."

The executioner cut off her feet but the shoes danced off with them into the dark woods. The man made her a pair of wooden feet and he cut two branches for her to use as crutches.

"Surely I've suffered enough," thought Karen. "I'll go to church and tell the people this." But when she was near the church door the red shoes danced in front of her so she turned away.

She was sad and lonely all the week so on Sunday she hobbled off to church. "I'm as good as anybody inside there," she whispered. "Some of them are proud and vain, I dare say, if they are really honest." At the churchyard gate she stopped. There were the red shoes dancing wildly in front of her again. Filled with horror she turned back and this time she knew she would never be proud again.

The wife of the church minister took pity on her and gave her some work. Karen worked well and the minister's children loved her dearly. She told such beautiful stories, they said, but they saw that she shook her head when they longed for expensive clothes, jewels and beautiful curly hair.

One Sunday they asked Karen to go to church with them, but she was afraid to see the red shoes again. When they had left, she sat alone in her little room reading her prayerbook. The wind softly carried the music from the church to her and she lifted up her head.

Suddenly her room was filled with bright light. The spirit she had seen once before stood by her but this time he held a bunch of roses. He touched the ceiling. It rose high in the air. He touched the walls, which opened wide until Karen could see the organ and the children singing sweetly. She saw many people smiling at her. The church had come to her! Someone whispered softly, "It is good that you are here, dear Karen." The sun streamed through the windows and Karen's heart was filled with peace and happiness at last.

THE RAT'S DAUGHTER

Eastern Traditional

There lived once in Japan a rat and his wife who came from an old and noble family. They had one beautiful and clever daughter of whom they were very proud. She could gnaw through the hardest wood and run like the wind. Her coat was a lovely soft silky brown and her pointed teeth shone like pearls. Many of the other young female rats envied her good looks.

Her proud parents expected her to marry well. Her father was a rat through and through and happily dreamed of his daughter marrying a handsome young rat from their own group. There was a particularly fine specimen that he thought would be suitable: a young rat with long moustaches that touched the ground and whose family was even nobler and older than his own.

The rat's mother had very different ideas, however. She despised all rats outside her own family and could not consider that any of them would be good enough for her own darling daughter.

"My daughter shall never marry a mere rat," she declared, holding her head high. "With her beauty and talents she has a right to marry someone better than *that*."

So the husband and wife quarrelled day and night about who would make a suitable husband for their child. But they never even thought to ask their daughter what she herself thought.

At last the wife said:

"I think only the mighty and powerful Sun is good enough for my child – let us pay him a visit."

The husband reluctantly agreed and they set off with their daughter to visit the Sun in his golden palace. Once there the wife looked up at the Sun and said bravely:

"Noble king, here is our precious daughter and we are offering her to you in marriage as we know that you are the most powerful being on earth, and only you will be worthy of her."

Now the Sun was amused at this proposal but he hadn't the slightest intention of marrying anybody, least of all a rat, so he said carefully:

"It is very kind of you to offer your beautiful daughter to me,

133

but I really cannot accept – after all I am not really the most powerful being on earth: the Cloud is. He can pass over me and stop my light whenever he wishes." At that moment the Cloud did indeed cover the Sun and he was blocked from view.

The husband and wife agreed to ask the Cloud immediately. Certainly, they thought, the Cloud was more powerful than the Sun, as at any time he could cover the Sun whether the Sun wanted this or not.

The Cloud was rather taken aback when the rats offered their daughter to him in marriage. He did not want to offend the couple, but he did not want to marry a rat – even a very beautiful one – and so he said:

"It is kind of the Sun to describe me as the most powerful being

in the world, but he really isn't right. The Wind is far more powerful than I am, watch this –" and at that moment a great gust of Wind blew the Cloud across the sky.

The husband and wife saw that the Wind was more powerful than the Cloud and asked him if he would like to marry their darling daughter. The Wind was secretly appalled at the idea – he was far too busy travelling around the world to be stuck in one place and married to a rat. So he said in a great booming voice:

"The Cloud is quite right – I am more powerful than he is but I am not more powerful than that Wall over there. He has the power to stop me in my flight. Ask him to marry your daughter."

The three rats all stared at the huge brick wall looming over them.

The wife said:

"Well, Wall, as you are the most powerful being, we can offer you the hand of our beautiful daughter in marriage."

The Wall was considering this proposal when all at once there was a terrible wailing noise. It was the young female rat.

"I don't want to marry a *Wall*!" she cried. "How can you all be so cruel and not consider my feelings? I would have married the Sun, or the Cloud or the Wind, because that was what you wished, but *not* an ugly old Wall!"

The Wall was somewhat hurt at this outburst and declared that he had no wish to marry a rat anyway.

"It is quite true," he said, "that I can stop the Wind, but there is someone who is more powerful than I – that is the rat who lives under me. He can reduce me to powder, simply by gnawing with his teeth. A fine young male rat would surely make the best companion for your daughter."

The young female rat was delighted at this suggestion and said she would love to marry the handsome young rat with the moustaches that touched the ground, whom her father had suggested in the first place. Her mother was happy to agree now that she knew how powerful rats really were.

So they all returned home. The lady rat married the handsome rat with the moustaches and a wonderful wedding celebration was enjoyed by all.

THE DEAD WIFE

North American Indian Traditional

Once there was a man and his wife who lived on the edge of a large forest. They were Red Indians, but after they were married they chose to live apart from the rest of their tribe who had settled many miles away.

They lived in quiet harmony together. He would catch fish in the river nearby or hunt for food in the forest, while his wife worked at home cooking and sewing.

One day, when the man returned from his hunting, he found his wife had fallen ill with a violent fever. He nursed her as well as he knew how, but after a few days she died in her sleep.

The man wept for many weeks, he could not get used to being without his wife. In the end he felt so lonely he made a wooden doll of about the same height and size as his wife had been and then he

dressed the doll with his wife's clothes. He carved a face out of the wood, and made-believe it was his wife come back to him. Night after night he would sit by the fire with the doll and talk gently to it as he used to talk to his wife. He looked after the doll carefully and would brush away any ashes that happened to fall on the doll from the fire.

He was always busy during the day now, as he had to cook and mend as well as go out hunting for food. But in the evenings he would sit quietly by the fire with the wooden doll and tell it of the day's happenings, and so a year passed by.

One evening he came back from hunting and found that some wood had been collected and left by his home, and he did not remember having done it himself. He thought he must have forgotten. But the next night when he returned home not only had there been wood gathered but there was a merry fire burning, and by the fire sat not the doll, but his own dear wife. He was too astonished to speak, but simply gazed at his wife in wonder. After a short while she said to him: "Dear husband, The Great Spirit took pity on you, because you could not be comforted after my death and you did not forget me. So he let me come back to you, but on one condition: you must not stretch out your hand and touch me till we have seen the rest of our people – if you do, I shall die."

The man's heart was filled with tender happiness, and he said: "Dear wife, we must go at once to our tribe."

However, snow fell thick and fast all that night, and they were not able to travel for several days. The man longed to hold his wife, but he remembered her words and did not go near her.

At last they started on their journey, having prepared some deer's flesh to take with them. They travelled for five days, and they had one more day's journey to complete, when once again, a terrible snow blizzard started. They stopped to rest for the night and lay down on their skins to sleep. But the heart of the man was stirred by his wife lying so close to him and he stretched out his arms to her. She waved him away and said, "We haven't seen our people yet. It is too early." But this time he did not listen and he put his arms around her – and found he was clutching the wooden doll.

When he saw what had happened, he pushed it away from him in horror and anger and ran and ran until he finally came upon his tribe, where he lay down and wept and told them his story. Some people doubted, so he took them to the place where they had rested and there lay the doll. They saw footprints left in the snow by two people – but the prints of one were like that of a doll.

GOLD TREE AND SILVER TREE

English Traditional

Once upon a time there lived a king whose wife was called Silver Tree. Their only child was a girl and they decided to call her Gold Tree. One day Queen Silver Tree and Princess Gold Tree went for a walk in the palace gardens and they came across a pretty stream with a tinkling waterfall. Under the clear water they saw a trout with glistening blue-green scales.

"What a bonny fish," said the queen, "but I am more beautiful, I think." To their surprise the trout answered politely, "I'm afraid you are not."

"I'm the most beautiful queen in the world," Silver Tree said crossly.

"Oh dear," the trout said calmly, "it is true you are beautiful Silver Tree but your daughter is more beautiful." With that he dived quickly under the water.

They went back to the palace and the queen went straight to bed!

"I promise that I'll never feel well again until I get the heart of Gold Tree," she said fiercely to herself.

When the king returned home, Gold Tree told him that her mother was ill, so he hurried to her room.

"What troubles you, my dear?" he asked in a kindly voice.

"You alone can help me," she said meekly. "If I can but get the heart of Gold Tree I will be well," and Silver Tree smiled a horrible smile which the king did not see. He was very upset for he loved his daughter and did not want to harm her.

By a happy chance, the son of a great king had come to his court that very day to ask Princess Gold Tree to marry him. Quickly the king agreed. He begged the happy couple to ride away secretly and as soon as they had gone he sent his huntsman to kill a deer and take out its heart. When he handed this to his wife she felt better at once and sprang out of bed, fit and well!

Several years later, Silver Tree went to the stream again and called to the trout, "Well, my fine fish, am I not the most beautiful queen in the world?"

"You are beautiful, it is true," said the fish, "but you are not the most beautiful, O Queen."

"Who is more beautiful?" she demanded. "Tell me at once."

"Your daughter, Gold Tree," was his reply.

"She no longer lives, stupid fish," said Silver Tree scornfully.

"I fear you are wrong," said the trout, "she married a prince and she lives over the sea in another land."

Silver Tree rushed home. She begged the king to let her use his royal ship. Then the queen sailed away and the winds blew the ship to the princess's home across the sea.

Gold Tree saw her father's ship coming into the harbour. She turned to the courtiers and said, "My mother is on that ship. She will kill me if she can, I must hide!" They hurried her away and locked her in a room and when the queen came ashore she went to the palace and began to shout, "Come and greet your mother. I've travelled a long way to see you." But Gold Tree called back, "I'm locked in, I fear."

"Well then," Silver Tree said, "will you please put your little finger through the keyhole so that your own mother may drop a kiss on it?"

Gold Tree put out her finger and the wicked queen stabbed it

with a poisoned dart. Instantly Gold Tree fell down dead.

When the prince came home he was overcome with sorrow to find his wife was dead. She looked so lovely that he did not bury her. Instead he locked her in a room and kept the key on a golden chain round his neck and he would not let anybody go in.

Now Princess Gold Tree had a lovely young daughter who desperately wanted to see her mother. She had seen what her father had done and so one day, when the prince forgot to put on his gold chain with the key, the girl picked it up and hurried to the locked room. She knelt down and whispered, "Oh, Mama, you are so beautiful." She saw the poisoned dart in her mother's finger so she pulled it out. At once Gold Tree stirred then rose up, alive and as lovely as ever and she kissed her daughter tenderly.

When the prince came home later that day, his daughter said:

"What is the finest present I could give you, dear father?"

"My beloved Gold Tree," he said at once.

"Go into that room," his daughter said, "you will find her there." What joy there was in the palace that night when the prince knew his wife was alive again.

A year later Silver Tree visited the trout in the stream again.

"I know I'm the most beautiful queen in the world," she boasted.

"I fear not," the fish said. "Gold Tree is more beautiful."

"But she's dead. I poisoned her myself," the queen screamed and she ran back to the palace. "Let me have your ship again," she said to the king.

She sailed away and Gold Tree was terrified when she saw her father's ship again.

"My mother is here. She'll try to kill me," she told her daughter. But she answered cheerfully, "Don't worry. Let's go down to meet her!"

Silver Tree met them on the shore and she held up a silver cup.

"See," she said, "I've brought a special drink for dear Gold Tree." Gold Tree's daughter stepped forward. "It is the custom in this country," she said, "that whoever offers a drink must first drink from the same cup." So Silver Tree lifted the cup and pretended to drink. As soon as she did this, the young girl knocked the cup so that the drink went down Silver Tree's throat! She fell at their feet, quite quite dead.

And the prince, his beautiful wife Gold Tree and their clever daughter lived happily and peacefully ever after.

SINBAD AND THE
OLD MAN OF THE SEA

Arabian Nights

In a Middle Eastern country there once lived a sailor called Sinbad. Whenever he set sail on a voyage he seemed to find adventures and wonderful things to see. On his sixth voyage he had many merchants on board his ship with valuable cargo to sell.

They sailed for some weeks across the sea until they came to a desert island. On the shore they found an enormous egg. There were tiny cracks in the shell and they could hear little squeaks and cheeps which showed that the young bird inside was ready to hatch out.

"Do not touch that egg," Sinbad warned the other sailors and merchants. "It is a roc's egg and the parent birds are dangerous." No one took any notice. Instead, they broke open the egg, lit a fire and roasted the young bird. As they were finishing their feast Sinbad saw two large black clouds in the sky.

"Here come the parent rocs," he shouted. "We'd better get back on board before they notice us, for they are sure to seek revenge."

Everybody scrambled on board and they set sail. They watched the rocs find the broken egg and heard their fearsome squawking before they flew off. The ship sailed as fast as it could but it was no use. The huge birds chased after it, holding enormous stones in their claws. The first one dropped its stone. It missed the ship. Then the second roc flew low and dropped its stone right in the centre of the boat which split from end to end. All the sailors and merchants sank under the waves and were drowned. But Sinbad seized a wooden plank and he managed to float on this to another island. He waded ashore and found trees and flowers growing everywhere. He wandered along until he saw an old man sitting on the banks of a clear stream.

"Hello there," called Sinbad cheerily, "were you shipwrecked too?" He did not answer but pointed to Sinbad's back. He showed that he wanted to get across the stream to pick fruit. Sinbad felt sorry for the weak old fellow so he hoisted him on his back and carried him over the water. Then he knelt down.

"There you are," said Sinbad, "you can get down now." Instead,

the old man slipped his arms round Sinbad's neck and pulled them tight. He was as strong as an ox, with hard leathery skin.

When Sinbad struggled to get free, he gripped his throat so tightly that poor Sinbad could not breathe and he fainted.

When he awoke the old man was still gripping his neck. He hit Sinbad with a heavy stick and kicked him.

"Get up, you lazy rascal," he shouted. "Carry me round these trees for I want to pick the best fruit."

Sinbad staggered round all day without food or rest and that night he dropped on the ground unable to walk any further. Even when Sinbad was asleep the old man lay down beside him and still held his throat in a hard cruel grip.

Next day the old man wanted to climb a nearby hill. Poor Sinbad struggled up the steep path in the blazing sun while the old man kicked him if he did not walk fast enough for him. Each day he was forced to carry this horrible fellow around. He was tired and very miserable. "How can I get rid of him?" he wondered.

Then one day the old man cackled: "Today we'll go wherever you want to go – so long as I come too!"

Sinbad walked slowly until he came across some empty gourds, and a plan formed in his mind. He cleaned out the largest one and squeezed the juice from several bunches of grapes into it. Then he left the juice in the gourd for some days. Next time he and the old man passed that way Sinbad found the gourd. He sipped the wine he had made from the grape juice. It tasted good so he drank some more and then a little more.

"What's that you're drinking?" the old man demanded.

"Grape juice, that's all," laughed Sinbad, "but it tastes very nice."

"Give me some," came the rough rude order. So Sinbad filled a small gourd and the old man drank it all down in one huge gulp. He had never drunk wine like this before and it made him feel sleepy and a little bit stupid!

Suddenly Sinbad found that the grip round his neck was much looser. Quickly he twisted round and threw the wicked creature to the ground. He picked up a heavy stone and with one blow, he killed him.

He raced to the seashore, shouting with joy. He was free at last! He met some sailors who were getting water from the stream. They were astonished to hear his sad story.

"How lucky you have been," they exclaimed. "You were captured by the Old Man of the Sea. He has killed hundreds of shipwrecked sailors. Nobody has ever escaped from him until now. He deserved to die."

The sailors took Sinbad back to Baghdad, where he settled down to a peaceful life.

"I've had enough adventures," he said, "I won't be going off to sea again."

Was this really Sinbad's last adventure? What do you think?

ENTER THE SWEEP

Richmal Crompton (from *William the Conqueror*)

illiam and the sweep took to one another at once. William liked the sweep's colouring, and the sweep liked William's conversation. William looked up to the sweep as a being of a superior order.

"Didn't your mother *mind* you being a sweep?" he said wonderingly, as the sweep unpacked his brushes.

"N-naw," said the sweep, slowly and thoughtfully. "Leastways, she didn't say nothin'."

"You don't want a partner, do you?" said William. "I wun't mind being a sweep. I'd come an' live with you an' go round with you every day."

"Thanks," said the man, "but p'raps your pa would have somethin' to say."

William laughed bitterly and scornfully.

"Oh, yes, *they'd* fuss. *They* fuss if I get a bit of mud on my boots. As if their old drawin'-room carpet mattered. Have you any little boys?"

"Yus, three," said the sweep.

"I s'pose *they'll* all be sweeps," said William gloomily, feeling that the profession was becoming overcrowded.

"Come *out* of that room, Master William," called cook, who, in the absence of William's parents, took what William considered a wholly unjustifiable interest in him. William extended his tongue in the direction of the voice. Otherwise he ignored it.

"I'd meant to be a robber," went on William, "but I think I'd as soon be a sweep. Or I might be a sweep first, an' then a robber."

"Come out of that *room*, Master William," called cook. William simulated deafness.

"I'd like to be a sweep an' a robber an' a detective an' a soldier, an' some more things. I think I'd better be them about a year each, so's I can get 'em all in."

"Um," said the sweep. "There's somethin' in that." Cook appeared in the doorway.

"Didn't you hear me telling you to *come* out of that room, Master William?" she said pugnaciously.

"You can't expect me to hear you when you go shoutin' about in the kitchen," said William loftily. "I just heard you *shoutin'*."

"Well, come out of this room, anyway."

"How can you expect me to know how it's done if I don't stay to watch? Wot's the good of me goin' to be a sweep if I don't know how it's done?"

"What's the good of me covering up all the furniture if you're going to stay here getting black as pitch? Are you coming out?"

"No," said William exasperated. "I've *gotter* stay an' learn. It's just the same as Robert goin' to college – my stayin' to watch the sweep. Wot's the *good* of me bein' a sweep if I don't learn? Folks prob'ly wun't pay me if I didn't know how to do it, and *then* what'd I do?"

"Very well, Master William," said the cook with treacherous sweetness, "I'll tell your pa when he comes in that you stayed in here with the sweep when your ma said most speshul you wasn't to."

William reconsidered this aspect of affairs.

"All right, Crabbie," he said grudgingly. "An' I hope that I jolly well *spoil* your chimney when I'm a sweep with not knowing how to do it."

He wandered round the house and watched through the window. It was a thrilling performance. He was lost in roseate dreams of himself pursuing the gloriously dirty calling of chimney sweep when the sweep appeared with a heavy sack.

"Where shall I put the soot?" he said.

William considered. There was a nice bit of waste ground behind the summer-house. He was looking carefully round to make sure that his arch-enemy cook was nowhere in sight.

"Jus' here," he said, leading the sweep round to the summer-house.

The sweep emptied the sack. It was a soft grey-black pile. William thrilled with the pride of possession.

"That's *mine*, isn't it?" he said.

"Well, it's not *mine*," said the sweep jocularly. "You can 'ave it to practise on."

He left William smiling proudly above his pile.

From over the wall behind the summer-house William could see the road. He waved his hand effusively to the sweep as he passed on his little cart.

"I say," called William.

The sweep drew up.

"Does the horse an' cart cost much?" said William anxiously.

"Oh no," said the sweep. "You can get 'em dirt cheap. I'll lend you this 'ere of mine when you go into the business."

With a facetious wink he drove on, and William returned to the contemplation of his pile of soot.

Soon a whistle that he knew roused him from his reverie and he peeped over the wall.

Ginger, William's lifelong friend and ally, as earnest and freckled and snub-nosed as William himself, was passing down the road. He looked up at William.

" 'Ello," said William, with modest pride. "I've gotter bit of soot in here."

But Ginger had a rival attraction. "They're ratting in Cooben's barn," he said.

William weighed the attraction of ratting and soot, and finally decided in favour of ratting.

"All right," he called, "wait a sec. I'll come."

He completely forgot his soot until tea-time.

Then, as he was going out of the house, he met Mr and Miss Arnold Fox coming in. They were coming to call on Mrs Brown. Both were very tall and very thin, and both possessed expansive smiles that revealed perfect sets of false teeth.

"Good afternoon, William," said Mr Fox politely.

"Afternoon," said William.

"A rough diamond, our William," smiled Mr Fox to his sister.

William glared at him.

She laid her hand on William's head.

"Manners maketh man, dear William," she said.

She then bent down and kissed William.

Mr Arnold Fox took off his hat and playfully extuinguished William with it. Then he laid it on the hall table and went into the drawing-room, leaving William boiling and enraged on the door-step.

That reminded William of his soot.

William and Ginger sat lazily upon the wall watching the passers-by. Absent-mindedly they toyed with handfuls of soot.

They were cheered by the sight of Mr Arnold Fox going down the road – his forehead beneath his hat suspiciously dark.

"That'll teach *him. He'll* take some washing," said William.

"Look!" said Ginger, excitedly, leaning over the wall. Along the road came three children in white, Geoffrey Spencer and Joan Bell with her little sister Mary. Geoffrey Spencer, in a white sailor suit, walked along mincingly, holding Joan Bell's little bag-purse for her. Mary toddled along holding her elder sister's hand.

William admired Joan intensely. Occasionally she conde-scended to notice his existence.

"Hello!" called William. "Where are you going?"

"Posting a letter," said Geoffrey primly.

"Come in an' play," said William; "we've got some soot."

"No," said Geoffrey piously. "Mother said I wasn't to play with you."

"You're so rough," explained Joan with a little fastidious sniff.

William flushed beneath his soot. He felt that this reflected upon his character. He was annoyed that anyone, even so insigni-ficant as Geoffrey, should be forbidden to play with him.

"Rough!" he said indignantly. Then, "Well, an' I'd rather be rough than an ole softie like you – you an' your ole white suit!"

"Come along, Joan," said Geoffrey with a superior smile. "I'm not going to talk to him."

William rolled white, angry eyes in his black face.

"Yah – boo, softie!" he called over the wall.

Yet he was depressed by the proceeding, and even Ginger's suggestion of trying the effect of the soot on the bed of arum lilies did not revive him much. However, the effect was certainly cheering. So they moved on to the white roses and worked with the pure joy of the artist on them till they heard the dulcet tones of Joan and Mary and Geoffrey returning from the post. Then they went back to the wall. Joan was growing bored with Geoffrey. She looked up almost longingly towards William's grimy face.

"Where *is* your soot, William?" she asked.

"Jus' here," said William. "It's jolly good soot."

"I'll come in an' *look* at it," she said condescendingly. "I won't come in an' play. I'll come in an' *look* at it. You can go on home, Geoffrey."

Geoffrey debated with his conscience. "I won't come in," he said, " 'cause mother says he's so rough. I'll wait for you out here."

So hand-in-hand Joan and Mary came round to the back of the summer-house. William and Ginger proudly introduced them to the soot.

"Ith lovely," said Mary. "Leth – leth danth round it – holding handth."

"All right," said William genially. "Come on."

Nothing loth, they joined hands and danced round it. Joan laughed excitedly.

"Oh, it's fun," she cried. "Faster."

"Father!" cried Mary.

They went faster and faster. William and Ginger, with the male's innate desire of showing off his prowess, began to revolve at lightning speed.

Then came the catastrophe.

Plop!

It was Mary who lost her balance and fell suddenly and violently on her face into the heap of soot.

Joan, with feminine inconsistency, turned upon William, stamping her foot.

"*You* did it! You nasty, rough, horrible boy!"

"I *didn't*!"

"You *did*!"

"He *didn't!*" cried Ginger.

"He *did!*"

"He *didn't!*"

Meanwhile Mary had arisen from the soot heap – hair, eyes, and mouth full of soot, soot clinging to her dress. Her voice joined in the general uproar.

"Ooh – it taths nathy, it taths nathy – oo – oo." Joan wept in angry sympathy.

"See how *you* like soot in your mouth, you nasty boy!" she screamed at William, seizing a handful of soot and hurling it at William's face.

That was the beginning of the battle.

Geoffrey, hearing the noise, came nobly to the rescue, to be received by a handful of soot from Ginger. It was a glorious battle. Ginger and William fought Geoffrey, and Joan fought everyone, and Mary sat on the soot heap and screamed. They threw soot till there was practically no soot left to throw. A butcher boy who was passing and heard the noise came in to arbitrate, but stayed to participate. Sheer lust of battle descended upon them all. Then came sudden sanity. In stricken silence they gazed at each other.

Joan seized Mary by the hand. She glared round at them all from a small black face framed with grimy curls.

"I *hate* you all!" she said, stamping a small black foot.

"*Hate* you all!" screamed Mary, whose tears were making white tracks down her black face.

"It wasn't me," said Geoffrey eagerly and ungrammatically.

"I hate *you*," said Joan, "worse than anyone – worse than William and worse than anybody, an' I'm going home to tell mother – so there."

"Tho' there," wailed Mary in concert.

With outraged dignity and clinging soot on every line of her figure, Joan led Mary from the garden.

It was more than Geoffrey could bear.

He followed them sobbing loudly, his white suit a cloudy grey-black.

Joan's voice floated out on the twilit air.

"An' I'm *goin'* to tell mother – *you'll* catch it, William Brown."

Ginger looked round uneasily.

"I'd best be going, William," he murmured.

Dejection descended upon William.

"A'right."

Then he looked at Ginger and down at himself.

"Funny how it gets all over you," he said, "and don't it make your eyes look queer?"

"Am I's bad as you?" said Ginger apprehensively.

"Worse," said William.

"Will it come off with cold water?"

"Dunno," said William.

"I'll give it," said Ginger, "a jolly good *try*. What'll your folks say?"

"Dunno," said William.

"Well, goo'night, William."

"Goo'night," said William, despondently. Dusk had fallen.

He crept round to the back door, hoping to slip up the back stairs unobserved. But the cook's strident voice came from the library.

"Mrs Bell wants you on the telephone at once, please'm. It's something about Master William."

William beat a hasty retreat to the laurel bushes. Then, hearing footsteps on the drive, he stood on tiptoe and peered out. He met the horrified gaze of the housemaid, who was returning from her afternoon out.

With a wild yell she ran like an arrow towards the back door.

"Oh lor! Oh lor!" she called. "I seed the devil. I seed 'im in the garding."

William among the laurel bushes smiled proudly to himself. Then he sat down cross-legged in his retreat, black face on black hands, gleaming white eyes gazing dreamily into the distance.

He was not building castles in the air; he was not repenting of his sins; he was not thinking about future retribution. He was merely deciding that he wouldn't be a sweep after all. It did taste so nasty.

SAINT GEORGE AND THE DRAGON

English Legend

Hundreds of years ago in about AD 400 a boy called George was born in Cappadocia where his father was a Roman officer. George was a Christian but at that time many people were tortured for their faith, so when he grew up he decided to travel the world and tell others all about his Christian beliefs.

After a few years, he travelled to North Africa where he rode into the town of Silene and soon found out about the troubles there: in an evil-smelling lake nearby, there lived a dragon. It had claws like a lion; a serpent's tail; huge sharp teeth; and fire spurted from its mouth.

The dragon had come into the town and killed many men with its fiery tongue and sharp teeth. The townsfolk tried to keep the dragon away from their houses by feeding it each day with two sheep. But before long they had only a few sheep left.

"What shall we do?" people cried. "The king must help us."

So the king had a meeting with all the important townspeople.

"This dragon will come into our town again if we're not careful," he told them. "So we must feed it somehow."

"What with?" asked the mayor. "We have only four sheep left in our fields."

They talked and they argued until one man said: "Dragons like eating children. So I say that each week one girl or boy from the town should be fed to the dragon."

Everybody shouted and screamed, then the king spoke, "Has anybody got a better idea?" There was silence, so the king went on, "We'll have a lottery. Each boy and each girl will be given a number and once a week a number will be pulled out of this velvet bag. Whoever holds that number will be given to the dragon. It will not matter if the child is rich, poor, a noble or a peasant, everyone must take part so that our town may be saved. That is the law now."

And so several children were fed to the dragon. Later on, the number of Princess Sabra was pulled out of the bag. She was the king's only child and she was both beautiful and gentle. The king was overcome with sorrow. He turned to the people and said, "She is my only daughter, a princess. Please, you cannot take her."

"You made the law," they replied. "You said everybody must take part. You cannot change the rules to save your daughter."

Sadly, the king went to Princess Sabra. "Alas, my dearest daughter," he said. "You must be handed over to the dragon three days from now."

As the time came close, the mayor came to the king and said: "We can see the dragon is breathing fire. It is hungry. Your daughter must go!"

Sabra put on her finest clothes as if her wedding day had come. Her father kissed her and he himself led her to the dragon's lair and left her to her fate. The poor girl stood there weeping bitterly and shaking with fear as she waited for the dreadful dragon to come.

Instead, she heard the sound of horse's hooves and the clink of armour. It was George of Cappadocia who came galloping up, his gleaming sword at his side and his spear in his hand. He had witnessed the town's sufferings and had now come to rescue the fair princess.

"Princess," George said, "have no fear. I shall save you."

But as he said this, a dark shadow came over them and the dragon rushed out. George made the Sign of the Cross to show he was

a Christian then he spurred on his horse, lifted his spear and charged! The dragon was taken by surprise and George's spear went deep into the monster's throat. It fell over and George leapt from his horse and plunged his sword under the green scales. The dragon lay on its side and gave up the battle.

"Tie your girdle round its head," George said to Sabra, "it cannot hurt you now." She did this and the dragon followed her like a pet dog. When the people saw the dragon they began to run away but George called out, "Do not be afraid. I think that God made me brave enough to overcome this dragon. See, it is dying, and will hurt you no more."

The king offered George gold and jewels but he would not take them. "Give this reward to the poor," he said, "and build a church on the spot where I defeated the dragon."

The king promised to do this and George set off on his travels again. He had many adventures but when he reached Palestine, the Roman Governor tortured him because he was a Christian and chopped off his head.

A splendid chapel was built over his grave but George's heart was taken out and carried to England. The Order of Saint George was founded in Windsor Castle and after that, George the Dragon-Slayer of Cappadocia was known as Saint George of England.

DEATH AND THE BOY

West African Traditional

A dreadful famine came over the land of West Africa many years ago. Every day the sun blazed down. The water holes grew smaller and smaller until they dried up altogether. The crops in the fields shrivelled and died while the poor animals staggered about looking for food and water. People in the villages spent every hour of every day digging in the hard earth where they hoped to find a few withered roots. They watched the sky and they prayed for the rain-clouds to come.

In one village a boy got tired of digging.

"Dear me," he sighed. "I've forgotten what meat tastes like. And I hate these horrible flies. They manage to find something to live on! I think I'll go into the jungle and try my luck there."

So the next day he slipped away from his home and wandered along the jungle paths. But he found no food and on the third day he was ready to give up. He was turning round to go home when he saw a strange sight. There were many thin black ropes lying by the side of the path. They stretched in different ways through the dry bushes. "What have we here?" the boy wondered. "I think I'll follow one of these ropes and find out where it leads."

He walked for at least a mile until he saw a small hill. He tramped towards it, keeping his eye on the rope all the time. But the hill wasn't a hill. It was a hut. The ropes weren't ropes. They were locks of hair. And that hair belonged to a giant! He was enormous and his teeth looked very sharp indeed.

"He looks very well fed," the boy said to himself, "I wonder how he gets his food in this terrible famine?"

He was wondering whether to stay or run away when the giant spoke.

"What are you? What are you doing here?"

"Please, sir," the boy said. "I'm a b-b-boy. I'm only looking for meat."

"You can work for me, if you like," the giant went on. "I'll give you plenty of meat but you must work hard and do as you're told."

"I'll work well," the boy promised. "What shall I do?"

154

"Sweep out the hut and chop wood for the fire," roared the giant.

The boy started working that very day and the giant kept his word and gave him as much meat as he could possibly eat.

The boy worked well for some months but he missed his parents and home. "May I go home for a while?" he asked the giant one day.

"Certainly," said the giant, "but I must have someone to do your work while you are away. You'd better find somebody for me."

"Of course I'll do that," the boy replied. He packed a bag full of meat and set off back to his village.

His family were happy to welcome him. "How well you look," they exclaimed. "So plump and we are all so thin!"

"I'd like to know exactly what you've been doing," said his brother.

"Well, it's like this," the boy replied. "I have the easiest job in the world and what's more, I get plenty of meat as well. How would you like a job the same as this?"

"I'd take it at once," his brother said. "Tell me about it."

"I met this man in the jungle," the boy explained, "and I look after his hut. He wants some help while I take my holiday."

"I'll go today," his brother said quickly as he saw the joints the boy was unpacking. "What do you call your master, did you say?"

"His name is Owuo." Everybody was silent suddenly. Owuo is a West African word which means Death!

The weeks went by and the boy was restless. There wasn't any meat at home. His father and mother wanted him to help in the sun-baked fields which was very hard work indeed. So one day he went back into the jungle with his bag and he followed the hair-ropes to the giant's hut. He looked around but to his surprise he could not see his brother anywhere.

"Oh," said the giant, "he was homesick so he went home. Didn't you meet him as you came through the jungle?"

"No, I wonder why he didn't wait here for me!" the boy said.

"Why worry about him?" the giant said quickly.

The boy swept and dusted the hut as usual. It was very easy work and the giant gave him so much meat that he grew round and fat. After a time he longed to see his family again and hear all the village news.

"Would you mind if I went home again for a while?" he asked.

"Not at all," the giant said, "but I wonder if you could find a girl to take your place this time? I'd like a wife."

The boy set off the next day, but when he arrived in his village he did not think his parents were so glad to see him. "You told your brother all about your wonderful job," they said. "He went into the jungle but he never came back. What happened to him? Tell us that."

The boy did not mention that the man he worked for was a giant because if he did, he knew they would not let him go back to the hut. That night, he was thinking about the giant's steaks when his sister sat down nearby. "Why are you fat and we are skinny?" she asked. The boy told her about Owuo. "He wants a wife," he added. "A wife?" his sister said. "If I married Owuo would I have to work hard in the fields? Would he give me plenty of meat?"

156

"I think so," said her brother, rather doubtfully.

"Tell me the way," his sister interrupted. "It's a wonderful chance for me. A husband and plenty of food too!"

She forced her brother to tell her how to find Owuo and next day she left the village, taking a servant with her as well for company.

This time, the boy did not stay long in his village. He did not understand why he felt uneasy but he could not stop thinking about his sister and her servant. He went back and followed the trail of the black hair-ropes to the giant's hut.

Owuo was sitting outside and at once the boy was worried. Owuo was gnawing a bone just like a dog. And he was all alone!

"I didn't expect you back so early," the giant said cheerfully.

"Well, I thought about my sister," the boy started to say, but Owuo spoke quickly, "I haven't seen her or her rascally servant for some days now. They'll turn up when they're hungry, never you fear," and he tossed the cleaned bone carelessly over his shoulder. "You must be hungry, my boy, after your long walk. What about getting yourself a nice supper?"

Somehow the boy did not feel at all happy but he thanked Owuo and went into a shady place where the meat was stored away from the sun and flies. He stepped over the piles of bones which were always left lying around then he stopped. His hair stood on end. His feet refused to move. His eyes opened as wide as dinner-plates. His blood seemed to turn into ice. A bracelet of red beads was fastened round one of the bones. He knew it at once – it belonged to his sister! He stared all around him. He felt sick suddenly as well as horrified.

As soon as it was dark he crept away from the hut. When he was far enough away from it, he raced through the jungle at a tremendous speed. He was breathless when he reached his village but he managed to call to his parents and he poured out his horrible story.

They were sorrowful at the loss of their children and servant but they were completely horrified when they and all their neighbours understood for what purpose Owuo had killed them. They were terribly angry as they set off to march through the jungle to take their revenge. Each of them carried a flaming torch. The boy was their guide but he felt very miserable. He blamed himself for all these deaths, you see.

Before long they found the hair-ropes. The boy stopped

suddenly. "I have a good idea," he cried. "Owuo is too big for us to fight. But this fire can help us." He seized the nearest torch and pushed it into all the hair-ropes. It was like lighting fireworks. The hair sizzled and frizzled through the bushes and the villagers followed as close as they dared. Owuo was fast asleep in his hut but when the flames reached him, he disappeared in a flash. The villagers rushed up and all they could find was a big heap of powder on the ground.

The boy kicked the ashes round the hut and he found a small bottle. There were a few drops of liquid inside. He guessed that the potion was magic and he rushed over to the food-store and carefully poured three drops on the bones. Instantly his brother, his sister and her servant came to life! Everybody laughed and danced with joy. "There's one drop left," the boy said. "What shall I do with it?"

"Nothing," said his father. "Wait!" cried his mother. "Idiot!" shouted everybody else as the boy poured that last drop over the giant's ashes.

There was a funny hiss and a thin grey smoke with a horrible smell twisted and turned. Slowly, slowly, the ashes turned into a huge eye which opened and shut with an evil look.

Back the boy jumped. He was terrified but nothing more grew out of the ashes. One magic drop was not enough to make a giant come alive!

The family and their neighbours went home. They never went near that place again.

Some people say that Owuo's eye is still blinking there and that there is so much dust it will never stop.

THE FOX AND THE STORK

Aesop's Fables

A Fox decided to ask a Stork to dinner one evening. The Fox thought he was being very clever when he provided some delicious soup in a shallow dish. The Fox watched, smiling to himself, as the Stork tried in vain to drink the soup – but was unable to because of her long and narrow bill. The poor Stork was as hungry at the end of the meal as she had been before it. The Fox pretended to be sorry that the Stork had not eaten more and said that perhaps the soup had had too much pepper in it. The Stork remained quiet, and then asked the Fox if he would be so good as to return her visit. The Fox readily agreed to dine with her the next day.

At the dinner, the Stork proudly presented the soup in a tall and elegant vessel with a narrow stem. The Stork reached in easily with her beautiful long neck and bill, but the Fox could only watch helplessly, as he was quite unable to reach the top of the tall glass.

THE CROW

Polish Traditional

There were once two princesses who were both young and pretty. Near to where the sisters lived there stood an old ruined castle set in a garden filled with flowers. The younger princess liked to walk alone in the garden and smell its rich fragrance.

One day she was walking under some lime trees, when a black crow hopped out of a rosebush in front of her. The poor bird was tattered and torn and was in considerable pain. The princess took pity on it at once. The crow felt this and said, "Do not be upset, little one. I am not really a crow at all, but an enchanted prince, doomed to spend my youth in misery. You may be able to save me if you wish to."

"I would dearly love to help you," said the princess eagerly.

"It will mean leaving your family and living in this ruined castle for a year," said the crow. "There is one habitable room in which there is a golden bed where you must sleep. There is one other very important thing I must tell you: whatever you may see or hear in the night, do not scream out – for if you give even a single cry my sufferings will become worse and the spell will never be broken."

The sweet princess at once left her home and went to live in the ruined castle.

When night came she went to lie down on the golden bed but found she could not sleep. Suddenly, she was startled by noises out in the passageway – she stiffened as the noises grew louder and then sat up in horror as her door was flung open and a troop of mysterious creatures entered her room. She watched in mute terror as they lit a fire in the big old fireplace and placed a cauldron of boiling water on it. Then these strange beings approached the poor princess and caught hold of her and dragged her towards the cauldron. The girl nearly fainted with fear – but she remained silent. Then suddenly the cock crowed and the beings vanished. The princess sank exhausted back on to her bed, still trembling, but thankful that she had not uttered a single cry.

The princess saw the crow in the garden that morning – his wounds had begun to heal and he thanked her for her courage.

And so time passed. Each night she suffered awful torments

from the strange spirits. But they always disappeared when the cock crowed and no harm ever came to her.

Then, a day before the year was up, the princess's older sister came to visit her. She begged to be allowed to spend the night with her sister in the golden bed and the soft-hearted princess gave in to her, telling her to remain silent, no matter what.

That night, the evil spirits appeared and danced before the bed. The sister screamed, and nothing would quieten her.

The next day, after her sister had departed, the young princess wept, thinking that she had broken her promise to the prince. Then, the black crow appeared. He was torn and bleeding, but he spoke softly to her, "If only you had stayed alone last night, I would now be a prince. There is only one thing that can save me now, and that is for you to go out and work as a kitchen-maid for a year and suffer many hardships."

So the princess went out into the world and served as a kitchen-maid. She endured a great deal, but she was never tempted to go back to her family, and she worked hard for her living.

One evening, when she was scrubbing some pans in the scullery, she heard a rustling noise. She looked up and there was the black crow at the window. He swooped down and was instantly transformed into a handsome young man. He knelt at her feet and kissed her weary little white hands. "Thank you, my sweet one, you have saved me. Come home with me now."

So they returned to the castle where they had endured so much. But the castle was transformed – it was now completely restored and looked magnificent surrounded by the fragrant flower garden. And there they lived in deep happiness for many, many years.

THE BOY
WHO FOUND FEAR

Turkish Traditional

In a faraway land there once lived a woman who had one son. She loved him dearly, but he was often lonely because their cottage was on the edge of a forest and nobody lived nearby. So the boy stayed at home and they kept each other company.

One wintry night when they were chatting by the fire, there was a sudden storm and the strong winds blew open the front door. The woman shook and shivered. She looked over her shoulder as if something horrible had been blown inside. "Shut the door," she said quickly. "I'm frightened. I don't know why."

"Frightened?" said her son. "What do you feel if you're frightened?"

"Frightened is frightened," his mother answered. "You're afraid of something and Fear takes hold of you. That's all I can say."

"How odd!" said her son. "I think I'll travel the world and look for Fear."

The next morning he set off before dawn and went through the forest until he came to a mountain. He climbed for some hours until he reached a rocky hollow where he saw a band of fierce robbers warming themselves round a lovely fire. The boy was tired and cold by this time so he went straight up to them and wriggled close to the flames.

"Good evening," he said cheerily.

The robbers were so surprised to see him that they stopped sharpening their knives and daggers. "Who are you?" their captain demanded. "Who has dared to enter our camp?"

"Don't worry," the boy replied, "I'm searching for Fear, that's all. Do you know where I can find it, please?"

"Fear is here with us," growled the captain.

"Is that so?" said the boy. "Where is it? I see nothing."

"Take this flour, sugar and butter down to the churchyard," the robber said. "Bake a cake for us in this pot, then come back here."

The boy felt warmer now so he agreed willingly and ran down the hill. When he reached the churchyard he found some sticks and made a fire. He filled the pot with water and when the water was bubbling he mixed flour, sugar and butter into a flat cake and put it into the pot. Before long it was nicely cooked so he put it on a stone to cool while he put out the fire. At that moment a thin white hand stretched up from a grave and a quivery ghostly voice asked:

"Did you make that cake for me?"

"Certainly not," laughed the boy. "I've made this cake for some living people, not for someone in his grave!" He picked up the cake, patted the outstretched hand and then he ran back up the mountain, whistling cheerfully.

"Did you find Fear?" the robbers asked when he gave them the cake.

"No," he said. "Was Fear in the churchyard? All I saw was a hand in a grave. He wanted my cake but I tapped the hand and said I'd made it for someone else. The hand vanished. That's all!"

He snuggled near the fire while the robbers looked at each other in surprise. Then one of them spoke to the boy.

"Well, you can try again. Follow that path over there until you come to a deep pool. You'll meet Fear on the way, I'm sure."

"That's good," the boy said as he jumped up and ran off.

It did not take him long to see the water sparkling in the

moonlight and when he got close he noticed a tall swing standing over the pool, and in the swing he saw a small boy who was sobbing bitterly.

"Fancy putting a swing over the water," the boy thought. "I'd better find out why that child is crying so much." He hurried forward just as a pretty girl ran in front of him and stopped him.

"Oh dear, my poor little brother," she cried. "I tried to lift him down but the swing is so high that I cannot reach it. Please will you stand close to the edge of the pool and let me stand on your shoulders? I'm sure I could reach him then."

"Of course," the boy said and in a flash the girl jumped on his shoulders. But instead of helping her brother out of the swing she pushed her feet hard against the older boy's neck. She pressed so hard that he started to choke and his feet slipped towards the water. He was angry with the girl so he gave a tremendous heave and threw her off backwards! Her bracelet flew off her arm as she reached the ground and he picked it up. "I think I'll keep this to remind me of tonight and the strange things that have happened," he said to himself. As he turned around, he saw that the girl, the child and the swing had all three vanished! He shrugged his shoulders and as dawn was breaking he went over the mountains to a little town. As he walked along the street, tired and hungry, he met a merchant who stopped him and said, "You're wearing my bracelet! Where did you get it?"

"It's mine," said the boy.

"No, it isn't. It's mine. Hand it over," cried the merchant, lifting his heavy stick.

"We'd better find the judge and tell him our stories," the boy declared calmly. "If he decides it is yours, you shall have it. If not, I'll keep it." The merchant agreed and lowered his stick. They went to the court and saw the judge. He listened carefully to both of them then he said seriously:

"Neither of you has a right to the bracelet, so it must remain in the court until you can bring another one to match it."

The boy and the merchant bowed and left the court. Both of them wondered where they could possibly find a second bracelet. The youth walked on until he found himself on the seashore. He saw that a ship had struck a hidden rock and was sinking fast. The crew were standing on deck screaming and shrieking, their faces deathly white. "Have you found Fear?" the boy called. Back came the loud answer, "Help! We are drowning. Don't ask questions but help us!" The boy did not pause for a second, he threw off his heavy clothes and swam to the ship.

"Our ship is going down. We'll all drown. We're frightened!" the boy heard the sailors shout, as he asked them to throw down a rope. "Fasten your end to the mast," he called while he fastened the other end safely around his waist. Then he dived down, down, down, until he touched the sea-bed and he looked all around. He spotted a mermaid tugging at an iron chain which she had somehow fastened to the ship above. She was dragging it little by little under the waves. He grabbed her arms and forced her to drop the chain. Immediately the ship stopped heaving about and the sailors managed to float it gently off the rock. The boy unfastened the rope around his waist and tied the mermaid to a rock to keep her out of mischief. Then he swam calmly up and away to the beach.

Quickly he dressed and wandered on until he reached a lovely garden. Many beautiful flowers were growing near a crystal-clear stream so he decided to rest awhile. He curled up under a bush and fell fast asleep. A soft cooing sound woke him and he saw three doves diving into the stream. Playfully they splashed each other, then they plunged deep into a pool. But what a surprise! When they came up, they had changed into three graceful girls. They carried golden goblets filled to the brim with sparkling liquid.

"Let us raise a toast, dear sisters," said one girl. "I'll drink to the youth who tapped my hand in the graveyard. I didn't manage to frighten him at all. Who will you drink to?"

"To the youth who threw me over his shoulders at the pool," said the second sister. "He wasn't scared even when I almost choked him to death."

"And I'll drink to the youth," said the third, "who tied me to a rock just as I was pulling a ship and its frightened crew under the sea."

They lifted their goblets and drank to the youth's health, but before they could put them down the youth stood in front of them. "I am that youth you've been chatting about, now you can give me the bracelet which matches the one I picked up. I deserve that for all the trouble you have caused me."

"Come with us," the sisters laughed. They led him into a hidden cave and quickly found the second bracelet which they fastened round the youth's arm. "Thank you, dear friends," he said. "I'll never forget you but I must be on my way. I cannot rest until I find Fear."

He claimed his bracelet from the judge and set off again on his travels. He did not meet Fear as he tramped along and when he came to a big town, the streets were so packed with people he could scarcely move.

"Why are there so many people here?" he asked a man standing nearby.

"Our king is dead," he answered. "He had no children but we must find another king, so every morning a sacred pigeon flies out of yonder tower: whoever it chooses to sit upon, that person will be our king. The pigeon will fly out at any moment so watch carefully, young man."

All eyes were turned to the tower and when the sun was exactly over it, a door opened and a beautiful pigeon stood there. Its feathers gleamed pink, grey, green and blue as it circled in the air. Once, twice, three times it circled then it swooped down and rested on the youth's head. There was a great shout, "Our king! Our king!" but he did not hear the shouts. Suddenly he saw himself sitting on a throne, listening to everybody. Some wanted to be rich, some wanted to be married, some had quarrelled with their neighbour. Every day he would be forced to settle these affairs. He could not have more adventures with robbers, graveyards or mermaids. He hid his face in his hands and groaned: "*No!*"

More pigeons flew from the tower and one by one they settled on his head and the crowds shouted louder and louder: "Our king!"

As the young man listened a sudden cold shiver that he did not understand, shook him from head to toe.

"This is the Fear you have been searching for," whispered a soft voice in his ear. And the young man lifted his head.

"On this day," he said to himself, "I have found Fear and it has brought me a kingdom."

THE SORCERER'S APPRENTICE

Russian Traditional

In Old Russia a small valley once nestled at the foot of a dark mountain. The people who lived there never climbed the steep paths up the mountain, for at the top there was a huge castle with high walls and gloomy towers. A Sorcerer lived there and he never allowed anybody to draw near or see inside his forbidding castle.

The villagers worked happily together in the fields. They helped each other with the farm animals and they always had enough to eat and drink.

One autumn they went to the fields to gather their crops as usual, laughing and joking as they walked along. But when they got there, the fields were empty. There was not a single ear of wheat nor any fruit on the trees or grapes on the vines. Everything had vanished.

"Our crops were here yesterday," said one farmer. "I saw them myself."

"They must have been stolen during the night," said another.

"Rascals! Thieves!" shouted another. "They've taken everything! I'll teach them to steal our harvest if I catch them."

The villagers trooped back home, then they hunted for the robbers. They looked at footprints on the paths, but their own boots had made them. They hunted for grain or a dropped apple, but they found nothing. "It's vanished. It's like magic," they muttered.

The villagers didn't starve because they had enough food in their barns left over from the year before. They planted seeds the next spring as usual and they were pleased to see that the crops were growing bigger and better than ever. When autumn came the villagers watched the harvest carefully. Every day the women walked around the fields and every night the men stood guard. Harvest Day came but, oh dear, all the crops disappeared again.

"They were fine when we left them at dawn," the men said.

"Well, they've gone now," one old woman said, "there must be an evil spirit about. Our valley is bewitched!" Children started to cry. Old people sobbed, "What will happen this winter? There's no food in the barns. We'll starve." What a sad sight it was. Then a boy called

Yuri stepped forward. "It's no use crying like this," he said. "I'm strong and healthy, so I'm going to try and solve this puzzle. I'll call on the Sorcerer and see what he has to say. Maybe I'll make my fortune at the same time. Who knows!" With a cheery wave Yuri ran over the fields to the mountain path and he was soon out of sight.

Yuri cut himself a fine walking stick from a tree he found, then he climbed swiftly upwards. The thick white mountain mist swirled all around and soon he could not see the valley far below. This was a real adventure, he thought, and he whistled a merry tune as he climbed.

"I must reach the mountain top before long," Yuri puffed.

"My dear young man, you are there already." A loud harsh voice sounded in Yuri's ear. Then the strangest old man came out of the mist and stood in front of him. Yuri held his breath. He'd never seen anyone like this before. His robes were dark and covered with strange jewels. He held a wand in one hand and a big black raven was sitting on his arm.

"This must be the Sorcerer," Yuri thought. "I hope he is the friendly kind."

"It is almost dark," the Sorcerer said, "you'd better spend the night in my castle." So Yuri followed him inside the huge castle walls. The Sorcerer hurried across the courtyard and Yuri saw barrels and sacks of food everywhere. The Raven flew off the Sorcerer's arm and perched on the boy's shoulder. "This food is from your valley," he croaked.

"He stole it, did he?" whispered Yuri. "How cruel! I could kill him."

"He'll kill you first," screeched the Raven. "I advise you to learn about his magic spells, then you can use them against him." At that moment the Sorcerer spun round. "I'm looking for an apprentice," he said. "You look to be a lively lad. What about it?" Yuri thought about the Raven's words then he said, "If you'll give me magic lessons, I'll help you with your work."

The Sorcerer showed Yuri around the castle and at last they went into the Great Hall. Yuri could see statues, armour, ancient books, and bottles filled with hissing bubbling liquids. A great iron cauldron almost as big as Yuri stood in the middle of the hall and the Sorcerer pointed to it and growled, "As my apprentice you must keep this cauldron filled to the brim or else there'll be trouble, serious trouble."

So next day Yuri began work as an apprentice. Each day he was given more and more work but he never had his magic lessons. The Raven often perched on Yuri's arm and one day he croaked, "Will you take me with you when you escape from here?"

"Escape!" laughed Yuri. "I can go home anytime. I'm not a prisoner!" He walked to the castle gate with the Raven. Then he stopped dead. He could not move an inch forward. The Sorcerer had put a spell on him! Yuri gritted his teeth. He'd beat the Sorcerer in the end!

But the Sorcerer made him work harder than ever. He mixed bowl after bowl of horrible-smelling liquid and he made Yuri carry heavy books of spells into the Great Hall, but the worst job was keeping that huge cauldron filled up. Yuri had to go down many stone steps and across rough cobblestones to reach the stream where he filled his buckets. He had to make trip after trip with the heavy buckets and his shoulders ached. "I wish I knew a few magic words," he said. "I'd make these buckets fly!"

"If you knew some magic we could get away from here," the Raven screeched grumpily. "Have you noticed that the clever old

fellow never lets us hear one single word when he makes his spells?"

"You're right," said Yuri. "We must find a way to overhear the magic words. Then we'll use them and set ourselves free."

But it wasn't easy. They crept behind the Sorcerer's back. They hid under the table. Yuri offered to hold the bottles of nasty liquid but it was no use. The Sorcerer gave Yuri more work both day and night but he didn't let out any secret spells at all.

One night Yuri was so tired he fell asleep in a dark corner of the Great Hall. The Sorcerer was so busy with his spells that he didn't notice him. Accidentally he knocked a glass bottle on to the floor. It broke into a thousand pieces with such a crash that it woke Yuri up. To his astonishment the Sorcerer clicked his fingers at a broom nearby. He said some all-important magic words and at once the broom scurried across the room by itself. It cleared up the glass quickly then hurried back to its place again.

After a time the Sorcerer went to bed. Yuri crept upstairs as well and he smiled as he practised the magic words he'd just heard.

Next day he told the Raven the good news. "Be careful," the bird croaked, "don't do anything until the Sorcerer is out of the

way." He flew to the top of the tower and watched until the old man disappeared from view. Yuri hopped with excitement. He said the magic words and ordered the broom to fetch the water for the cauldron. He could not believe his eyes! Two long thin brown arms shot out of the broom handle and grabbed the two buckets. In a twinkling it dashed through the Great Hall; it jumped down the steps and cobbles to the stream. Yuri and the Raven could not keep up with the broom and in no time at all the big cauldron was full. Yuri was very pleased. That was a big part of his work finished in a short time. But it wasn't finished! The broom went back to the stream and filled the buckets again. Bucketful after bucketful it brought back and before long, water was pouring out all over the floor.

"Help," screeched the Raven. "Stop it, Yuri, or we'll be flooded."

"I can't," shouted Yuri. "I only know the magic words to begin spells."

The broom poured more and more water into the cauldron. Soon tables, chairs, papers, books, floated gaily around the hall. Yuri grabbed an axe and chopped the broom in two. To his horror, the

second half grew arms and carried two more buckets! Soon the castle was flooded and water flowed down the stairs into the courtyard. Then there was a clap of thunder and the sky grew dark. The Sorcerer had returned. He was so furious that sparks flew off his robes. He screamed some words and at once the broom went back to its place and the water disappeared. The Sorcerer turned angrily to deal with his apprentice but Yuri was smiling! At last he'd heard the magic words to stop spells!

"Beat that boy," bellowed the angry old man to the broom. Yuri waited calmly. The broom was ready to hit him, then he shouted the magic words and at once the broom slunk away.

"I know your secrets now," laughed Yuri. "Your wicked spells are finished, Sorcerer. You let slip the magic words." He danced around. But the Sorcerer smiled a horrible smile and called Yuri to him.

"You're a clever young fellow," he said smoothly. "I'm not surprised that you've learnt so much. You're the best apprentice I know."

"Take care," the Raven croaked fearfully. "Beware this smiling old man!" In a trice, the Sorcerer turned into a growling bear. He gave Yuri a nasty swipe with his large paw and Yuri hid under the table. The bear broke it with one blow. He pushed the boy into a corner and lifted his paw. The raven flew down. "Bears hate snakes," he screeched. "Turn yourself into a snake with the magic words."

Yuri had been so frightened that he'd forgotten that he knew them! The next moment he turned into a snake slithering towards the bear who promptly turned into an eagle. The eagle caught the snake in its cruel talons and the Raven flew about shouting and cawing: "Change, Yuri, change."

In a flash Yuri changed himself into a wildcat. Spitting and snarling, he leapt at the eagle but he only managed to pull out a tuft of his tail feathers before he spread his wings and escaped. Round and round the Great Hall the eagle flapped until at last he flew outside the castle with the wildcat chasing swiftly after him. Like lightning, the eagle dropped down by the stream and then he vanished. The wildcat raced to the water. He peered over the edge but he could see nothing. He crouched down and blinked.

Then a pretty silver fish swam into sight and a gentle little voice said, "Hello there. You're not so clever after all, my bonny fellow. My magic is better than yours. You'll never find me in this stream." The Sorcerer had turned himself into this gleaming fish!

"If I turn myself into a fisherman," whispered Yuri to the Raven. "I can wade in the water and catch him."

The Raven shook his glossy feathers, "You'll have to be very clever and cunning to catch that fish. Why don't you try doing this?" And he flew down and whispered something into Yuri's ear.

Yuri changed back into his real self then he stood on the bank and called, "Sorcerer, prove that your magic is greater than mine. Can you change yourself into anything, anything at all?"

"Just you wait," boasted the old man. "I'm a small fish now but I can turn myself into the highest mountain in the world. That's how strong my magic is."

"That's easy enough," said Yuri scornfully. "Anybody can grow big. It's much harder to change into something really small."

The little fish flapped in the water. "Tell me what you want. I'll soon show you, stupid apprentice, who is the greatest wizard of all."

"Well then," said Yuri, "turn yourself into a drop of water."

There was a flash of lightning and the Sorcerer's magic words sounded like thunderbolts. To be truthful, Yuri and the Raven were scared! Then the big booming voice died away. There was silence everywhere except in the little stream. It tinkled and bubbled through the castle gardens and onto the mountainside. It gurgled down the path into a sparkling waterfall then it flowed into a river and finished in the sea.

Yuri and the Raven laughed and danced with joy by the stream. Yuri sang, and the Raven cawed: "He's gone. He'll be swallowed up in the sea. The Sorcerer was too clever in the end! We're free. At last I can fly anywhere in the wide world."

"Let's go home," said Yuri. "Please come with me, dear friend. You helped me so much. Everybody will want to thank you."

So the Raven nestled on Yuri's arm and they hurried down the mountain path without looking back at the gloomy castle.

All the villagers rushed out to welcome them. They gave a wonderful feast with lots of music and dancing. For many weeks afterwards, Yuri and the Raven were kept busy telling about their adventures. Yuri remembered the magic words and he used them for the good of the whole village. Soon the valley was the happiest place in the whole of Old Russia. "I promise that the magic words will only be used to bring happiness," said Yuri, "never evil things."

"I'll make sure you keep that promise," croaked his friend the Raven from his golden perch in Yuri's splendid new house. And he did too!

ORPHEUS IN THE UNDERWORLD

Greek Legend

Thousands of years ago in the sunny Greek islands there lived a band of men called the Argonauts. They were famous warriors, but there was one of them who did not carry a sword, spear, bow and arrow, or even a shield. His name was Orpheus and he carried a lyre. He was the son of a king, and Calliope, his mother, was the goddess of poetry. Apollo, the god of music, had given Orpheus his lyre and he made such wonderful music that everybody listened in delight. Birds flew round his head; trees bent down to listen and wild animals gathered at his feet. Even the hard rocks became soft when Orpheus played and sang his sweet songs.

Orpheus helped Jason, a famous Argonaut, to take the Golden Fleece by singing a lullaby to a fierce dragon and when he returned from this adventure a lovely nymph called Eurydice came to listen to his music. She loved his songs and Orpheus soon loved her. She promised to marry him and they were wonderfully happy together.

But one day Orpheus was practising his music at home and Eurydice went for a walk in the woods with a friend of theirs called Aristeus. He was jealous of Orpheus and, once he was alone with Eurydice, began to make fun of him. At first, Eurydice thought he was joking but soon she saw that he really meant all the unkind things he was saying about her husband. She was frightened and upset. She turned away from Aristeus and ran back towards her house. He ran after her for, truth to tell, he was sorry he had teased her and he wanted her to forgive him. But when she heard him crashing along Eurydice ran even faster. She wanted to get back to Orpheus. In her hurry she did not look where she was going so she did not see a bright green snake coiled up in the grass. Her foot caught its tail. Instantly it reared up and sank its forked tongue into her ankle. She hardly felt the pain but went on running until she felt giddy. Her legs were as heavy as lead. She screamed then everything went black. Orpheus rushed out of the house but he could not help her now. Eurydice was dead.

Orpheus went wild with grief. For a time he would not leave the house, neither would he eat nor drink. Then one day as dawn was breaking, he put on the dress of the Argonauts and left his house. He carried his lyre, but now he played such sad music that trees and stones wept when they heard him. Alone he wandered until one day he went into a temple and begged Zeus, the most powerful of the gods, to help him.

"I beg you to let me go to the Underworld," he said, "so that I may find Eurydice. I cannot live without my beloved wife."

"You may go," said Zeus, "but your path will be difficult. You will meet many perils. Think carefully before you go."

Orpheus did not wait. His journey took many weary months as he travelled over mountains, across deserts, through wild forests. He battled against blinding snowstorms and scorching sun until he came to a wide ocean where he found a tiny boat. He sailed on and on until he reached the shores of the Underworld. Everything looked grey and gloomy and not a sound could he hear. He walked on till he saw a pair of big black gates. He peered through into a dark cave. A watchdog called Cerberus lumbered towards him. It had three heads and three sets of sharp black fangs. One head began to growl. The second head started to howl and the third one snapped its strong jaws greedily. Slowly Orpheus lifted his lyre and played enchanting music. The howling stopped and one head after the other drooped until Cerberus sank to the ground. Orpheus played and sang until the monster was fast asleep then he stepped over its sleeping body into the cave.

He walked along a sandy path which went deep down into the earth. Silver flames flickered on the walls and he heard the sound of water. To his surprise he saw a river black as night, and an old man standing by a low flat boat which looked like a fish. He was holding two oars painted with butterflies and he glared at Orpheus. "Who are you?" he demanded. "I wasn't expecting anyone today. You're not dead!" He poked Orpheus in his ribs. "You're alive!"

"What is your name, old man?" asked Orpheus, "and what is your work?"

"I am Charon," was the reply, "I run the ferry over the River Styx to the Underworld. But I cannot take a live man."

"I must go across," said Orpheus. "I cannot swim over because the water is flowing too fast. Please ferry me, I beg you."

"Impossible!" said Charon.

Then Orpheus lifted his lyre again and played until the ferryman's heart was softened and he agreed to row Orpheus to the other bank.

Orpheus went along another path away from the River Styx. He was now in a ghostly grey land and in the distance he noticed the dim grey shape of a castle. He walked towards it and all the time he played and sang for he hoped Eurydice would hear him. On the way he passed many strange sights. He saw a man standing in a river under a bunch of juicy grapes. This was the wicked King Tantalus who was for ever hungry and thirsty in the Underworld. Whenever he stooped to drink the water it flowed out of his hands. When he wanted to pick but a single grape the whole bunch swung out of his reach. As Orpheus passed by, Tantalus listened to the sweet music and forgot his terrible punishment for a few moments.

Orpheus came to a man called Sisyphus who had betrayed Zeus. As a punishment he was forced to push a great stone up a steep hill. When he was almost at the top, the stone always rolled back to the bottom and Sisyphus had to climb down and roll it up all over again. He was startled to hear sweet music in the Underworld and he rested for a moment to forget his troubles, but Orpheus passed him without a look.

Soon he reached the fifty wicked daughters of Danaus who had killed their husbands. Their punishment was to fill a bottomless barrel with water. They could never do this hopeless task, but they stopped when they heard the lyre. Orpheus only thought about Eurydice and did not look at them.

There were many more horrid cruel sights by the path until at last, Orpheus reached the castle. He strode through the open black gates and found himself in a circular hall. It had black walls and a black marble floor but no furniture except for two silver thrones. There staring at him, sat a man and a woman. They wore black robes and their faces were hidden by black shadows like masks.

"Who are you, mortal man? Why have you come here?" the man demanded.

"My name is Orpheus, an Argonaut," came the quiet reply.

"Do you know who I am?" interrupted the man. "I am Hades, King of the Underworld and this is my wife, Persephone. Only dead people pass through the gates of my kingdom so if you value your life, you'd better offer me a good reason for your visit."

"I have come for my wife," said Orpheus.

"Your wife!" exclaimed Hades, "who may she be?"

"She is the nymph, Eurydice," said Orpheus. "We lived happily together, then a poisonous snake bit her. She died at once but the great Zeus allowed me to travel here to get her back."

"That's impossible," Hades said loudly, "nobody ever leaves this kingdom."

Orpheus sank to his knees. "Your Majesty," he pleaded, "I left my home and my friends. For years I've travelled all over the world and suffered great hardship. I faced that monster dog Cerberus. I charmed Charon and I've seen many fearful sights all round this castle. I've endured these things for Eurydice. Give her back to me I pray, for I love her above all else."

"Love!" Hades said coldly. "There is no love here. Tell me about it."

Once more, Orpheus played his lyre, and sang these words: "O Hades, you brought your queen, Persephone, here from the world above. Have you forgotten the love you felt for her? You said you could not live without Persephone. Let me take Eurydice, my wife, home with me. Give her to me or keep me here with you for I cannot live without her!"

There was silence as he finished his song. Then Persephone leaned forward. Orpheus saw the tears on her cheeks as she whispered to her husband. Hades nodded and said gently, "Your song has touched my wife's heart. Indeed, you've reminded me of the happy world above. Your wish is granted. Eurydice is nearby in the resting place we call the Elysian Fields. You may take her back home, but remember my words well: take the same path and play your lyre so that she may hear the music and follow you. But there is one condition." Hades stopped while Orpheus held his breath until he went on: "You must not speak nor turn round until you are standing in the sunlight. Do not look at Eurydice for if your eyes fall upon her before you reach your world she will be lost to you for ever!"

Orpheus thanked Hades and his queen and left the black hall. He played his lute and the music sounded like the sweetest laughter in the world. Out he went and as he crossed the grey lands to reach the cave he looked neither right nor left. He heard nothing except the sound of his lyre. "I pray my wife is following me," he thought. "I cannot hear her footsteps, surely Hades would not play any cruel tricks on me?"

He reached the cave and walked down to the dark river. Charon was waiting to row him across. "I don't think Cerberus will let you out," he cackled, but Orpheus dared not answer. He did not hear his wife jump into the boat. It had not rocked with the weight of an extra person. There could be no harm in making sure – but at the last moment he made himself stare straight ahead. His eyes and neck began to ache. His fingers were bleeding as he plucked the strings of his lyre but he kept on playing softly, sweetly.

He reached the other bank and climbed up the path. He saw the faint glimmer of light beyond the black gates. He had arrived at the door to the outside world. Would the three-headed monster let Eurydice walk out? But the three heads were still fast asleep. Orpheus walked over them into the warm sunshine. He was free! Then a sudden fear made him shiver. Perhaps Cerberus was only pretending to be asleep. What if the monster would not let her pass? What if the iron gates clanged shut before she got out? Was she frightened? He must help her. He turned. He called her name. She was only a few feet away, so pale and so lovely.

"Farewell," she murmured, then she vanished down the dark

path while a ghostly voice whispered, "Why did you speak? Why did you turn? You've lost her. She has gone for ever."

Orpheus dropped his lyre. He held out his arms to the empty air and the gates to the Underworld shut in his face. He kicked and he shook them but they did not move. He shouted to Hades for help but there was not a sound anywhere. He wept with sorrow and Zeus took pity on him. He sent the Argonauts to find their friend and they took him back to Greece.

Orpheus never played a happy tune on his lyre again. Over the countryside he wandered for many years and his songs were so sad that the rocks and the hardest stones wept when they heard them.

Orpheus died on the Greek island of Lesbos and people say that the loveliest music ever written in the world was sung and played there in his memory.

THE GROUND GIVES WAY

Tom King (from *Stig of the Dump*)

If you went too near the edge of the chalk-pit the ground would give way. Barney had been told this often enough. Everybody had told him. His grandmother, every time he came to stay with her. His sister, every time she wasn't telling him something else. Barney had a feeling, somewhere in his middle, that it was probably true about the ground giving way. But still, there was a difference between being told and seeing it happen. And today was one of those grey days when there was nothing to do, nothing to play, and nowhere to go. Except to the chalk-pit. The dump.

Barney got through the rickety fence and went to the edge of the pit. This had been the side of a hill once, he told himself. Men had come to dig away chalk and left this huge hole in the earth. He thought of all the sticks of chalk they must have made, and all the blackboards in all the schools they must have written on. They must have dug and dug for hundreds of years. And then they got tired of digging, or somebody had told them to stop before they dug away all the hill. And now they did not know what to do with this empty hole and they were trying to fill it up again. Anything people didn't want they threw into the bottom of the pit.

He crawled through the rough grass and peered over. The sides of the pit were white chalk, with lines of flints poking out like bones in places. At the top was crumbly brown earth and the roots of the trees that grew on the edge. The roots looped over the edge, twined in the air and grew back into the earth. Some of the trees hung over the edge, holding on desperately by a few roots. The earth and chalk had fallen away beneath them, and one day they too would fall to the bottom of the pit. Strings of ivy and the creeper called Old Man's Beard hung in the air.

Far below was the bottom of the pit. The dump. Barney could see strange bits of wreckage among the moss and elder bushes and nettles. Was that the steering wheel of a ship? The tail of an aeroplane? At least there was a real bicycle. Barney felt sure he could make it go if only he could get at it. They didn't let him have a bicycle.

Barney wished he was at the bottom of the pit.

And the ground gave way.

Barney felt his head going down, and his feet going up. There was a rattle of falling earth beneath him. Then he was falling, still clutching the clump of grass that was falling with him.

"This is what it's like when the ground gives way," thought Barney. Then he seemed to turn a complete somersault in the air, bumped into a ledge of chalk half-way down, crashed through some creepers and ivy and branches, and landed on a bank of moss.

His thoughts did those funny things they do when you bump your head and you suddenly find yourself thinking about what you had for dinner last Tuesday, all mixed up with seven times six. Barney lay with his eyes shut, waiting for his thoughts to stop being mixed up. Then he opened them.

He was lying in a kind of shelter. Looking up he could see a roof, or part of a roof, made of elder branches, a very rotten old carpet, and rusty old sheets of iron. There was a big hole, through which he must have fallen. He could see the white walls of the cliff, the trees and creepers at the top, and the sky with clouds passing over it.

Barney decided he wasn't dead. He didn't even seem to be very much hurt. He turned his head and looked around him. It was dark in this den after looking at the white chalk, and he couldn't see what sort of a place it was. It seemed to be partly a cave dug into the chalk, partly a shelter built out over the mouth of the cave. There was a cool, damp smell. Woodlice and earwigs dropped from the roof where he had broken through it.

But what had happened to his legs? He couldn't sit up when he tried to. His legs wouldn't move. "Perhaps I've broken them," Barney thought. "What shall I do then?" He looked at his legs to see if they were all right, and found they were all tangled up with creeper from the face of the cliff. "Who tied me up?" thought Barney. He kicked his legs to try to get them free, but it was no use, there were yards of creeper trailing down from the cliff. "I suppose I got tangled up when I fell," he thought. "Expect I would have broken my neck if I hadn't."

He lay quiet and looked around the cave again. Now that his eyes were used to it he could see further into the dark part of the cave.

There was somebody there!

Or Something!

Something, or Somebody, had a lot of shaggy black hair and two bright black eyes that were looking very hard at Barney.

"Hullo!" said Barney.

Something said nothing.

"I fell down the cliff," said Barney.

Somebody grunted.

"My name's Barney."

Somebody-Something made a noise that sounded like "Stig".

"D'you think you could help me undo my feet, Mr Stig?" asked Barney politely. "I've got a pocket-knife," he added, remembering that he had in his pocket a knife he'd found among the wood-shavings on the floor of Grandfather's workshop. It was quite a good knife except that one blade had come off and the other one was broken in half and rather blunt.

"Good thing I put it in my pocket," he thought. He wriggled so he could reach the knife, and managed to open the rusty half-blade. He tried to reach the creepers round his legs, but found it was difficult to cut creepers with a blunt knife when your feet are tied above your head.

The Thing sitting in the corner seemed to be interested. It got up and moved towards Barney into the light. Barney was glad to see it was Somebody after all. "Funny way to dress though," he thought, "rabbit-skins round the middle and no shoes or socks."

"Oh puff!" said Barney, "I can't reach my feet. You do it, Stig!"

He handed the knife to Stig.

Stig turned it over and felt it with his strong hairy hands, and tested the edge with a thumb. Then instead of trying to cut the creepers he squatted down on the ground and picked up a broken stone.

"He's going to sharpen the knife," thought Barney.

But no, it seemed more as if he was sharpening the stone. Using the hard knife to chip with, Stig was carefully flaking tiny splinters off the edge of the flint, until he had a thin sharp blade. Then he sprang up, and with two or three slashes cut through the creeper that tied Barney's feet.

Barney sat up. "Golly!" he said. "You *are* clever! I bet my Grandad couldn't do that, and he's *very* good at making things."

Stig grinned. Then he went to the back of the cave and hid the broken knife under a pile of rubbish.

"My knife!" protested Barney. But Stig took no notice. Barney got up and went into the dark part of the cave.

He'd never seen anything like the collection of bits and pieces, odds and ends, bric-à-brac and old brock, that this Stig creature had lying about his den. There were stones and bones, fossils and bottles, skins and tins, stacks of sticks and hanks of string. There were motor-car tyres and hats from old scarecrows, nuts and bolts and bobbles from brass bedsteads. There was a coal scuttle full of dead electric light bulbs and a basin with rusty screws and nails in it. There was a pile of bracken and newspapers that looked as if it were used for a bed. The place looked as if it had never been given a tidy-up.

"I wish I lived here," said Barney.

Stig seemed to understand that Barney was approving of his home and his face lit up. He took on the air of a householder showing a visitor round his property, and began pointing out some of the things he seemed particularly proud of.

First, the plumbing. Where the water dripped through a crack in the roof of the cave he had wedged the mud-guard of a bicycle. The water ran along this, through the tube of a vacuum-cleaner, and into a big can with writing on it. By the side of this was a plastic football carefully cut in half, and Stig dipped up some water and

offered it to Barney. Barney had swallowed a mouthful before he made out the writing on the can: it said WEEDKILLER. However, the water only tasted of rust and rubber.

It was dark in the back of the cave. Stig went to the front where the ashes of a fire were smoking faintly, blew on them, picked up a book that lay beside his bed, tore out a page and rolled it up, lit it at the fire, and carried it to a lamp set in a niche in the wall. As it flared up Barney could see it was in fact an old teapot, filled with some kind of oil, and with a bootlace hanging out of it for a wick.

In the light of the lamp Stig went to the very back of the cave and began to thump the wall and point, and explain something in his strange grunting language. Barney did not understand a word but he recognized the tone of voice – like when grown-ups go on about: "I'm thinking of tearing this down, and building on here, and having this done up . . ." Stig had been digging into the wall, enlarging his cave. There was a bit of an old bed he had been using as a pick, and a baby's bath full of loose chalk to be carried away.

Barney made the interested sort of noises you are supposed to make when people tell you that they are going to put up plastic wallpaper with pictures of mousetraps on it, but Stig reached up to a bunch of turnips hanging from a poker stuck in the wall. He handed Barney a turnip, took one for himself, and began to eat it. Barney sat down on a bundle of old magazines done up with string and munched the turnip. The turnip at least was fresh, and it tasted better to him than the cream of spinach he'd hidden under his spoon at dinner time.

Barney looked at Stig. "Funny person to find living next door to you," he thought. Stig did not seem much bigger than himself, but he looked very strong and his hands looked cleverer than his face. But how old was he? Ten? Twenty? A hundred? A thousand?

"You been here long?" asked Barney.

Stig grinned again. "Long," he said. "Long, long, long." But it sounded more like an echo, or a parrot copying somebody, than an answer to his question.

"I'm staying at my Grandmother's house," said Barney. Stig just looked at him. "Oh well," thought Barney, "if he's not interested in talking I don't mind." He stood up.

"I better go now," he said. "Thank you for having me. Can I have my knife back, please?"

Stig still looked blank.

"Knife," said Barney, and made cutting movements with his

hand. Stig picked up the sharp worked flint from the floor of the cave and gave it to Barney.

"Oo, can I have that!" exclaimed Barney. "Thank you!"

He looked at the stone, hard and shiny, almost like a diamond and much more useful. Then he put it in his pocket, said goodbye again, and went out of the low door of the shelter.

It was getting late in the autumn evening, and it was already dark and gloomy in the pit. Barney knew there was a way out right at the other end of the pit, and by going a long way round he could get back to the house. There were rustlings in dry leaves and muffled sounds from the middle of bramble patches, but somehow Barney found he didn't mind. He felt the hard stone in his pocket and thought of Stig in his den under the cliff. You weren't likely to find anything stranger than Stig wherever you looked. And, well, Stig was his friend.

HOW THE CAMEL GOT HISHUMP

Rudyard Kipling

Now this is the next tale, and it tells how the Camel got his big hump.

In the beginning of years, when the world was so new-and-all, and the Animals were just beginning to work for Man, there was a Camel, and he lived in the middle of a Howling Desert because he did not want to work; and besides, he was a Howler himself. So he ate sticks and thorns and tamarisks and milkweed and prickles, most 'scruciating idle; and when anybody spoke to him he said "Humph!" Just "Humph!" and no more.

Presently the Horse came to him on Monday morning, with a saddle on his back and a bit in his mouth, and said, "Camel, O Camel, come out and trot like the rest of us."

"Humph!" said the Camel; and the Horse went away and told the Man.

Presently the Dog came to him, with a stick in his mouth, and said, "Camel, O Camel, come and fetch and carry like the rest of us."

"Humph!" said the Camel; and the Dog went away and told the Man.

Presently the Ox came to him, with the yoke on his neck, and said, "Camel, O Camel, come and plough like the rest of us."

"Humph!" said the Camel; and the Ox went away and told the Man.

At the end of the day the Man called the Horse and the Dog and the Ox together, and said, "Three, O Three, I'm very sorry for you (with the world so new-and-all); but that Humph-thing in the Desert can't work, or he would have been here by now, so I am going to leave him alone, and you must work double-time to make up for it."

That made the Three very angry (with the world so new-and-all), and they held a palaver, and an *indaba*, and a *punchayet*, and a pow-wow on the edge of the Desert; and the Camel came chewing milkweed *most* 'scruciating idle, and laughed at them. Then he said "Humph!" and went away again.

Presently there came along the Djinn in charge of All Deserts, rolling in a cloud of dust (Djinns always travel that way because it is Magic), and he stopped to palaver and pow-wow with the Three.

"Djinn of All Deserts," said the Horse, "*is* it right for any one to be idle, with the world so new-and-all?"

"Certainly not," said the Djinn.

"Well," said the Horse, "there's a thing in the middle of your Howling Desert (and he's a Howler himself) with a long neck and long legs, and he hasn't done a stroke of work since Monday morning. He won't trot."

"Whew!" said the Djinn, whistling, "that's my Camel, for all the gold in Arabia! What does he say about it?"

"He says 'Humph!'" said the Dog; "and he won't fetch and carry."

"Does he say anything else?"

"Only 'Humph!'; and he won't plough," said the Ox.

"Very good," said the Djinn. "I'll humph him if you will kindly wait a minute."

The Djinn rolled himself up in his dustcloak, and took a

bearing across the desert, and found the Camel most 'scruciatingly idle, looking at his own reflection in a pool of water.

"My long and bubbling friend," said the Djinn, "what's this I hear of your doing no work, with the world so new-and-all?"

"Humph!" said the Camel.

The Djinn sat down, with his chin in his hand, and began to think a Great Magic, while the Camel looked at his own reflection in the pool of water.

"You've given the Three extra work ever since Monday morning, all on account of your 'scruciating idleness," said the Djinn; and he went on thinking Magics, with his chin in his hand.

"Humph!" said the Camel.

"I shouldn't say that again if I were you," said the Djinn; "you might say it once too often. Bubbles, I want you to work."

And the Camel said "Humph!" again; but no sooner had he said it than he saw his back, that he was so proud of, puffing up and puffing up into a great big lolloping humph.

"Do you see that?" said the Djinn. "That's your very own humph that you've brought upon your very own self by not working. Today is Thursday, and you've done no work since Monday, when the work began. Now you are going to work."

"How can I," said the Camel, "with this humph on my back?"

"That's made a-purpose," said the Djinn, "all because you missed those three days. You will be able to work now for three days without eating, because you can live on your humph; and don't you ever say I never did anything for you. Come out of the Desert and go to the Three, and behave. Humph yourself!"

And the Camel humphed himself, humph and all, and went away to join the Three. And from that day to this the Camel always wears a humph (we call it "hump" now, not to hurt his feelings); but he has never yet caught up with the three days that he missed at the beginning of the world, and he has never yet learned how to behave.

THE LAWYER
AND THE GHOST

Charles Dickens

I knew a man – forty years ago – who took an old, damp, rotten set of chambers, in one of the most ancient Inns, that had been shut up and empty for years and years before. There were lots of stories about the place, and it certainly was far from being a cheerful one; but he was poor, and the rooms were cheap, and that would have been quite a sufficient reason, if they had been ten times worse than they really were.

The man was obliged to take some mouldering fixtures, and, among the rest, was a great lumbering wooden press for papers, with large glass doors, and a green curtain inside; a pretty useless thing, for he had no papers to put in it; and as to his clothes, he carried them about with him, and that wasn't very hard work either.

Well, he moved in all his furniture – it wasn't quite a truck-full – and had sprinkled it about the room, so as to make the four chairs look as much like a dozen as possible, and was sitting down before the fire at night, drinking the first glass of two gallons of whisky he had ordered on credit, wondering whether it would ever be paid for, if so, in how many years' time, when his eyes encountered the glass doors of the wooden press. "Ah," says he, speaking aloud to the press, having nothing else to speak to; "if it wouldn't cost more to break up your old carcase, than it would ever be worth afterwards, I'd have a fire out of you in less than no time."

He had hardly spoken the words, when a sound resembling a faint groan appeared to issue from the interior of the case; it startled him at first, but thinking that it must be some young fellow in the next chamber, who had been dining out, he put his feet on the fender, and raised the poker to stir the fire.

At that moment, the sound was repeated: and one of the glass doors slowly opening, disclosed a pale figure in soiled and worn apparel, standing erect in the press. The figure was tall and thin, and the countenance expressive of care and anxiety, but there was something in the hue of the skin, and gaunt and unearthly appearance of the whole form, which no being of this world was ever seen to wear.

"Who are you?" said the new tenant, turning very pale; poising the poker in his hand, however, and taking a very decent aim at the countenance of the figure. "Who are you?"

"Don't throw that poker at me," replied the form: "If you hurled it with ever so sure an aim, it would pass through me, without resistance, and expend its force on the wood behind. I am a spirit!"

"And, pray, what do you want here?" faltered the tenant.

"In this room," replied the apparition, "my worldly ruin was

worked, and I and my children beggared. In this room, when I had died of grief, and long-deferred hope, two wily harpies divided the wealth for which I had contested during a wretched existence, and of which, at last, not one farthing was left for my unhappy descendants. I terrified them from the spot, and since that day have prowled by night – the only period at which I can re-visit the earth – about the scenes of my long misery. This apartment is mine: leave it to me!"

"If you insist upon making your appearance here," said the tenant, who had had time to collect his presence of mind, "I shall give up possession with the greatest pleasure, but I should like to ask you one question, if you will allow me."

"Say on," said the apparition, sternly.

"Well," said the tenant, "it does appear to me somewhat inconsistent, that when you have an opportunity of visiting the fairest spots of earth – for I suppose space is nothing to you – you should always return exactly to the very places where you have been most miserable."

"Egad, that's very true; I never thought of that before," said the ghost.

"You see, sir," pursued the tenant, "this is a very uncomfortable room. From the appearance of that press, I should be disposed to say that it is not wholly free from bugs; and I really think you might find more comfortable quarters: to say nothing of the climate of London, which is extremely disagreeable."

"You are very right, sir," said the ghost politely, "it never struck me till now; I'll try a change of air directly."

In fact, he began to vanish as he spoke: his legs, indeed, had quite disappeared!

"And if, sir," said the tenant, calling after him, "if you *would* have the goodness to suggest to the other ladies and gentlemen who are now engaged in haunting old empty houses, that they might be much more comfortable elsewhere, you will confer a very great benefit on society."

"I will," replied the ghost, "we must be dull fellows, very dull fellows, indeed; I can't imagine how we can have been so stupid."

With these words, the spirit disappeared, and what is rather remarkable, he never came back again.

THE BUTTERFLY WHO SANG

Terry Jones

A butterfly was once sitting on a leaf looking extremely sad.

"What's wrong?" asked a friendly frog.

"Oh," said the butterfly, "nobody really appreciates me," and she parted her beautiful red and blue wings and shut them again.

"What d'you mean?" asked the frog. "I've seen you flying about and thought to myself: that is one hell of a beautiful butterfly! All my friends think you look great, too! You're a real stunner!"

"Oh *that*," replied the butterfly, and she opened her wings again. "Who cares about *looks*? It's my singing that nobody appreciates."

"I've never heard your singing; but if it's anywhere near as good as your looks, you've got it made!" said the frog.

"That's the trouble," replied the butterfly, "people say they can't hear my singing. I suppose it's so refined and so high that their ears aren't sensitive enough to pick it up."

"But I bet it's great all the same!" said the frog.

"It is," said the butterfly. "Would you like me to sing for you?"

"Well . . . I don't suppose my ears are sensitive enough to pick it up, but I'll give it a try!" said the frog.

So the butterfly spread her wings, and opened her mouth. The frog gazed in wonder at the butterfly's beautiful wings, for he'd never been so close to them before.

The butterfly sang on and on, and still the frog gazed at her wings, absolutely captivated, even though he could hear nothing whatsoever of her singing.

Eventually, however, the butterfly stopped, and closed up her wings.

"Beautiful!" said the frog, thinking about the wings.

"Thank you," said the butterfly, thrilled that at last she had found an appreciative listener.

After that, the frog came every day to listen to the butterfly sing, though all the time he was really feasting his eyes on her beautiful wings. And every day, the butterfly tried harder and harder to impress the frog with her singing, even though he could not hear a single note of it.

But one day a moth, who was jealous of all the attention the butterfly was getting, took the butterfly on one side and said: "Butterfly, your singing is quite superb."

"Thank you," said the butterfly.

"With just a little more practice," said the cunning moth, "you could be as famous a singer as the nightingale."

"Do you think so?" asked the butterfly, flattered beyond words.

"I certainly do," replied the moth. "Indeed, perhaps you already *do* sing better than the nightingale, only it's difficult to concentrate on your music because your gaudy wings are so distracting."

"Is that right?" said the butterfly.

"I'm afraid so," said the moth. "You notice the nightingale is wiser, and wears only dull brown feathers so as not to distract from her singing."

"You're right!" cried the butterfly. "I was a fool not to have realized that before!" And straight away she found some earth and rubbed it into her wings until they were all grey and half the colours had rubbed off.

The next day, the frog arrived for the concert as usual, but when the butterfly opened her wings he cried out: "Oh! Butterfly! What have you done to your beautiful wings?" And the butterfly explained what she had done.

"I think you will find," she said, "that now you will be able to concentrate more on my music."

Well, the poor frog tried, but it was no good, for of course he couldn't hear anything at all. So he soon became bored, and hopped off into the pond. And after that the butterfly never *could* find anyone to listen to her singing.

THE OLD HOUSE

Hans Andersen

In the far North there was once a beautiful old house. It had strange figures carved over each little window and rainwater splashed from the roof into gutters shaped like curling dragons. Above the front door the builder had written a poem, and flowers and leaves were carved on every scrap of wood. The other houses in the street were new. They were neat and straight with smooth big windows. "That old house is a disgrace," they muttered angrily at night, "with its fancy decoration and big old-fashioned steps. It ought to be pulled down!"

Across the street in the newest house of all there lived a happy little boy. He liked the old house. "I expect horses and carriages would draw up to those wide steps," he thought dreamily.

Sometimes the owner of the house looked out into the street. The boy always gave a little nod and the owner nodded back. He wore a coat with brass buttons, wide baggy trousers and a wig on his head. He never had any visitors except for an old servant who came each day to clean and do the shopping. "Our poor old neighbour must get very lonely," the young boy's mother said to him one day. This worried him so he packed a little parcel and when he saw the servant walking along the street, he rushed out and handed it to him.

"Please give this to your master," he said shyly. "I've heard that he is very lonely so I would like him to have my tin soldier to keep him company."

The servant smiled. He took the parcel to his master and later he went across the street and spoke to the boy's parents. "My master," he said, "would be very pleased if you would allow your son to visit him this afternoon." They agreed willingly so the boy ran over to the house. All the carved figures seemed to smile at him as he went up the stone steps into the hall where the walls were covered with paintings of knights in armour and ladies in lovely gowns. He went up the winding stairs into a room full of old furniture. The walls were covered with leather which had pretty gold flowers painted on it. "Leather lasts for ever," the walls whispered. "Sit down, little boy," called the chairs in a creaky cracking way.

Then the master of the house came forward. His wig was crooked but his voice was kind. "Thank you for the tin soldier," he said, "and thank you for coming to visit me. Would you like to look at my little treasures? They keep me company you see, and they remind me of happy days and old friends."

"But aren't you lonely?" the little boy asked.

"Oh no, I chat to my friends in my dreams about old times." Then he hobbled away to fetch some sweets and fruit. The boy wandered about the room. He looked at the pictures, then he saw the tin soldier standing on a beautifully painted box.

"Take me back," the soldier wailed, "I'm so lonely here. There's no lovely noise, no toys to talk to, only all these old sticks of furniture to look at! That old man never gets a hug or smile from anybody."

"He has pleasant dreams and happy thoughts."

"They're no use to me," yelled the soldier. "I can't bear it here."

"Don't be so unkind," the boy whispered as the old man came back with a tray of nice things to eat. Later on, the boy went home, but now he waved and bowed to the old man every day.

Then the old man asked the boy to pay him another visit.

The chairs still creaked, the clock chimed, the leather walls sang

195

their little song. Nothing had changed. Every hour, every day was always the same. "Take me back," yelled the tin soldier when he spotted the boy. "I'm dreaming now about your house and the happy time I had with you and the family. I'll be like the old man soon. Dreams! Dreams! Dreams! Send me to the wars. If I lose an arm or a leg it will show I'm alive! I can't stand living here."

"I gave you away as a present," the boy said. "I can't take you back. You must stay here."

This time the old man opened drawer after drawer filled with funny little toys. The boy and the old man were laughing happily, when the tin soldier started to jump furiously up and down on the wooden chest. "I'm going into battle," he screamed. Then he fell onto the floor.

"Wherever has he gone?" the boy said, and together they looked around. "Don't worry," the old man said, "my servant will find him." But he never did. The tin soldier had fallen through a crack in that old wooden floor and nobody spotted him at all.

The boy went home and once more, he and the old man waved to each other through the window. The weeks went by and soon it was winter. Thick ice formed on the windows and snowdrifts covered the roads. One day the boy scraped a small hole in the ice on the window. Some men were carrying a coffin out of the old house. The kind lonely old man had died. No friends followed the coffin, so the boy blew a kiss across the street.

"Goodbye, old friend," he whispered.

When spring came the furniture was sold. The old walls crumbled and the leather on the walls flapped in the wind. Then the house was torn down. "Good," said the other houses. "This will be a smart street now." A new house was built, with big windows and square walls, but this time a garden was planted in front of the house.

The boy grew up and when he got married he moved into the new house. One day his bride was planting flowers in the garden when something pricked her finger. It was the tin soldier! The wife showed it to her husband who exclaimed, "It looks like the one I gave to a lonely old man long ago." He told his wife the story and her eyes filled with tears. "I shall keep this soldier," she said, "to remind me about the old house." She polished the soldier but she left a tiny scrap of leather that was stuck on his back.

"I'm so happy that I haven't been forgotten," the soldier whispered and the scrap of leather murmured, "I said that leather lasts for ever, didn't I!"

THE MILKMAID AND HER PAIL

Aesop's Fables

Amilkmaid was returning home one fine morning, carrying a pail of frothy white milk upon her head. The sky was blue, the birds were singing in the trees and she felt a joy in her heart. Soon her mind began to wander:

"The milk in this pail will provide me with cream. From the cream I can make butter and take this to market to sell. With the money I will buy some eggs, and these on hatching will produce chickens. After a time I shall have a large poultry yard. Then, I shall sell some of the poultry and with the money I shall buy myself a pretty dress, which I shall wear to market. All the young men will admire me and want to kiss me. But I shall toss my head and ignore them!"

And with that, she tossed her head up high, forgetting all about the pail, and, alas, all the milk was spilt and all her dreams were broken.

THE ENVIOUS NEIGHBOUR

Japanese Traditional

In Japan hundreds of years ago, an old couple lived in a little house in a village. They had no children, but they had a small dog whom they loved, and they looked after it very well.

One morning the man was digging in his garden and his dog was playing around as usual. Then the dog raced over to his master and barked loudly. It ran back to the spot where it had been scratching and then it came over to his master again. The old man grew curious and he carried his spade and followed the dog which barked happily and chased his tail in excitement. He began to dig, and soon his spade struck something hard. He bent down and dragged out a great box full of shining gold pieces. It was so heavy that his wife rushed out to help him carry it home. What a wonderful supper they all had that night!

All the villagers heard about the old couple's good fortune and were very happy for them. But their next-door-neighbour was so jealous of their good luck that he could not work or sleep. He thought of nothing except how to get hold of some of that gold for himself. So he went and knocked on the couple's front door.

"I'm wondering if your dog could find a fortune for me?" he boldly asked. "Could you let me have him for a few days?"

"You know that we love him very much," the old man said. "We have never let him out of our sight. How can you ask such a thing?"

Their neighbour went home but day after day he badgered them until they agreed to lend him their pet for one night.

"I'll take great care of him," he promised, but when he returned home, he put the dog out into the garden and left him there.

The man waited impatiently all night for the dog to find something, when he saw the dog running to the foot of a tree. The man seized a spade and rushed outside. He pushed the dog roughly aside and started to dig. His eyes gleamed as he thought about the gold he hoped to find, but what did he uncover? Nothing but a pile of old bones! He was furious.

"You've played a fine trick on me," he bellowed, "so take that." He hurled an axe at the poor dog and killed it with one blow.

"What story can I tell my neighbours?" he wondered. He went indoors and found a large and, it must be said, not very clean, handkerchief then he knocked on the old couple's door. He pretended to cry when they opened it.

"Oh, my dear neighbours," he sobbed. "Your sweet dog suddenly dropped dead although I looked after him most carefully. I thought I'd better tell you at once."

The old man and his wife burst into real tears for they had loved their pet so much. Then the old man brought the dead dog home and buried it under the tree where it had found the treasure.

Several nights later, the old man had a curious dream. His dog seemed to be standing by his bed and it told him to chop down the treasure tree and make a bowl for cleaning rice out of its roots. When he awoke he told his wife about the strange dream. He did not want to lose the tree, but his wife did not hesitate.

"Our dog gave us good advice before," she said. "We must follow it again."

So the tree was cut down and its roots were carved into a beautiful bowl. When the rice crop was ready, the couple took down this bowl and heaped the stalks inside, ready to pound them and take out the grains of rice. In a flash the grains turned into gold pieces! Husband and wife looked at each other and exclaimed: "Our faithful dog has helped us again. Let us give a feast and share our good fortune with our friends."

Before long, the same neighbour hurried over to visit them. He wanted to get a share of their good fortune somehow.

"I wonder if you have a strong bowl you might lend me?" he asked. "I want to take the rice off the stalks today."

The couple were unhappy. They did not want to part with their precious bowl. "Yet," said the husband, "we must not be greedy. We must be neighbourly." So he handed it over and the man raced back home and threw enormous handfuls of rice into the bowl. But no gold pieces appeared. His rice turned into berries that had a truly horrible smell. The man was enraged. He chopped up that lovely bowl and then set fire to the pieces of wood. Then he had to rush outside to get away from the terrible smell!

He went next door and made up a long story, but the old couple were most upset and somehow they did not quite believe his excuses.

That very night the dog came to his master in a dream and told him to collect the ashes of the burnt bowl and bring them home. Then he must find out when the daimio, a Japanese word which means great lord, was visiting the city. On that day the old man should carry the ashes and as soon as he saw the daimio coming, he must climb into the cherry trees along the road and sprinkle the ashes over them.

The old man was puzzled, but he trusted his old dog now and at dawn he went quietly to his neighbour's garden and took away the wood-ashes. He put them carefully into a pretty jar and when he got back home he asked his wife when the daimio was coming to the city.

"Today!" she told him. "It's a pity it has been so cold for there will be no cherry blossom on the trees to welcome him."

At once her husband hurried to the road holding the jar very carefully. Many people were waiting there as well and he saw that his wife was right: not a leaf or flower could be seen on the cherry trees. He did not have long to wait before he heard a lot of noise and he saw clouds of dust in the distance. He knew the daimio and his men must be approaching. As they came closer, the crowds all round bowed very low and the procession passed by. The old man did not bow. He looked straight at the great lord.

"Who is that old man?" the daimio demanded angrily. "He is staring so rudely at me. Why is he disobeying the old custom by not

bowing to me, the mighty daimio? Bring him in front of me at once."
The old man saw a guard coming towards him so he awkwardly
climbed into the nearest tree and scattered the ash in every direction.
At once, the buds on every tree burst into flower. The pink and white
flowers looked so lovely that the daimio's heart was touched. Cherry
blossom in bloom for him, he thought. Instead of a scolding or worse,
he gave many presents to the old man and he invited him and his wife
to visit him in his splendid castle.

Naturally, before long, the envious neighbour heard all about
the old couple's good fortune. He rushed to the spot where he had
burned the wooden bowl and was overjoyed to find a small heap of
ashes which had been left behind by his neighbour. He scooped these
up and went off to stand by the roadside, hoping to see the daimio, as
he knew he was expected again that day. "I can scatter these ashes
over many more trees," he gloated to himself, "for I'm far stronger
than the old man. Why should he have all the luck anyway? Am I not
just as worthy?"

His eyes became tired with staring along the road but at last he
caught sight of the soldiers and servants marching in front of the
great lord. Swiftly he clambered up the tallest tree and took careful
aim. He waited until the daimio was almost underneath him then he
threw out some ash. His handful of ashes turned into a great cloud
which blew straight into the eyes and mouth of the great lord himself
as well as the soldiers! They shrieked in pain for the ash was red-hot
and burned them. Every tree seemed to be covered with soot but not a
single flower-bud or leaf opened. The envious man threw out his last
handful of dust and as he did so he fell headlong out of the tree, right
at the foot of the angry daimio!

"You've injured my soldiers and ruined my robes," he said
angrily. "What is your excuse, miserable man?"

"I only wanted the cherry blossoms to come out early to make the
road beautiful for you, noble lord," the man whined.

But some villagers muttered and grumbled and one called out:
"Do not believe him, daimio. He killed the old couple's pet dog. He
burnt their rice bowl because he was jealous of their good fortune and
even worse, he is now telling lies to you."

The daimio cast him into prison and when he was set free the
people in his village did not welcome him because he had not changed
his ideas. He was still envious and jealous of everybody and in the
end, he became a miserable, lonely old man.

THE PRACTICAL PRINCESS

Jay Williams

Princess Bedelia was as lovely as the moon shining upon a lake full of waterlilies. She was as graceful as a cat leaping. And she was also extremely practical.

When she was born, three fairies had come to her cradle to give her gifts as was usual in that country. The first fairy had given her beauty. The second had given her grace. But the third, who was a wise old creature, had said, "I give her common sense."

"I don't think much of that gift," said King Ludwig, raising his eyebrows. "What good is common sense to a princess? All she needs is charm."

Nevertheless, when Bedelia was eighteen years old, something happened which made the king change his mind.

A dragon moved into the neighbourhood. He settled in a dark cave on top of a mountain, and the first thing he did was to send a message to the king. "I must have a princess to devour," the message said, "or I shall breathe out my fiery breath and destroy the kingdom."

Sadly, King Ludwig called together his councillors and read them the message. "Perhaps," said the Prime Minister, "we had better advertise for a knight to slay the dragon? That is what is generally done in these cases."

"I'm afraid we haven't time," answered the king. "The dragon has only given us until tomorrow morning. There is no help for it. We shall have to send him the princess." Princess Bedelia had come to the meeting because, as she said, she liked to mind her own business and this was certainly her business.

"Rubbish!" she said. "Dragons can't tell the difference between princesses and anyone else. Use your common sense. He's just asking for me because he's a snob."

"That may be so," said her father, "but if we don't send you along, he'll destroy the kingdom."

"Right!" said Bedelia. "I see I'll have to deal with this myself." She left the council chamber. She got the largest and gaudiest of her state robes and stuffed it with straw, and tied it together with string.

202

Into the centre of the bundle she packed about fifty kilos of gunpowder. She got two strong young men to carry it up the mountain for her. She stood in front of the dragon's cave, and called, "Come out! Here's the princess!"

The dragon came blinking and peering out of the darkness. Seeing the bright robe covered with gold and silver embroidery, and hearing Bedelia's voice, he opened his mouth wide.

At Bedelia's signal, the two young men swung the robe and gave it a good heave, right down the dragon's throat. Bedelia threw herself flat on the ground, and the two young men ran.

As the gunpowder met the flames inside the dragon, there was a tremendous explosion.

Bedelia got up, dusting herself off. "Dragons," she said, "are not very bright."

She left the two young men sweeping up the pieces, and she went back to the castle to have her geography lesson.

The lesson that morning was local geography. "Our kingdom, Arapathia, is bounded on the north by Istven," said the teacher. "Lord Garp, the ruler of Istven, is old, crafty, rich, and greedy." At that very moment, Lord Garp of Istven was arriving at the castle. Word of Bedelia's destruction of the dragon had reached him. "That girl," said he, "is just the wife for me." And he had come with a hundred finely-dressed courtiers and many presents to ask King Ludwig for her hand.

The king sent for Bedelia. "My dear," he said, clearing his throat nervously, "just see who is here."

"I see. It's Lord Garp," said Bedelia. She turned to go.

"He wants to marry you," said the king.

Bedelia looked at Lord Garp. His face was like an old napkin, crumpled and wrinkled. It was covered with warts, as if someone had left crumbs on the napkin. He had only two teeth. Six long hairs grew from his chin, and none on his head. She felt like screaming.

However, she said. "I'm very flattered. Thank you, Lord Garp. Just let me talk to my father in private for a minute." When they had retired to a small room behind the throne, Bedelia said to the king, "What will Lord Garp do if I refuse to marry him?"

"He is rich, greedy, and crafty," said the king unhappily. "He is also used to having his own way in everything. He will be insulted. He will probably declare war on us, and then there will be trouble."

"Very well," said Bedelia. "We must be practical."

She returned to the throne room. Smiling sweetly at Lord Garp, she said, "My lord, as you know, it is customary for a princess to set tasks for anyone who wishes to marry her. Surely you wouldn't like me to break the custom. And you are bold and powerful enough, I know, to perform any task."

"That is true," said Lord Garp smugly, stroking the six hairs on his chin. "Name your task."

"Bring me," said Bedelia, "a branch from the Jewel Tree of Paxis."

Lord Garp bowed, and off he went. "I think," said Bedelia to her father, "that we have seen the last of him. For Paxis is fifteen hundred kilometres away, and the Jewel Tree is guarded by lions, serpents, and wolves."

But in two weeks, Lord Garp was back. With him he bore a chest, and from the chest he took a wonderful twig. Its bark was of rough gold. The leaves that grew from it were of fine silver. The twig was covered with blossoms, and each blossom had petals of mother-of-pearl and centres of sapphires, the colour of the evening sky.

Bedelia's heart sank as she took the twig. But then she said to herself, "Use your common sense, my girl! Lord Garp never

travelled three thousand kilometres in two weeks, nor is he the man to fight his way through lions, serpents, and wolves."

She looked carefully at the branch. Then she said, "My lord, you know that the Jewel Tree of Paxis is a living tree, although it is all made of jewels."

"Why, of course," said Lord Garp. "Everyone knows that."

"Well," said Bedelia, "then why is it that these blossoms have no scent?"

Lord Garp turned red.

"I think," Bedelia went on, "that this branch was made by the jewellers of Istven, who are the best in the world. Not very nice of you, my lord. Some people might even call it cheating."

Lord Garp shrugged. He was too old and rich to feel ashamed. But like many men used to having their own way, the more Bedelia refused him, the more he was determined to have her.

"Never mind all that," he said. "Set me another task. This time, I swear I will perform it."

Bedelia sighed. "Very well. Then bring me a cloak made from the skins of the salamanders who live in the Volcano of Scoria."

Lord Garp bowed, and off he went. "The Volcano of Scoria," said Bedelia to her father, "is covered with red-hot larva. It burns steadily with great flames, and pours out poisonous smoke so that no one can come within a metre of it."

"You have certainly profited by your geography lessons," said the king, with admiration.

Nevertheless, in a week, Lord Garp was back. This time, he carried a cloak that shone and rippled like all the colours of fire. It was made of scaly skins, stitched together with golden wire as fine as a hair; and each scale was red and orange and blue, like a tiny flame.

Bedelia took the splendid cloak. She said to herself, "Use your head, miss! Lord Garp never climbed the red-hot slopes of the Volcano of Scoria."

A fire was burning in the fireplace of the throne room. Bedelia hurled the cloak into it. The skins blazed up in a flash, blackened, and fell to ashes.

Lord Garp's mouth fell open. Before he could speak, Bedelia said, "That cloak was a fake, my lord. The skins of salamanders who can live in the Volcano of Scoria wouldn't burn in a little fire like that one."

Lord Garp turned pale with anger. He hopped up and down,

unable at first to do anything but splutter.

"Ub – ub – ub!" he cried. Then, controlling himself, he said, "So be it. If I can't have you, no one shall!"

He pointed a long, skinny finger at her. On the finger was a magic ring. At once, a great wind arose. It blew through the throne room. It sent King Ludwig flying one way and his guards the other. It picked up Bedelia and whisked her off through the air. When she could catch her breath and look about her, she found herself in a room at the top of a tower.

Bedelia peered out of the window. About the tower stretched an empty, barren plain. As she watched, a speck appeared in the distance. A plume of dust rose behind it. It drew nearer and became Lord Garp on horseback.

He rode to the tower and looked up at Bedelia. "Aha!" he croaked. "So you are safe and snug, are you? And will you marry me now?"

"Never," said Bedelia, firmly.

"Then stay there until never comes," snarled Lord Garp.

Away he rode.

For the next two days, Bedelia felt very sorry for herself. She sat wistfully by the window, looking out at the empty plain. When she was hungry, food appeared on the table. When she was tired, she lay down on the narrow cot and slept. Each day, Lord Garp rode by and asked if she had changed her mind, and each day she refused him. Her only hope was that, as so often happens in old tales, a prince might come riding by who would rescue her.

But on the third day, she gave herself a shake.

"Now then, pull yourself together," she said sternly. "If you sit waiting for a prince to rescue you, you may sit here for ever. Be practical! If there's any rescuing to be done, you're going to have to do it yourself."

She jumped up. There was something she had not yet done, and now she did it. She tried the door.

It opened.

Outside, were three other doors. But there was no sign of a staircase, or any way down from the top of the tower.

She opened two of the doors and found that they led into cells just like hers, but empty.

Behind the fourth door, however, lay what appeared to be a haystack.

From beneath it came the sound of snores. And between snores,

a voice said, "Sixteen million and twelve . . . *snore* . . . sixteen million and thirteen . . . *snore* . . . sixteen million and fourteen . . ."

Cautiously, she went closer. Then she saw that what she had taken for a haystack was in fact an immense pile of blond hair. Parting it, she found a young man, sound asleep.

As she stared, he opened his eyes. He blinked at her. "Who – ?" he said. Then he said, "Sixteen million and fifteen," closed his eyes, and fell asleep again.

Bedelia took him by the shoulder and shook him hard. He awoke, yawning, and tried to sit up. But the mass of hair made this difficult.

"What on earth is the matter with you?" Bedelia asked. "Who are you?"

"I am Prince Perian," he replied, "the rightful ruler of – oh dear! Here I go again. Sixteen million and . . ." His eyes began to close.

Bedelia shook him again. He made a violent effort and managed to wake up enough to continue, "– of Istven. But Lord

Garp has put me under a spell. I have to count sheep jumping over a fence, and this puts me to slee – ee – ee –"

He began to snore lightly.

"Dear me," said Bedelia. "I must do something."

She thought hard. Then she pinched Perian's ear, and this woke him with a start. "Listen," she said. "It's quite simple. It's all in your mind, you see. You are imagining the sheep jumping over the fence – no! don't go to sleep again!

This is what you must do. Imagine them jumping backwards. As you do, *count* them backwards, and when you get to *one*, you'll be wide awake."

The prince's eyes snapped open. "Marvellous!" he said. "Will it work?"

"It's bound to," said Bedelia. "For if the sheep going one way will put you to sleep, their going back again will wake you up."

Hastily, the prince began to count, "Six million and fourteen, six million and thirteen, six million and twelve . . ."

"Oh, my goodness," cried Bedelia, "count by hundreds, or you'll never get there."

He began to gabble as fast as he could, and with each moment that passed, his eyes sparkled more brightly, his face grew livelier, and he seemed a little stronger, until at last he shouted, "Five, four, three, two, ONE!" and awoke completely.

He struggled to his feet, with a little help from Bedelia.

"Heavens!" he said. "Look how my hair and beard have grown. I've been here for years. Thank you, my dear. Who are you, and what are you doing here?"

Bedelia quickly explained.

Perian shook his head. "One more crime of Lord Garp's," he said. "We must escape and see that he is punished."

"Easier said than done," Bedelia replied. "There are no stairs in this tower, as far as I can tell, and the outside wall is much too smooth to climb."

Perian frowned. "This will take some thought," he said. "What we need is a long rope."

"Use your common sense," said Bedelia. "We haven't any rope."

Then her face brightened, and she clapped her hands. "But we have your beard," she laughed.

Perian understood at once, and chuckled. "I'm sure it will reach almost to the ground," he said. "But we haven't any scissors to cut it off with."

"That is so," said Bedelia. "Hang it out of the window and let me climb down. I'll search the tower and perhaps I can find a ladder, or a hidden staircase. If all else fails, I can go for help."

She and the prince gathered up great armfuls of the beard and staggered into Bedelia's room, which had the largest window. The prince's long hair trailed behind and nearly tripped him.

He threw the beard out of the window, and sure enough the end of it came to within a metre of the ground.

Perian braced himself, holding the beard with both hands to ease the pull on his chin. Bedelia climbed out of the window and slid down the beard. She dropped to the ground and sat for a moment, breathless.

And as she sat there, out of the wilderness came the drumming of hoofs, a cloud of dust, and then Lord Garp on his swift horse.

With one glance, he saw what was happening. He shook his fist up at Prince Perian.

"Meddlesome fool!" he shouted. "I'll teach you to interfere."

He leaped from the horse and grabbed the beard. He gave it a tremendous yank. Head-first came Perian, out of the window. Down he fell, and with a thump, he landed right on top of old Lord Garp.

This saved Perian, who was not hurt at all. But it was the end of Lord Garp.

Perian and Bedelia rode back to Istven on Lord Garp's horse.

In the great city, the prince was greeted with cheers of joy – once everyone had recognized him after so many years and under so much hair.

And of course, since Bedelia had rescued him from captivity, she married him. First, however, she made him get a haircut and a shave so that she could see what he really looked like.

For she was always practical.

THE MAULVI
AND THE DONKEY

Pakistani Traditional

In a village in Pakistan long ago, there lived a Muslim teacher, or Maulvi as he is known in Pakistan, whose classes were filled with young boys. Some of them were bright and some were slow to learn. Sometimes the Maulvi lost his temper when the slower boys had not understood their lessons and he used to shout loudly at them, "You don't understand? It's as clear as daylight! You're stupid, that's what it is. Stupid like donkeys. Well, I've turned donkeys into men before now. And I'll do it again."

While he was shouting at the poor boys, a dhobi, or clothes-washer, passed the open schoolroom door. He stopped open-mouthed as he listened to the Maulvi. He rushed home and called excitedly to his wife, "Wonderful news! Our Maulvi can turn donkeys into men. We can get the son we've longed for. Let us take our best donkey to the Maulvi and ask him to change it into a man." His wife agreed so off they went to the school. "Er, um," they said anxiously, "please use your power and change our donkey into a man for us."

"Impossible," the Maulvi said in great astonishment. "I can't do that."

"You can," said the dhobi, "I know you can. Please try very hard."

"Quite impossible," the Maulvi replied. "I'm a teacher, not a magician."

The dhobi and his wife did not believe him. They begged and they pleaded and the Maulvi started to think they were out of their minds.

"I must get rid of them," he thought, so aloud he said, "Very well. It will cost you four hundred rupees and it will take four months. It's very hard to do this, you know."

"That's fine," the couple exclaimed and they rushed home to collect the money and the donkey. Then back they went to the schoolroom.

"That's a splendid animal," the Maulvi said. "It will make a fine man." When the dhobi had left, the Maulvi called to one of his students, "Lead this donkey deep into the jungle. Tie him up and leave it there."

Four months to the day, the dhobi returned.

"Have you managed everything? Where is my man?" he asked.

"Your man!" the Maulvi answered, "Haven't you heard the news? Your donkey is now very important. He is a government officer. He is the Kazi of Karachi. You'll have to go there to find him now."

"That's wonderful," said the dhobi, "but do you think he'll recognize me, his old master, now that he is famous?"

"I'm sure he will," laughed the Maulvi. "But if you take my advice, you'll show him the gunny bag you used to put his feed in. He'll remember that, then he'll be sure to recognize you as well."

The dhobi was so happy. He set off for the city at once.

Now a Kazi listens to people who are worried or need help in some way. On the day when the dhobi arrived in the city, the Kazi was extra busy and his courtroom was packed with people. The dhobi pushed near to the front until he could just see the top of the

211

Kazi's head and he called and he waved happily. The Kazi did not pay any attention because he was so busy with his work.

"Hey, I'm over here," he shouted. The Kazi went on writing quietly. The dhobi was desperate. He remembered the Maulvi's advice about the feeding bag. He pulled out the bag and waved it happily backwards and forwards.

The Kazi stopped writing. He peered over the top of his desk and at once the dhobi smiled and waved the feeding bag furiously above his head! The Kazi was puzzled. He wondered what this funny man was doing. Why was he smiling? And whatever was he waving at him? He said crossly, "What do you think you are doing?"

"Doing?" came the answer. "Don't you know who I am, you silly donkey, you? I'm your master, the clothes-washer!" Then he held the feeding bag right under the great man's nose. "Didn't I give you a feed every morning out of this bag? Didn't my wife and I look after you well? The Maulvi in our village turned you into a man but you'd better not forget you were once a donkey."

The Kazi had had enough by this time and ordered his guards to throw him outside. The dhobi was furious. He shook his fist and waved the feeding bag when the guards pushed him away. "You think you're so important but you're nothing but a donkey. I'd rather have my old donkey than an ungrateful man! Is this how you repay me?" he bellowed.

In a fearful temper he went straight back to the Maulvi.

"I'll give you another four hundred rupees if you'll change that Kazi back into our donkey," he shouted.

"Very well, bring the money here tomorrow," he was told.

The teacher sent a boy to bring the donkey back from the jungle where it had been happily grazing all this time. Next day the dhobi handed over the four hundred rupees to the Maulvi, who then led out the donkey and gave it to the dhobi. He gave one look and knew at once it was his best donkey!

He took him home and the dhobi and his wife treated him kindly. After all, they told themselves, not many people own a donkey who has been an important man like the Kazi of Karachi!

THE PASSING OF KING ARTHUR

Arthurian Legend

King Arthur and his Knights of the Round Table lived in the West Countrie hundreds of years ago. They fought many battles in aid of anyone who was troubled by wicked and cruel overlords. But the king's last battle, when he met Mordred, the worst traitor of all, was the fiercest one he had ever had to fight. Every man fought to the death and the battle raged all day. First one side seemed to be winning then the other. Arthur's knights picked out someone to attack but then they themselves were laid low and the only noise to be heard was the clashing of swords.

Knight after knight perished and still King Arthur battled on until at last he and the traitor Mordred came face to face.

"Ha, Mordred. Prepare to meet your death," cried Arthur and he whirled his famous sword Excalibur above his head.

"Think you to defeat me, Arthur Pendragon?" Mordred answered. "Never! It is your last hour which has come."

Then they charged. Arthur was much older than Mordred but his skill with the sword was still greater. Their horses were weary but back and forth they carried the two men. King Arthur fought the best fight of his life, for he raised his arm and charged Mordred so fiercely that his lance pierced right through Mordred's armour and he fell from his horse on to his knees. Arthur got down from his weary horse and even at that moment he was ready to forgive his old enemy. He held out his hand but Mordred struck Arthur a terrible blow before he fell back to the ground.

"I have killed the traitor, but I fear he may have killed me also," Arthur whispered as blood poured out of the wound from Mordred's sword. Sir Bedevere, one of the few knights still alive, managed to catch the king as he fell.

Mordred's men ran away when they saw their leader was dead and Arthur's men were the winners. The king was carried gently to the castle nearby where someone had hoisted the royal flag upon a tower to welcome him.

Wise men and good wives tried to stop the flow of blood from Arthur's wound but it was a hopeless task. He lay back on his pillows as nobles told him that the battle had been won and another enemy had been defeated again. He could not rejoice over the victory as he listened to the names of knight after knight who had been killed.

"This circle of the bravest and best knights, the Knights of the Round Table, has been broken," he said sadly. "It was a heavy price to pay for victory. I pray that your next ruler will think it was worth it."

"Do not say such things," said Sir Bedevere. "You are our only king!"

"No, good and loyal knight," Arthur murmured, "another king will follow me, for I fear Mordred dealt me a death-blow and my end is fast approaching."

He rested for a time then he feebly raised his head and said, "Bedevere, my time has come. I command you to carry me to the lake where Merlin the Magician led me to find Excalibur, my trusty sword."

Bedevere did not want to move the injured king but he had to obey. Carefully he took the king on his back with Excalibur by his side. "Which way shall I take, Sire?" he asked and Arthur pointed this way and that, clearly and directly. The way seemed easy to find and soon they reached the huge lake in the centre of a silent forest.

"Lay me down," said Arthur. "I fear I am too weak so I must ask you to do this for me, gentle knight. Take Excalibur and throw it far into the water. And on your return, tell me what you saw."

Bedevere took the sword and walked to the water's edge. He looked at Excalibur carefully and he saw the two messages 'Keep me' and 'Cast me away' engraved on each side of the blade. He admired the jewels on the handle and even as he lifted his arm to throw the sword away he had a sudden thought. "This is too good to waste. Why shouldn't I keep it and use it in battle myself?" So he hid it under some rushes and went back to the king.

"Your sword has been cast away, Sire," he said.

"What did you see? What did you hear?" the king asked.

"I heard the ripple washing in the reeds, and the wild waters lapping on the crag," said Bedevere.

"You are lying," Arthur said, "go back, Bedevere. Do as I commanded."

The knight walked back to the lake and pulled out the sword from its hiding place. Its jewels sparkled even in that gloomy place and Bedevere said to himself, "What a pity if nobody sees this lovely sword ever again. It is my duty to keep Excalibur!" For himself perhaps? He put it back in its hiding-place and went back to the king.

"What did you see?" he asked. His voice was weak and weary.

"Something wonderful," Bedevere replied. "A wild swan swooped down and carried off your sword."

"You are lying," said Arthur. "You are the last of my knights yet I cannot trust you. Go, and if you fail me a third time even though I am dying I will kill you, for you will have dishonoured the name of the Knights of the Round Table." He closed his eyes in pain.

Bedevere was ashamed for he really loved the king. He pulled out Excalibur and though he wanted to keep it, he hoisted the famous sword over his head and threw it with all his might to the centre of the lake. The waters opened and a hand covered with white silk rose up and caught the sword. Then the hand sank slowly beneath the water, taking the shining sword down, down, down. With a light heart, Bedevere ran to the dying king. "I closed my eyes so that I should not see the jewels," he said. "I threw Excalibur, then I saw a white arm rise from the lake. It grasped Excalibur and the waters closed around the arm as they sank together."

"The Lady of the Lake has taken back her sword," Arthur said faintly. "But I am cold. It is time for me to die, so good Bedevere, do one last thing for me. Carry me to the water's edge."

Tenderly, Bedevere lifted the king and as he did so he saw a black boat move silently across the lake. Six ladies wearing black gowns and veils sat inside the boat and when it reached the shore Bedevere noticed jewelled crowns glinting under their veils. The six queens carried Arthur into the boat and laid him silently on a richly embroidered cloth of gold.

Tears streamed down Bedevere's cheeks as he saluted the king. He stood there while the boat sailed silently back across the lake and out of his sight. Then he went sadly back to the castle, ready to serve his new king – whoever it was to be.

But nobody saw King Arthur die. And the story goes that he is not really dead but is waiting to come back if his beloved West Countrie is in real danger again.

BRER FOX INVITES BRER RABBIT TO DINNER

Joel Chandler Harris

Many years ago, on a plantation in America, an old servant called Uncle Remus used to tell tales of Brer Rabbit to a little boy.

"There was one particular time," said Uncle Remus one evening, "that Brer Fox got mighty close to having Brer Rabbit for his dinner."

And this is how the story went:

One day, Brer Rabbit came trotting along the road, looking as plump and healthy as you ever did see. Brer Fox just happened to be coming along down the opposite side of the road and he licked his lips at the sight.

"Hold on Brer Rabbit," says Brer Fox.

"I ain't got time, Brer Fox," says Brer Rabbit.

"I just want to have a quick confab with you," says Brer Fox.

"All right, Brer Fox, but holler from where you stand. I'm monstrous full of fleas this morning," says Brer Rabbit.

"I saw old Brer Bear this morning. He says you and me should be more neighbourly and I said I'd come and see you."

Brer Rabbit, he scratches one ear kinda dubiously, and says, "Why don't you drop round tomorrow and take dinner with us? I expect we can get up some sort of meal for you."

"Well, that's a fine gesture, Brer Rabbit, I'd be sure happy to come." And off runs Brer Fox, grinning from ear to ear.

Next day, Brer Rabbit and Missis Rabbit, they prepare a mighty good supper. The little Rabbits, they keep an eye out for the guest, and soon enough one of them rabbits comes running in crying, "Ma! Pa! I see Mr Fox a-coming!"

Brer Rabbit, he takes the little ones by the ears and tells them to sit down and stay quiet, and he and Missis Rabbit, they wait and they wait, but no guest shows up.

By and by, Brer Rabbit, he goes to the door and peeps out. And there, sticking out from behind the corner of the house is the tip of Brer Fox's bushy tail. Then Brer Rabbit, he shuts the door and bolts it firmly and makes sure all them windows are fastened mighty tightly and he and Missis Rabbit and the little Rabbits, they stay in and stay quiet. But I tell you, no guest came that night.

Next day, Brer Fox sends word by Brer Mink and excuses himself – saying he had been too sick to come to dinner. He asks if Brer Rabbit would come and take dinner with him, and Brer Rabbit sends back word that he'd be right agreeable.

By and by, Brer Rabbit, he brushes up his coat and saunters down to Brer Fox's house. As he gets near he can hear some mighty strange groaning noises. He peeps in through the door and there he sees Brer Fox in a rocking chair, all wrapped around with blankets and looking kinda weak.

Brer Rabbit, he looks round, but he don't see no dinner. He just sees an empty pan and a carving knife right by it.

"Looks like you going to have chicken," says Brer Rabbit.

"Yes, Brer Rabbit – nice juicy and tender," says Brer Fox, licking his lips.

Then Brer Rabbit, he say, "You ain't got no calamus root, have you, Brer Fox? I just can't eat no chicken without no calamus root." And Brer Rabbit, he leaps out of the door as quick as you please and hides behind some bushes. It ain't long after, when old Brer Fox comes a-creeping out of that house and he looks no more ill than you or I. But Brer Rabbit, he leaps up before Brer Fox can spot him, and hollers, "Oh, Brer Fox! I'll just put your calamus root on this here stump. Get it while its fresh!" and with that he gallops off home, and there ain't nothing Brer Fox can do.

Uncle Remus leant back in his chair and looked at the little boy. "Well, Brer Fox ain't caught Brer Rabbit yet, and what's more, honey, he ain't a-going to."

TOAD OF TOAD HALL

Kenneth Grahame (from *The Wind in the Willows*)

It was a bright morning in the early part of summer; the river had resumed its wonted banks and its accustomed pace, and a hot sun seemed to be pulling everything green and bushy and spiky up out of the earth towards him, as if by strings. The Mole and the Water Rat had been up since dawn, very busy on matters connected with boats and the opening of the boating season; painting and varnishing, mending paddles, repairing cushions, hunting for missing boat-hooks, and so on; and were finishing breakfast in their little parlour and eagerly discussing their plans for the day, when a heavy knock sounded at the door.

"Bother!" said the Rat, all over egg. "See who it is, Mole, like a good chap, since you've finished."

The Mole went to attend the summons, and the Rat heard him utter a cry of surprise. Then he flung the parlour door open, and announced with much importance, "Mr Badger!"

This was a wonderful thing, indeed, that the Badger should pay a formal call on them, or indeed on anybody. He generally had to be caught, if you wanted him badly, as he slipped quietly along a hedgerow of an early morning or a late evening, or else hunted up in his own house in the middle of the wood, which was a serious undertaking.

The Badger strode heavily into the room, and stood looking at the two animals with an expression full of seriousness. The Rat let his egg-spoon fall on the tablecloth, and sat open-mouthed.

"The hour has come!" said the Badger at last with great solemnity.

"What hour?" asked the Rat uneasily, glancing at the clock on the mantelpiece.

"*Whose* hour, you should rather say," replied the Badger. "Why, Toad's hour! The hour of Toad! I said I would take him in hand as soon as the winter was well over, and I'm going to take him in hand today!"

"Toad's hour, of course!" cried the Mole delightedly. "Hooray! I remember now! *We'll* teach him to be a sensible Toad!"

"This very morning," continued the Badger, taking an arm-chair, "as I learnt last night from a trustworthy source, another new and exceptionally powerful motor-car will arrive at Toad Hall on approval or return. At this very moment, perhaps, Toad is busy arraying himself in those singularly hideous habiliments so dear to him, which transform him from a (comparatively) good-looking Toad into an Object which throws any decent-minded animal that comes across it into a violent fit. We must be up and doing, ere it is too late. You two animals will accompany me instantly to Toad Hall, and the work of rescue shall be accomplished."

"Right you are!" cried the Rat, starting up. "We'll rescue the poor unhappy animal! We'll convert him! He'll be the most converted Toad that ever was before we've done with him!"

They set off up the road on their mission of mercy, Badger leading the way. Animals when in company walk in a proper and sensible manner, in single file, instead of sprawling all across the road and being of no use or support to each other in case of sudden trouble or danger.

They reached the carriage-drive of Toad Hall to find, as the Badger had anticipated, a shiny new motor-car, of great size, painted a bright red (Toad's favourite colour), standing in front of the house. As they neared the door it was flung open, and Mr Toad,

arrayed in goggles, cap, gaiters, and enormous overcoat, came swaggering down the steps, drawing on his gauntleted gloves.

"Hullo! come on, you fellows!" he cried cheerfully on catching sight of them. "You're just in time to come with me for a jolly – to come for a jolly – for a – er – jolly –"

His hearty accents faltered and fell away as he noticed the stern unbending look on the countenances of his silent friends, and his invitation remained unfinished.

The Badger strode up the steps. "Take him inside," he said sternly to his companions. Then, as Toad was hustled through the door, struggling and protesting, he turned to the *chauffeur* in charge of the new motor-car.

"I'm afraid you won't be wanted today," he said. "Mr Toad has changed his mind. He will not require the car. Please understand that this is final. You needn't wait." Then he followed the others inside and shut the door.

"Now, then!" he said to the Toad, when the four of them stood together in the hall, "first of all, take those ridiculous things off!"

"Shan't!" replied Toad, with great spirit. "What is the meaning of this gross outrage? I demand an instant explanation."

"Take them off him, then, you two," ordered the Badger briefly.

They had to lay Toad out on the floor, kicking and calling all sorts of names, before they could get to work properly. Then the Rat sat on him, and the Mole got his motor-clothes off him bit by bit, and they stood him up on his legs again. A good deal of his blustering spirit seemed to have evaporated with the removal of his fine panoply. Now that he was merely Toad, and no longer the Terror of the Highway, he giggled feebly and looked from one to the other appealingly, seeming quite to understand the situation.

"You knew it must come to this, sooner or later, Toad," the Badger explained severely. "You've disregarded all the warnings we've given you, you've gone on squandering the money your father left you, and you're getting us animals a bad name in the district by your furious driving and your smashes and your rows with the police. Independence is all very well, but we animals never allow our friends to make fools of themselves beyond a certain limit; and that limit you've reached. Now, you're a good fellow in many respects, and I don't want to be too hard on you. I'll make one more effort to bring you to reason. You will come with me into the smoking-room, and there you will hear some facts about yourself; and we'll see whether you come out of that room the same Toad that you went in."

He took Toad firmly by the arm, led him into the smoking-room, and closed the door behind them.

"*That's* no good!" said the Rat contemptuously. "*Talking* to Toad'll never cure him. He'll *say* anything."

They made themselves comfortable in armchairs and waited patiently. Through the closed door they could just hear the long continuous drone of the Badger's voice, rising and falling in waves of oratory; and presently they noticed that the sermon began to be punctuated at intervals by long-drawn sobs, evidently proceeding from the bosom of Toad, who was a soft-hearted and affectionate fellow, very easily converted – for the time being – to any point of view.

After some three-quarters of an hour the door opened, and the Badger appeared, solemnly leading by the paw a very limp and dejected Toad. His skin hung baggily about him, his legs wobbled, and his cheeks were furrowed by the tears so plentifully called forth by the Badger's moving discourse.

"Sit down there, Toad," said the Badger kindly, pointing to a chair. "My friends," he went on, "I am pleased to inform you that Toad has at last seen the error of his ways. He is truly sorry for his misguided conduct in the past, and he has undertaken to give up motor-cars entirely and for ever. I have his solemn promise to that effect."

"That is very good news," said the Mole gravely.

"Very good news indeed," observed the Rat dubiously, "if only – *if* only –"

He was looking very hard at Toad as he said this, and could not help thinking he perceived something vaguely resembling a twinkle in that animal's still sorrowful eye.

"There's only one thing more to be done," continued the gratified Badger. "Toad, I want you solemnly to repeat, before your friends here, what you fully admitted to me in the smoking-room just now. First, you are sorry for what you've done, and you see the folly of it all?"

There was a long, long pause. Toad looked desperately this way and that, while the other animals waited in grave silence. At last he spoke.

"No!" he said a little sullenly, but stoutly; "I'm *not* sorry. And it wasn't folly at all! It was simply glorious!"

"What?" cried the Badger, greatly scandalized. "You backsliding animal, didn't you tell me just now, in there –"

"O, yes, yes, in *there*," said Toad impatiently. "I'd have said anything in *there*. You're so eloquent, dear Badger, and so moving, and so convincing, and put all your points so frightfully well – you can do what you like with me in *there*, and you know it. But I've been searching in my mind since, and going over things in it, and I find that I'm not a bit sorry or repentant really, so it's no earthly good saying I am; now, is it?"

"Then you don't promise," said the Badger, "never to touch a motor-car again?"

"Certainly not!" replied Toad emphatically. "On the contrary, I faithfully promise that the very first motor-car I see, poop-poop! off I go in it!"

"Told you so, didn't I?" observed the Rat to the Mole.

"Very well, then," said the Badger firmly, rising to his feet. "Since you won't yield to persuasion, we'll try what force can do. I feared it would come to this all along. You've often asked us three to come and stay with you, Toad, in this handsome house of yours; well, now we're going to. When we've converted you to a proper point of view we may quit, but not before. Take him upstairs, you two, and lock him up in his bedroom, while we arrange matters between ourselves."

"It's for your own good, Toady, you know," said the Rat kindly, as Toad, kicking and struggling, was hauled up the stairs by his two faithful friends. "Think what fun we shall all have together, just as we used to, when you've quite got over this – this painful attack of yours!"

"We'll take great care of everything for you till you're well, Toad," said the Mole; "and we'll see your money isn't wasted, as it has been."

"No more of those regrettable incidents with the police, Toad," said the Rat, as they thrust him into his bedroom.

"And no more weeks in hospital, being ordered about by female nurses, Toad," added the Mole, turning the key on him.

They descended the stair, Toad shouting abuse at them through the keyhole; and the three friends then met in conference on the situation.

"It's going to be a tedious business," said the Badger, sighing. "I've never seen Toad so determined. However, we will see it out. He must never be left an instant unguarded. We shall have to take it in turns to be with him, till the poison has worked itself out of his system."

They arranged watches accordingly. Each animal took it in turns to sleep in Toad's room at night, and they divided the day up between them. At first Toad was undoubtedly very trying to his careful guardians. When his violent paroxysms possessed him he would arrange bedroom chairs in rude resemblance of a motor-car and would crouch on the foremost of them, bent forward and staring fixedly ahead, making uncouth and ghastly noises, till the climax was reached, when, turning a complete somersault, he would lie prostrate amidst the ruins of the chairs, apparently completely satisfied for the moment. As time passed, however, these painful seizures grew gradually less frequent, and his friends strove to divert his mind into fresh channels. But his interest in other matters did not seem to revive, and he grew apparently languid and depressed.

One fine morning the Rat, whose turn it was to go on duty, went upstairs to relieve Badger, whom he found fidgeting to be off and stretch his legs in a long ramble round his wood and down his earths and burrows. "Toad's still in bed," he told the Rat, outside the door. "Can't get much out of him, except, 'O, leave him alone, he wants nothing, perhaps he'll be better presently, it may pass off in time, don't be unduly anxious,' and so on. Now, you look out, Rat! When Toad's quiet and submissive, and playing at being the hero of a Sunday-school prize, then he's at his artfullest. There's sure to be something up. I know him. Well, now I must be off."

"How are you today, old chap?" inquired the Rat cheerfully, as he approached Toad's bedside.

He had to wait some minutes for an answer. At last a feeble voice replied, "Thank you so much, dear Ratty! So good of you to inquire! But first tell me how you are yourself, and the excellent Mole?"

"O, *we're* all right," replied the Rat. "Mole," he added incautiously, "is going out for a run round with Badger. They'll be out till luncheon-time, so you and I will spend a pleasant morning together, and I'll do my best to amuse you. Now jump up, there's a good fellow, and don't lie moping there on a fine morning like this!"

"Dear Rat," murmured Toad, "how little you realize my condition, and how very far I am from 'jumping up' now – if ever! But do not trouble about me. I hate being a burden to my friends, and I do not expect to be one much longer. Indeed, I almost hope not."

"Well, I hope not, too," said the Rat heartily. "You've been a fine bother to us all this time, and I'm glad to hear it's going to stop. And in weather like this, and the boating season just beginning! It's too bad of you, Toad! It isn't the trouble we mind, but you're making us miss such an awful lot."

"I'm afraid it *is* the trouble you mind, though," replied the Toad languidly. "I can quite understand it. It's natural enough. You're tired of bothering about me. I mustn't ask you to do anything further. I'm a nuisance, I know."

"You are, indeed," said the Rat. "But I tell you, I'd take any trouble on earth for you, if only you'd be a sensible animal."

"If I thought that, Ratty," murmured Toad, more feebly than ever, "then I would beg you – for the last time, probably – to step round to the village as quickly as possible – even now it may be too late – and fetch the doctor. But don't you bother. It's only a trouble, and perhaps we may as well let things take their course."

"Why, what do you want a doctor for?" inquired the Rat, coming closer and examining him. He certainly lay very still and flat, and his voice was weaker and his manner much changed.

"Surely you have noticed of late –" murmured Toad. "But no – why should you? Noticing things is only a trouble. Tomorrow, indeed, you may be saying to yourself, 'O, if only I had noticed sooner! If only I had done something!' But no; it's a trouble. Never mind – forget that I asked."

"Look here, old man," said the Rat, beginning to get rather alarmed, "of course I'll fetch a doctor to you, if you really think you want him. But you can hardly be bad enough for that yet. Let's talk about something else."

"I fear, dear friend," said Toad, with a sad smile, "that 'talk' can do little in a case like this – or doctors either, for that matter; still, one must grasp the slightest straw. And, by the way – while you are about it – I *hate* to give you additional trouble, but I happen to remember that you will pass the door – would you mind at the same time asking the lawyer to step up? It would be a convenience to me, and there are moments – perhaps I should say there is *a* moment – when one must face disagreeable tasks, at whatever cost to exhausted nature!"

"A lawyer! O, he must be really bad!" the affrighted Rat said to himself, as he hurried from the room, not forgetting, however, to lock the door carefully behind him.

Outside, he stopped to consider. The other two were far away, and he had no one to consult.

"It's best to be on the safe side," he said, on reflection. "I've known Toad fancy himself frightfully bad before, without the slightest reason; but I've never heard him ask for a lawyer! If there's nothing really the matter, the doctor will tell him he's an old ass, and cheer him up; and that will be something gained. I'd better humour him and go; it won't take very long." So he ran off to the village on his errand of mercy.

The Toad, who had hopped lightly out of bed as soon as he heard the key turned in the lock, watched him eagerly from the window till he disappeared down the carriage-drive. Then, laughing heartily, he dressed as quickly as possible in the smartest suit he could lay hands on at the moment, filled his pockets with cash which he took from a small drawer in the dressing-table, and next, knotting the sheets from his bed together and tying one end of the improvised rope round the central mullion of the handsome Tudor window which formed such a feature of his bedroom, he scrambled out, slid lightly to the ground, and, taking the opposite direction to the Rat, marched off light-heartedly, whistling a merry tune.

It was a gloomy luncheon for Rat when the Badger and the Mole at length returned, and he had to face them at table with his pitiful and unconvincing story. The Badger's caustic, not to say brutal, remarks may be imagined, and therefore passed over; but it was painful to the Rat that even the Mole, though he took his friend's side as far as possible, could not help saying, "You've been a bit of a duffer this time, Ratty! Toad, too, of all animals!"

"He did it awfully well," said the crestfallen Rat.

"He did *you* awfully well!" rejoined the Badger hotly. "However, talking won't mend matters. He's got clear away for the time, that's certain; and the worst of it is, he'll be so conceited with what he'll think is his cleverness that he may commit any folly. One comfort is, we're free now, and needn't waste any more of our precious time doing sentry-go. But we'd better continue to sleep at Toad Hall for a while longer. Toad may be brought back at any moment – on a stretcher, or between two policemen."

So spoke the Badger, not knowing what the future held in store, or how much water, and of how turbid a character, was to run under bridges before Toad should sit at ease again in his ancestral Hall.

THE GREY STONE

Alison Uttley

One fine day in winter, when the snow had forgotten to fall, and the wind had fallen asleep in the bare woods, eight little boys and a girl ran along a lane on their way home from school.

The little boys carried canvas dinner bags on their backs, but the little girl, who wore a red velvet cap, carried a basket. They trotted along, all talking at once, kicking the stones with their iron-tipped boots. The little girl had kicked a grey stone all the way from the village, where she had found it near the school gate, and now she was so intent on taking it home that she lagged behind the others.

"I'm going to have rabbit pie tonight," said one boy, "because my father killed a rabbit yesterday."

"I'm going to have a bantam egg," cried another. "Our bantam laid a tiddley egg this morning, and my muvver is boiling it for my tea."

"I'm going to have chitterlings," cried a third.

Then they all shouted what they were going to have, but some didn't know, so they just invented.

"I 'specks I'll have a gingerbread man with two currant eyes," said a romantic little boy.

"What are you having, Amanda?" they called to the girl, who was busy following her stone across the road.

"I'm going to have Mimsey-cake!" she said proudly.

When they came to a group of cottages they separated, the boys running shouting through their wicket gates, banging at the doors, calling across the red-tiled floors to their mothers. The little girl went farther on, still kicking the stone, until she, too, came to a small cottage set back from the road in a garden. She dribbled her stone up the path to the door, and then went in to have her Mimsey-cake.

The stone lay by the boot-scraper and stared about. This was the greatest luck! For years without end it had lain in the roads, kicked hither and thither by careless feet, ever since it had been quarried out of the great frowning cliff, and broken up by the roadman.

It had hoped to go to school, but, although it had been up and down the village street and into the lanes, it had never been as close to a door as this.

Always it had wanted to see the inside of a house, where those merry little feet lived, but the doors were closed. It had envied its brothers built into walls, but of course they had lost their freedom.

The door was flung open, but a rough little wind, which came curling down the valley, banged it to again.

"Prop the door open, Amanda," cried a voice, and Amanda stepped outside.

She picked up the stone and put it inside the cottage, leaning against the door. The stone was actually inside the house! "This is real life!" it thought.

It pushed hard and kept the door open, whilst Amanda's mother went out with a clothes basket, and returned with a pile of little garments. Then someone closed the door, and it was safe inside!

It squatted unnoticed in a corner, listening to the chatter, watching the baby in the cradle, and the cat and dog on the hearth.

Nothing escaped the stone, and it enjoyed everything, from the familiar feel of Amanda's boots, which were kicked off and flung on top of it, to the scorch of hot tea, which the brimming teapot spilled over it.

When all the household had gone to bed, and the lamp was put out, and the fire damped down, the stone listened to the voices talking, the voices which were silent in the daytime, but audible in the quiet of night.

Mice ran over it, crickets leapt upon it, the grandfather clock ticked out a long history of things it had seen, the table grunted, the chairs squeaked, the canary awoke and peeped down through the bars of his cage at the stranger.

"They'll turn you out," cried the clock, "and you haven't heard half my story."

"But I don't want to go," replied the stone. "I've been waiting for this for thousands of years, and I want a little comfort in my old age."

"They'll throw you out," repeated the clock, grimly, and all the little voices echoed, "Throw you out."

"What shall I do?" asked the stone, anxiously.

"Suppose you disguise yourself," suggested the big armchair, and all the voices said, "Disguise yourself."

So the mice dragged Amanda's velvet cap, which lay on a stool, and pulled it over the top of the stone, and the two boots moved in front of it, and a scarf fell down from behind the door and wrapped itself round its middle.

"What am I like?" asked the stone in a muffled tone, for it was smothered with clothes.

"Like Amanda," cried everything at once. So the stone sat still with the cap on its head, and the scarf round its body, and the two boots with their iron tips in front, and it hoped it would be taken for Amanda.

"This is adventure!" it muttered, and rejoiced it had left the road.

But when Amanda came down in the morning she hunted for her boots to clean, and there they were beside her cap and scarf!

"Who threw my cap and scarf down there?" she demanded, as she kicked the stone under the sofa. But the clock ticked solemnly on, and the fire flickered, and her mother said, "You must have done it yourself, Amanda, you are so very careless."

All day the stone hid, and at night it joined the family party.

Again the clock warned it of its fate.

"They'll throw you out," it said.

Sure enough the next morning a sweeping brush dragged it into the light.

"What's that stone doing there?" asked Amanda's mother as it rolled over towards the fire.

"It's the door-stop," exclaimed Amanda.

How proud the stone felt, for it was the first time it had ever had a title!

Amanda's father stooped down and picked it up. He held it as if he would fling it through the open door, into the road beyond the garden.

The clock ticked, "Goodbye, goodbye," the chairs creaked, and a little mouse behind the wainscot gave a cry, which the cat heard, for she sprang up and walked towards the wall.

Then he changed his mind. He examined the stone carefully, first on one side, and then on the other. He fetched a hammer and gave it a tap.

Horrors! A piece flew off, and the pale stone turned even paler. Was it going to be made into dust?

He chipped off another piece.

"Whatever are you doing, Father?" asked his wife, and Amanda stared up at him.

"See here," he cried. "Yon's a fossil."

Inside the stone was a group of dark ferns, perfect in their exquisite grace, their tiny fronds as clear as if they had been pressed in the stone that day.

"The place for this is on the chimney-piece," he continued, impressively. "I thought there was something in this bit of stone as soon as I saw it. It's the best fossil I've ever found in all my born days, and I'm a quarryman and ought to know."

So they placed it on the mantelpiece along with a shell in which the sea roared, and two china dogs with chains round their necks.

Every time a visitor came it was taken down and displayed in all its beauty. Every day it listened to the children's talk, as they came in from school to look at Amanda's fossil. But every night it listened to the secret voices which wove romantic stories out of the mists of past ages.

ROMULUS AND REMUS

Roman Legend

Long ago in Italy there lived two brothers, Numitor and Amulius. Numitor was king of a place called Alba Longa, where he ruled wisely and well. His brother was jealous of him and plotted to overthrow him.

Amulius mounted an armed attack on the good king and forced him to flee into the country with his three children. However, this did not satisfy Amulius. He wanted to make sure that his son would rule after him, so he sent some men to kill the two sons of Numitor. Then he ordered that Ilia, his daughter, should be shut up in a temple. The boys were killed and Ilia was imprisoned.

But while in the temple, Ilia gave birth to twin sons. They were called Romulus and Remus and folk said that the powerful God of War, Mars, was their father. Amulius was very angry when he heard about the baby boys. He ordered two servants to get into the temple and steal the babies from Ilia.

"When you have done this," he snarled, "toss the babies into the river. Neither of these boys will ever be king if I can help it!"

The two men stole the babies, but when they reached the river Tiber they could not bear to kill the infants so the men left the cradle on the bank.

It happened that the river became flooded and the waters rushed over the bank and carried the cradle away. Romulus and Remus slept peacefully until at last their cradle was washed into a little sandy bay at the foot of the Palatine mountains. The babies woke up and started to cry for they were very ungry and cold. A woodpecker flew down when it heard the noise and hopped over to the cradle.

"Babies!" it chirped. "I'd better bring my friend the she-wolf here," and it flew into the wood and asked the she-wolf to follow it. She licked the river mud off the howling boys and fed them with her own milk. Then she carried them to her den and looked after them with her own cubs.

Some time later, a shepherd called Faustulus, who worked for Numitor, found the little boys playing happily with some wolf-cubs

in a cave. The she-wolf was away so he picked them up and ran back quickly to his wife. He handed them over with great joy to her, for they had no children of their own.

Romulus and Remus, who were really royal princes, were brought up as shepherd boys. They were strong, handsome and brave and before long they were able to attack bands of robbers on the Palatine mountainside. They gave whatever they took from these robbers to their foster-parents.

One day some robbers managed to catch Remus and they led him to Numitor who owned the farms around there.

"Good sir," they whined, "we found this fellow stealing your sheep." Before Remus could say anything, Romulus sprang in front of him. He lifted his spear and said fearlessly: "This is my brother: he would not steal! I demand that you let him go, my lord."

The people around murmured. These young men were shepherds but they looked like lords! Numitor looked closely at them. "Put down your spear," he said. "I should like to hear about your parents and your family."

"Oh sir," said Romulus, "Faustulus found us in a wolf's cave.

He and his wife cared for us but we do not know who our real parents are."

"How old are you?" asked Numitor and after he had asked a few more questions, tears came into his eyes. "You are Ilia's children," he cried. "You are my grandsons!" He hugged them both. Then he turned to the crowds and said proudly: "Here are the rightful princes of the kingdom, Romulus and Remus."

They stayed with their grandfather now and learned to be soldiers as well as princes. After some time they planned to attack their grandfather's enemy, Amulius. They made their soldiers promise to keep their secret so when they attacked, Amulius was taken by surprise. He was killed in the fierce fighting. Then the young princes proudly led their grandfather Numitor back to the city of Alba Longa. He was the rightful king once more and he sent messengers to the temple where his daughter Ilia was a prisoner. They brought her back to Alba Longa and she cried with joy when she saw her children.

After a while the twin boys thought it was time to live in their own home. They liked the River Tiber and the lovely Palatine hills so they decided to build a new city there for themselves. Workers started to dig roads on the hillside and the brothers were very happy until one day a worker came to them and said, "Young masters, from whom shall we take our orders? Which of you is our king? Romulus or Remus?" The brothers looked at each other. "I'd like to be king," Remus thought, while Romulus said to himself, "I'm sure I'd be a better king than Remus." For the first time in their lives, the brothers had a fierce quarrel. Their grandfather heard about their troubles and sent this message: "You must visit the wise men in the temple. They will tell you what to do."

Romulus and Remus visited the sacred temple and they were told by the wise men that Romulus was to be king. Sad to say, from that time on they were no longer friends but became bitter enemies.

Romulus set to work on the plans for streets and houses but Remus would not let the workers get on with their work, and one day he was shouting and mocking them when he fell over a wall. He was killed on the stones and his body was buried under the city walls.

So Romulus was the king of the new city. He was wise and kind to all his people and he wrote down the laws he wanted them to obey. From that time onwards the city was called Rome in honour of King Romulus and before long it was the greatest and most beautiful city in Italy.

HUDDEN, DUDDEN AND DONALD O'LEARY

Irish Traditional

In a far corner of Ireland there once lived two farmers, Hudden and Dudden. They had hens clucking in their yards, woolly sheep on the hills and fine fat cows in the meadows near the river. But were they happy? No, they were not and all because of a poor farmer called Donald O'Leary. He had a hovel for his house and a strip of grass which only just kept his miserable cow Daisy from starving. She did her best but seldom did Donald get the sight of a pat of butter or a wee drink of milk from the poor creature.

And what was it that kept Hudden and Dudden awake at nights? Sure and they were jealous of Donald's bit of land. Daisy, poor bag of bones, they kicked aside. All they wanted was his land.

One day Hudden met Dudden. "'Tis a shame we can't get rid of that vagabond O'Leary," grumbled Hudden. "His farm is a disgrace, so it is."

"Let's kill Daisy," said Dudden, "that will shift him away for certain."

"Right," said Hudden and away they crept to Daisy's little hut. They didn't wait until it was decently dark but attacked the poor beast as she tried to chew the cud with only enough grass passing her lips to cover your hand. When Donald came to tuck her up for the night, didn't she lick his hand the once before she died, poor thing.

Donald was dumbfounded but he was a canny sort of fellow. "I'm wondering if I can get any good out of Daisy's death," he says to himself and the next day he set off early for the fair. Daisy's hide was slung over his shoulders and every penny he owned in the world was jingling in his pockets. Just before he got to the fair didn't he make several slits in the hide and didn't he push a penny into each slit. Then he walked into the best inn in the town, as bold as brass, as if it belonged to him. Carefully he hung the hide on a nail and sat down.

"It's your best whisky I'll be having," he called to the landlord. But the landlord wasn't too sure that he liked Donald's looks!

"Is it afraid you are that I won't pay?" asked Donald. "Why, this old hide here gives me all the money I want, so it does." He whacked it with his stick and a penny popped out. The landlord's eyes almost popped out too.

"What'll I give you for that hide?" he asked.

"Nothing, my good man. It isn't for sale."

"How about taking a gold piece for it?"

"It's not for sale, I'm telling you. Hasn't it kept me for years?" and Donald whacked the hide again so that out dropped a second penny.

Well, the landlord begged and Donald scratched his head. "It's kind I'm feeling today so maybe I'll let the hide go for a bag of gold."

That night who else but Donald should walk up to Hudden's farm.

"Good evening, Hudden," he says, "I'm after borrowing your good pair of scales."

"What's he wanting scales for?" thought Hudden as he handed them over.

In his broken-down hovel Donald weighed all the pieces of gold but that suspicious Hudden had stuck a pat of butter at the bottom of the scales so that the last piece of gold stuck fast there when Donald took them back to Hudden.

"Ghosts and Ghoulies!" exclaimed Hudden when Donald's back was turned and he pelted away to Dudden's farm. "That vagabond," he panted. "Bad luck to him."

"Is it Donald O'Leary you mean?" asked Dudden.

"Who else should I mean?" Hudden shouted. "He's in his hut counting sacks and sacks and sacks of gold! Look for yourself. Here's one piece that was stuck on my scales. *My* scales, if you please!"

Together they rushed to Donald's door. In they walked without a single by your leave. Then all they could say was, "Well, I never."

"Good evening, kind friends," said Donald. "I was just counting the last of my gold pieces and I'm thinking of the good turn you did me even though you thought you'd played a smart trick! My dear Daisy's hide was more valuable dead than alive. Cow hides are worth their weight in gold in the market right now."

Hudden nudged Dudden. Dudden winked at Hudden. Then the two of them tore out of that hovel like bees after honey.

"Goodnight, dear friends," called Donald. "Dear kind rogues that you are!"

Well, next day, not a cow, not a calf stayed on the two farms for were not their hides going to the fair, packed upon Hudden's biggest cart pulled by Dudden's strongest pair of horses.

When they reached the fair each one threw a hide over his arm and didn't the pair of them march along the street yelling, "Hides to sell. Plenty of fine hides to sell."

"What are you wanting for them?" a tanner asked.

"Their weight in gold for sure," the farmers said.

"Is it drunk you are so early in the morning?" the tanner laughed and he went back to his yard.

"Hides to sell. Dozens of best hides to sell," the men bawled.

"How much are you asking?" said a cobbler.

"To you, their weight in gold, a bargain," came the reply.

"Is it making fun of me you are?" shouted the cobbler. "Then you can be taking this for your pains," and he hit Hudden quite hard. He staggered back and folk came running from all corners of the fair. "What's happening? What's to do?" they cried.

"Sure and these vagabonds are trying to rob me," said the cobbler.

"Hold them. Hold them," puffed the innkeeper, "and isn't one of them the very villain who tricked me out of my gold yesterday?"

Hudden and Dudden got more kicks than pennies before they set off for home and alas, they met Donald O'Leary on the road!

"Whatever's the matter?" said he. "Your poor hats are knocked in. Your coats are torn. And it's bruised you are. Is it fighting you've been?"

"Fighting, is it?" roared they. "You deluded us with your lying taradiddle."

"Lies. What lies?" asked he. "You saw my gold with your own eyes."

But it was no use the three of them arguing. Donald had to pay for his trick. There was a grain sack lying nearby so Hudden and Dudden popped Donald inside. They tied him up tightly, pushed a pole through the knot then they carried him off like a pig in a poke. "To the Brown Lake of the Bog with him," they shouted and down the road they jogged.

But the Brown Lake was far away. The road was dusty and hard on their feet. The pole holding the sack was rock hard and made their shoulders ache. Then they spotted a friendly roadside inn. "I'm thinking we deserve a drink," said Hudden. "I'm parched."

"It's heavy he is even though he's so little," said Dudden. They dumped the sack like a sack of potatoes outside the inn. "You don't mind waiting, Donald old friend," they laughed then they raced inside the inn to get a drink.

Donald kept quiet for some time then he heard Hudden and Dudden clinking their glasses. "I'm thinking they'll be there for a while yet," he thought, so he called loudly: "I won't have her. I tell you I won't have her." But nobody took any notice. "I won't have her. I simply refuse to have her," he shouted more loudly. Nobody listened to him so he shouted at the top of his voice: "I won't have her. I won't have her. I won't have her."

"And who is it you won't have if you don't mind my asking?" said a farmer. He had just arrived with a fine drove of sleek cattle and was going into the inn for a drink. "Oh," says Donald from inside the sack. "It's the king's daughter herself. It's bothering me day and night they are, to get me to marry the girl."

"Marry a princess!" exclaimed the farmer. "Well, aren't you the luckiest fellow! I'll gladly change places with you."

"Are you saying that now?" says Donald in a muffled voice. "It

would be a fine thing I suppose, for a farmer to marry a princess all dressed in gold and jewels."

"Gold? Jewels, did you say? Ah now, couldn't you be taking me along with you?" asked the farmer.

"I'll be truthful with you," says Donald, "you sound like an honest fellow to me. The king's daughter is beautiful. She's covered with jewels from top to toe but I just don't care for her. You shall have her. I give her freely to you. But pray undo this cord and let me out. They tied me up tightly for they knew I'd run away from her and it's carrying me to the king's court they are!"

Donald crawled out; the farmer crawled in.

"Don't mind the shaking you'll get," says Donald, "just lie still. They'll maybe call you names because they'll think you don't want the king's daughter but don't bother about them. You'll get some bumps and thumps but it's only rumbling over the palace steps you'll be." Then he sighed, "It's a great deal I'm giving up for you."

"Take my cattle, I shan't need them," says the farmer. And Donald lost no time in driving them back home, I can tell you.

Out came Hudden and Dudden. One held one end of the pole and the other the other. "He's heavier, I'm thinking," says Hudden.

"Ach, don't fuss," says Dudden, "it's only a wee step to the Brown Lake."

"I'll have her. I'll have her now," yelled the farmer in the sack.

"You'll have it right enough," cried Hudden. "You'll not be playing your tricks on us much longer. What say you, Dudden?"

239

"True words," says he. "Here's the Brown Lake. Now a good heave-ho and he'll be gone." With that they pitched the sack into the water!

Off they went, arm in arm, whistling merrily. But when they were almost home who should they meet but Donald O'Leary. Worse still, there were fine cows grazing all round him and calves gambolling in the sun! "Is this you, Donald?" asked Dudden feebly. "Faith and you must have run quickly for you've beaten us home."

"Very true," said Donald. "I must thank you both for your good deed – even if your thoughts were evil," he said under his breath. "My old granny used to say that the Brown Lake led to the Land of Promise but I laughed at her. But it's true, true as my word! Take a look at these cattle." Hudden stared and Dudden gasped. The cattle were fine and fat. They couldn't believe their eyes.

"These aren't the best cattle either," Donald went on, "faith, I couldn't bring them for they wouldn't be driven away from the rich grass."

"Donald," said Hudden. "We know you're a decent fellow. You'll be showing us the way to find the cattle, won't you?"

"I don't know about that," said Donald, "to be sure there are plenty of cows down there. And why shouldn't I keep them all for myself?"

"You wouldn't want to keep all the good luck to yourself," said Dudden. "You were always our good neighbour and kind friend!"

"It was a bad example you set me, Hudden and Dudden, but I'll not be thinking of the past. There's plenty for all, I'm sure, so you can come along with me if you wish."

Back they went with light steps and cheerful hearts. When they came to the Brown Lake the sky was full of fluffy white clouds which were reflected in the clear lake water below. "Ah now, can you see them?" cried Donald as he pointed to the clouds in the lake. "Look, there they are."

"Where? Where? Show me," cried Hudden.

"Get out of my way, vagabond," cried Dudden and he elbowed Hudden aside. He jumped his hardest for he wanted to get the fattest cows for himself but Hudden wasn't far behind.

They never came back. Some folk say the farmer was waiting for them, and on stormy days they say he is chasing them under the lake. Others think they grew too fat like the cattle!

As for Donald O'Leary, he had enough cattle and sheep to last for the rest of his life. But he never forgot Daisy, his dear first cow!